PRIESTESS
OF
NKU

MILTON J. DAVIS

MVmedia, LLC
Fayetteville, GA

MVmedia, LLC
PO Box 1465
Fayetteville, GA 30214

Publisher's Note: This is a work of fiction. Names, characters, places, and incidents are a product of the author's imagination. Locales and public names are sometimes used for atmospheric purposes. Any resemblance to actual people, living or dead, or to businesses, companies, events, institutions, or locales is completely coincidental.

Book Layout ©2017 BookDesignTemplates.com

Ordering Information:
Quantity sales. Special discounts are available on quantity purchases by corporations, associations, and others. For details, contact the "Special Sales Department" at the address above.

Priestess of nKu/ Milton J. Davis. -- 1st ed.

Contents

To Shakira Rivers
Thank you for the inspiration and your generosity.

GLOSSARY

Awere – The Kashite colony
Bindamu – nKu word for outsider
Bintifalme – Princess
Bodantu – Kashite word for barbarian
Bwa – sir
Chuiku – Leopard Clan
Dumaku - Cheetah
Farasiku – Horse Clan
Fisiku – Hyena Clan
Jikubwa – Chuiku home city
Kibebeku – Tigerfish Clan
Kibokoku – Hippo Clan
Kipanga – Kashite riding eagles
Mambaku – Crocodile Clan
Maron - Chuiku warrior
Nguruweku – Bush pig Clan
Nyaniku – Baboon Clan
Nyatiku – Buffalo Clan
Mtemi – Mayor
nKu – Clan
Paaku – Antelope Clan
Pundaku – Donkey Clan
Simbaku – Lion Clan
Taiji – title
Tambiko – totem
Temboku – Elephant Clan
Vifaruku – Rhino Clan

BOOK ONE
THE NEW CLAN

ONE

Nandi ran as fast as she could but could not catch baba. She dodged the vines and shrubs as agile as any beast born to the bush, her breath easy and measured, but no matter how she tried she could not shorten the distance between them. For a moment she thought of dropping her spear, throwing down her bow, unfastening her waist belt, discarding her short sword and abandoning her arrow filled quiver. With less weight she could run faster, but a Hunter should never be without her weapons. It was the first lesson she learned.

"Baba!" she shouted. "Slow down!"

Baba kept running as if he did not hear her although she knew he did. Baba had the hearing of a bat fox. He was ignoring her.

"Baba!"

Nandi's frustration turned to anger as baba disappeared into a dense stand of trees. It was then she realized what he was doing. This was not a hunt. This was a lesson. She stopped running then slumped over to catch her breath. She began to pursue baba again, but this time she walked. Baba waited for her and she would track him. She just hoped she could find him before he surprised her and delivered another painful lesson. Nandi took a few steps before halting and crouching when she heard the crunch of dry leaves. She smiled; she was no longer hunting baba; baba was hunting her.

Nandi shut her eyes and let her other senses take over. She listened, the gentle breeze rustling loose leaves and pushing saplings into one another. Her nostrils filled with the aromas of the forest. Through her senses she touched the pulse of the woodland, sensing its rhythms. Only after she'd attain such a state did she open her eyes, seeking angles that did not align with those natural to the old growth forest in which she stood.

Nandi knew baba could approach her as if almost invisible; such was his skill. But this was a training lesson so he would do something to attract attention. She turned her head slowly, studying the natural lines of the bush, seeking that which broke the pattern. To her right a small bird flittered about its nest; just on the edge of her peripheral vision a bush deer stood just as still as she, aware of something amiss in its home. The sounds that reached her ears matched the movement she observed. She was about to move when a faint acrid smell alarmed her. She spun about, her sword drawn. Baba stood before her, his spear raised. He grinned as she lowered her sword.

"I'll never be as good as you!" she whined.

"You'll be better," baba said. "You have already surpassed my skills when I was your age."

They sat together, baba taking a strip of dried meat from his provision pouch and sharing it with her.

"Do you think I'll be good enough to become First Hunter?"

"Do you want to be?" he asked.

"Of course!"

"Are you sure? Some things look better at a distance than they do up close."

Baba's words confused her. "What does that mean?"

"It means some things seem easier when you're looking at them than when you actually have to do them."

"Like finding you," Nandi said.

Baba laughed. "Yes, like finding me."

Baba finished his meal then stood.

"Come now *chuikidogo*," he said. "It's time I got you back home."

Nandi pouted. "Why can't you live in the village with me and mama?"

"Because it is our way," baba replied.

He turned his back then squatted before her.

"Hop on," he said.

"I'm too big to ride," she said.

"I'll be the one to decide that. Now hop on."

Nandi climbed onto baba's back. He grunted as he staggered to stand.

"See, I told you!"

Baba laughed. "I'm just teasing."

The ground jolted under baba's feet. This time his staggering was not playful. He grabbed a nearby tree, holding tight as the world shook. Moments later it stopped.

"Earthquake," Nandi said.

"No," baba replied. "That was something different."

He squatted and Nandi jumped off his back. Baba ran and she ran behind him, nervousness keeping her legs moving despite her fatigue. That tiredness transformed to fear as she realized where they were going.

"Baba!" she shouted. "Baba, stop!"

Baba either did not hear her or didn't care. Nandi watched him run through the pines then scramble down the steep hill leading to the Hagosa River.

"Baba no!" she screamed.

Baba splashed into the river, high-stepping through the shallows until he reached the opposite bank. Baba was in Taikuland; if Taiku warriors discovered him they would attack immediately. Nandi paced, uncertain what to do. Should she go back to the city and tell mama, or should she try to find more marons to help? Both options would take too much time, she decided. She took out her sword then ran down the hill, almost falling. Nandi waded across the river then plunged into the bush after baba. She had run a short distance when someone grabbed her around her waist then covered her mouth before she could scream.

"What are you doing?" whispered baba. He uncovered her mouth.

"Following you," she whispered back.

Baba looked frustrated. "I can't send you back now. Stay close"

She nodded then followed baba through the bush. They traveled deep into Taikuland, Nandi anticipating an attack any minute.

"This is not right," Baba said.

"What, baba?" Nandi asked.

"We've seen no warriors."

"I would think that is a good thing."

"It is, but it is not normal."

They traveled until nightfall then made camp in the middle of a dense stand of trees. Baba shared his provisions with Nandi. They ate in darkness, careful not to make a fire. The next morning, they woke with the sunlight and continued their trek across Taikuland. By midday they reached the farthest limits, the towering mountains that formed the boundary of their world.

"Look," Baba said as he pointed at the mountains. Nandi gazed in the direction which her father gestured then gasped. There was a gaping hole at the base of the mountain. A cluster of dwellings pressed near the rim of the hole, a wooden palisade forming a barrier between the hastily built huts and the grasslands. Nandi thought they looked strange, and baba confirmed her suspicions.

"That is not Taiku," he said. "This is something different."

"How could that be?" she asked.

Baba looked at her in a way she'd never seen before.

"I don't know."

There was another blast and the ground trembled. Nandi saw dust rising behind the dwellings.

"What are they doing?" she asked.

Baba shook his head. "I don't know."

They gazed at the dwellings, baba shifting his eyes back to her. He took a breath then sat.

"We must get closer," he said. "I need to know what's happening and share this with your mama."

Nandi knew she was the reason he hesitated.

"I'm ready baba," she said. "I won't be a burden. I promise."

"I should take you back and gather the marons," he said. "That way if there was a fight, we would be ready."

Baba stared at her a moment longer then turned his attention back to the city before the hole.

"We will wait until dusk then get closer," he said. "You must stay close to me. Do everything I do."

"I will," Nandi said.

"This is no game *dama*," he said. "If you make a mistake, you will die."

Baba's words and demeanor sent a chill through Nandi.

"I understand baba," she said.

Nandi hid with baba the remainder of the day, the two eating little. They watched the city, noting the coming and going of its inhabitants. The longer they observed, the more they were convinced that whoever these people were, they were not nKu. As the sun settled below the mountains, Nandi spotted movement beyond the city.

"Baba, look," she said.

"I see it," he replied. "Taiku."

The quiet was shattered by the blaring of horns. The Taiku appeared from the surrounding forest as if summoned from air. The mountainside writhed as hundreds of Tai leapt from their perches, bearing their armed riders.

"It's an attack," baba said. "Let's go!"

Baba jumped to his feet and Nandi followed. Even though he ran slower for her to keep pace, Nandi still struggled. Soon they were close enough to hear the Taiku war cries as they surged toward the city palisades. The strange folks fled in desperate yet orderly fashion as if used to the threat. They were within the walls well before the Taiku reached the outlying homes. Baba and Nandi drew closer to the Taiku, keeping a good distance just in case they were seen and had to escape. They stopped when they reached the forest edge and watched the Taiku run toward the villages. The city defenders appeared when the Taiku were only a few strides away. They were armored from head to toe, their heads covered by helmets with eye slits and nostril holes. The warriors carried shields and long swords that glinted in the sunlight. Taiku and strangers met and a furious battle ensued. The Taiku were faster, but the strange warriors' armor protected them from the deadly assault. The strangers weren't invincible; they died like the Taiku, just not as quickly. Moments later the airborne Taiku arrived, their flying mounts diving down to attack with beaks and claws. Their riders threw their spears into the rear of the warriors, driving them back into the homes.

"Look!" Baba said. He pointed to the walls.

Rows of archers formed behind the palisades, holding bows like Nandi had never seen. Nandi looked at the swirling tais then shook her head.

"They are going to try to shoot them," she said. "They will miss."

Baba looked at her with a grim expression.

"Most of them will. All of them won't."

The strangers released their arrows. Like Baba said, most of the arrows missed, but enough reached their targets. The tais tumbled from the skies, their riders screaming as they fell. The arrows that did not strike the birds fell into the fighters below, killing friend and foe alike. Nandi had never seen so much death before. So many people dying at one time, each trying to protect their homes and those they loved. Except the people in the city were not nKu. They were Bindamu, strangers. They did not belong.

"Let's go," Baba finally said. "We have seen enough."

Baba was standing when the Tai warrior charged out of the bush.

"Baba!" Nandi shouted.

Baba spun and the man smashed into him. They fell on the ground and wrestled, grunting and snarling as they fought. Nandi grabbed her spear, charging toward them. She was about to plunge her spear into the Tai when another warrior appeared, running with his sword raised. He did not see Nandi, for he ran toward the wrestlers without looking her way. Nandi veered in his direction, staying silent until she was almost upon him. She screamed and the Taiku warrior jerked his head toward her as the spear plunged into his abdomen. The man grimaced as the spear burst from his back. Still, he managed to lunge at Nandi before his spirit fled. He staggered sideways then fell into the brush. Nandi stared at the man as his breathing slowed and then ceased. She held onto the spear shaft, unable to move. Sounds of fighting behind her stopped, but Nandi could not turn to see who won. A hand touched her shoulder, followed by a familiar voice.

"Let go," Baba said.

Nandi opened her hands and the spear fell to the ground. Baba moved her aside then grasped the spear shaft. He jerked it free of the warrior then handed it back to Nandi.

"You saved my life," he said.

Nandi didn't answer. She continued staring into the lifeless eyes of the Taiku.

"We must go," Baba said. "Others will come soon."

Nandi turned away from the dead warrior then ran behind Baba. She took one last look at the man before they entered woods too thick for her to see. They ran until they were deep into Chuikuland, safe from any Taiku ambushes. Baba set up camp near a small creek, gathering wood and making a fire. There was always the possibility another maron would approach them and challenge Baba, but most would concede once they saw Nandi. Children were precious to the Chuiku, and no maron would want to be accused of killing another in the presence of their child, especially a *dama*.

But Nandi's mind drifted far from such thoughts. She sat near the fire staring at her spear. The death of the Taiku warrior played over and over in her mind. Each time her stomach ached more as she recalled his blank stare before he collapsed to the ground and the sound of baba pulling the spear from his body. She heaved, spewing vomit on the ground and on the spear. Tears welled in her eyes as she fell onto her hands and knees, vomiting again and again until there was nothing left. She didn't notice Baba's hands rubbing her back until he lifted her up, preventing her from falling into the mess she'd created.

"Drink this," he said. "It will soothe your stomach."

Nandi took the cup from Baba's hand and drank. Whatever was inside was not water. The elixir felt warm in her throat; her stomach calmed a few minutes later. She drank all of it then extended the cup to Baba.

"Can I have some more?" she asked.

Baba grinned. "That is enough. Wait and see."

Moments later Nandi felt drowsy. She lay on the ground then rested her head on her band. She slept as soon as she closed her eyes. When she awoke it was daylight and Baba was breaking camp.

Nandi rubbed her eyes, stretched, and then began putting her things away as well.

"You did a brave thing yesterday," baba said. "I know it was not easy."

Nandi stopped banding. "I couldn't let him hurt you."

Baba opened his arms and Nandi ran to him, hugging him tight.

"It was terrible!" she said.

"Yes, it was," Baba replied. "But if you wish to be First Hunter, you must be prepared for more. A First Hunter must defend our people. She must fight other Hunters to maintain our territory, and sometimes lead us into war."

"I'm not sure I can do that," Nandi said.

"It is not my place to encourage you," Baba said. "That is your mother's task. I'm only a maron."

"You are First Maron!" Nandi said. She hugged baba again. "And you are my Baba."

"And as your baba I must get you home before your mama begins to worry."

They trekked for three days before the woods began to thin. Nandi's worries faded away as she saw the signs they were close to home. Her pace quickened as she thought of her home and her soft bed. Baba reached out, grabbing her shoulder. She turned to face him, a broad smile on her face.

"This is as far as I go," he said. "Ask your mama if she will come to speak with me. I will wait until dark. If she does not come, I will leave."

Nandi almost protested until she remembered marons were not allowed beyond the sweet tree ring. She looked about and saw the broad leaf plants, their branched laden with bright yellow fruit. It was a natural boundary that all marons respected except during the wet season celebrations or permission from the Matriarchs.

"She will come," Nandi said. "I'll make her."

Baba laughed. "No one makes your mama do anything."

"We'll see," Nandi replied.

She kissed Baba on the forehead then turned and ran toward home. Nandi sped through the forest with the confidence of familiarity. She knew these woods; every rock, tree, creek, lake and valley. She spent most of her life among them under the training of mama and the other Matriarchs, as all young girls did. Once they reached initiation age, the girls were separated. Those who showed Hunter skills continued to train in the forest, while those that did not were taught other skills. Nandi's mother decided to go beyond the normal training; allowing her to spend time living with Baba to learn the ways of the marons. It was a life she would never experience otherwise, and if she was to be First Hunter, she would need to be familiar with it. Baba taught her well; he also taught her the fighting skills of the marons. Combined with the martial tactics of the Matriarchs, Nandi became more skilled that the other Hunter candidates.

The forest opened to cultivated fields of sorghum, yams, okra and greens. Nandi made her way to the nearest road, her pace increasing without obstructions. Chuiku women worked the fields and tended the herds. Nandi called out and they answered; some smiling and waving as they recognized the Matriarch's daughter. She stopped briefly at one farm, drinking water and resting before continuing her run. The painted walls of Jikubwa, broke the horizon and Nandi laughed. She was home.

She waved at everyone as she entered the city, racing to her house.

"Mama! Mama!" she called out.

Mama came to the door and Nandi's smile grew wider. She wore a simple dress decorated with bright flowers, her dark brown braided hair brushing her shoulders. A curious look occupied her face until she saw Nandi. She opened her arms and met her daughter with a generous hug.

"My little chui has returned," she said.

Nandi took a moment to catch her breath.

"We saw the new nKu!" Nandi said.

Mama's expression changed from curiosity to puzzlement.

"New nKu? What are you talking about?"

Nandi grabbed mama's hand. "Baba will tell you. He needs to talk to you."

Mama's eyebrows rose and her forehead crinkled. "Your baba is here?"

Nandi nodded. "Yes!"

Mama frowned. "Let's go then."

Nandi's returned to the grove was much slower than her leaving. Mama refused to run and had to issue a number of commands as they left Jikubwa. She gathered a group of Hunters as protection before leaving the city, which furthered slowed them down. It was almost dusk when they finally reached the perimeter. Baba was standing as if she left only moments ago, munching on sweet tree fruit. To her surprise there were other marons as well. One of them caught her attention. He was very young, almost her age. It took her a moment to recognize him. It was Etana. She smiled at him and he smiled back.

Mama let go of her hand as she approached Baba and the marons, her Hunter guards close behind.

"Kondo, what is this nonsense about a new nKu?"

Baba bowed to mama.

"Adia, it is good to see you. How have you been?"

Mama folded her arms across her chest.

"Answer my question, Kondo."

"We were near Taikuland when we heard a loud sound like thunder. We went to see what was going on when we saw it. There was a hole in the mountain.."

"A hole? What do you mean a hole?"

"It is as baba said," Nandi replied. A hole in the mountains. And there is a city in front of the hole. The people in this city are not nKu."

The hunters gasped. Mama gave them a stern look and they quieted.

"Are you sure these people are not Taiku?"

"I am sure," Baba answered. The Taiku attacked them, but these people beat them back. We tried to get closer but we were attacked by Taiku. Which is the other reason I am here. Nandi was blooded."

Again, the Hunters reacted, but this time it was f nods and smiles of approval. Mama smiled as well.

"Now that is news I understand," Mama said. "It is sooner than I expected, yet no surprise. We will leave this issue of new people from beyond the mountains to the Taikubu."

"The Taiku are not doing a good job with their problem," Baba said.

"Then we will have new enemies to kill,"
Mama said. She scanned all the marons before
speaking again.

"Keep an eye on our new 'neighbors.' And try
not to kill each other as you do."

The marons knelt before Mama and dispersed into the woods, all except Baba.

"Is there something else?" Mama asked him.

"No, Aida," he said. "I am looking a bit longer, so I can carry your memory with me as I depart."

Nandi grinned as she saw mama hold back a
smile. It took a moment for her to regain her composure before she spoke.

"Go, Kondo," she finally said. "And may the
Priestesses watch over you."

Baba smiled then knelt. He came to his feet
then kissed Nandi on the head.

"Your time has come," he whispered. "Do not
bring shame to our name."

Nandi hugged his neck. "I won't Baba."

She let him go and he trotted into the forest.
When she turned around mama beheld her proudly.

"And when were you going to tell me you
were blooded?"

"I was too excited about the bindamu," Nandi said.

Mama waved her hand as if swatting an er-
rant bug. "That is not our concern. If the Taiku
don't deal with this new nKu, that is their failure."

Mama put her arm around Nandi's shoulders
then smiled.

"Come, daughter. We must prepare for your
initiation."

Nandi hugged mama's waist. The time had
come for her to become a hunter. Everything else
could wait.

Priestess of nKu

T W O

Tahnk An stood emotionless as the savages fled back to their mountain hovels. Her warriors cheered and the people celebrated, but Tahnk found no joy in their victory. She took this assignment because she wanted a change and because it was supposed to be a simple matter with the exception of the completion of the tunnel. This island was supposed to be barren. None of the scrolls mentioned inhabitants, and certainly not hostile ones. The first settlers had been wiped out soon after the breach; it was ten years before new settlers arrived, this time with warriors to protect them. Tahnk was among those settlers, appointed by the Na-Set to build the city and make the colony successful. For two years they suffered within the breach, attempting to fight their way out. Only when the Na-Set sent his elite warriors, the Medji, were they able to break out of the tunnel and into the open sky.

Tahnk descended the ramparts then climbed into her waiting chariot. She guided it through the cluttered streets followed by her personal guard. Healers tended the wounded, while priests said words over the dead before ordering the bodies wrapped. She would not insult Menuite people by entombing them in this cursed land. The bodies would be stored in the city crypt until they could be shipped back to Menu-Kash for proper burial.

"Honored One!"

Tahnk turned in the direction from which the call came. Three Medji trotted to her holding their shields and curved swords. She guided her chariot toward them. The warriors dropped to one knee; their heads bowed.

"Speak," she said.

The Medji officer, a bronze-skinned man with triple copper bands circling his bicep raised his head.

"We have captured one of the bird folk," he said. "He seems to be of high rank."

"Take me to him."

The men stood then marched away. Tahnk and her guards followed them back to the city walls then through the gates into the farmland. More Medji gathered a few strides away.

"Make way for the Honored One!" her guards shouted.

The Medji parted, revealing a dozen bird folk warriors squatting, their hands tied behind their backs. One was separated from the others. He wore a crown of feathers on his head; the look on his face defiant. Tahnk reined her horses still. A grin came to her face; she wondered how long it would take to break him.

"Bring him to my compound."

Her guards circled the man, drew their warclubs then beat him into unconsciousness before lifting him from the ground. Tahnk turned her chariot then headed back to the city; her guards and the subdued bird folk leader close behind. Tahnk's anger flared as she traveled back to her compound. This was useless suffering, something beneath her and her people, all for the whim of a Na-Set chasing a myth. But it was not her place to question, only to obey. As a Menuite noble, she possessed her own powers and alliances, but they were no match for the Na-Set. Her family had ruled Menu-Kash for millennia, and there was no clear rival in the fore-seeable future. If this folly was successful, it would only add to their power.

The gates of the compound opened, the entrance flanked by scores of warriors. They knelt in unison as Tahnk An rode through the gate followed by the Medji and her captive. The handlers waited as she arrived at her palace. She stepped from the chariot, absently handing the reins to a boy wearing a red tunic with a shaved head. As she entered the palace she spoke.

"Take him to the breaking room," she said. "I will be there momentarily."

The Medji dragged the man down a corridor that veered left from the main hall. Tahnk continued down the hall, her servants converging on her as she proceeded to the baths. Her attendants opened the doors and Tahnk entered, taking off her clothes as she neared the warm soothing waters of the baths. She descended into the bath, the warm water taking the edge off her anger. The spiced liquid lifted her body and she floated, her face barely breaking the surface. After a few moments of meditation, she washed, ridding herself of the filth of battle. When she emerged from the baths her servants waited with her clothes. She dressed then made her way to the breaking room.

The Medji stationed outside the breaking room bowed then opened the doors as. Tahnk An approached. The Birdman sat on the granite floor, his hands and feet untied. A gold band had been placed around his head. He raised his head as Tahnk An came closer. He grinned then jumped to his feet, charging toward her with balled fists. This was the part she enjoyed the most. She lifted her hand then twisted the gold band encircling her wrist. The man stopped as if he'd ran into a wall, his face twisted with pain as he reached for the gold band crushing his skull. Tahnk twisted the band again and the man screamed as he fell to his knees.

Tahnk An stood beside the writhing man. He managed to reach out and grab her dress; Tahnk removed his hand as if picking lint.

"You didn't think it would be that easy, did you Birdman?" she said. "I have questions. The sooner you answer, the shorter this session will be. I will release you and you'll have the honor of serving me the rest of your life. Or you can be defiant and lose your mind before you die. It's your choice."

Tahnk An stepped away from the man as she twisted the band. The man's writhing subsided until he lay still, a moan slipping through his lips. Tahnk waited for the man to regain some strength before asking her first question.

"What is your name?" she asked.

The prisoner's eyes cracked open.

"Durobe," he said.

Tahnk paced. "So, Durobe, what do your people call themselves?"

"We are Taiku."

Tahnk tilted her head. "Taiku?"

Durobe managed to sit up. "Yes. We are nKu. Tai is our totem."

"Tai? What is this Tai?"

"Tai is our protector, our bond to the spirits."

Tahnk eyes brightened. "Ah, the creatures you ride. They are Tai."

Durobe nodded.

"Tell me, Durobe, are you the only people of this land?"

Durobe shook his head. "There are other nKu. They have their own totems."

"Are these other . . . nKu your allies?"

Durobe's eyes narrowed before he spoke. "No."

Tahnk smiled. This was interesting information. Rivalries were the perfect way to gain allies.

"Who are these others?"

"Water," Durobe said.

"Water? There is a nKu of water?"

Durobe managed to laugh. "No, I need water if you wish me to continue talking."

"You must think this is a friendly chat," Tahnk replied. "I'm still trying to decide whether to kill you or let you live."

"I was dead the moment your warriors captured me," Durobe replied. "I am no fool. You think you will torture me until I tell you what you need to destroy my nKu. That will not happen. You may as well kill me know."

"That can be arranged."

"Or you can let me live, and I can assure you that you will never fight the Taiku again."

Tahnk strolled up to Durobe then clasped her hands behind her back. An opportunity to stop the fighting was interesting, at least for now. She could expand the city beyond its meager boundaries and set about the real reason she and the others had come to this worthless speck.

"I'm listening," she said.

"There are fourteen nKu," he said. "Dumaku, Frasiku, Fisiku, Kibebeku, Kibokoku, Mambaku, Natiku, Paaku, Pundaku, Simbaku, Temboku,

Viraruku, and Taiku. Some we only know through teaching, but others we know very well. We have no allies."

"And what nKu are the enemies of the Taiku?" Tanhk asked.

"The Chuiku," Durobe replied.

Tanhk heard the bitterness in Durobe's voice.

"There marons cross the river and raid our towns. They kill our warriors and steal our goods. It is they who forced us into the mountains. Whenever we venture forth, they return."

"It seems they are great fighters," Tahnk said.

Durobe did not answer.

"Durobe, we did not come here to fight your people," Tanhk said. "We came seeking something that is of great value to our people. When we find it, we will leave."

"What is it you seek?" Durobe asked. His eyes were wide with interest.

"That I cannot say," Tanhk said. "I can tell you that it is something that is probably of little value you. It may probably be dangerous."

"You seek the burning rock," Durobe said.

Tanhk eyes went wide. For once she was intrigued.

"What is this burning rock?"

"It is a blue stone," Durobe said. "It is cool to the touch, yet it sears the skin like fire. An nKu cannot touch it, but a priestess can. They use it to communicate with the Ancestors and to protect us from the Wild Winds."

"Does the burning rock exist in Taikuland?" Tahnk asked.

Durobe shook his head.

"No. It is far beyond our borders."

"Where?"

"I don't know," Durobe said. "That is a question for the elders."

"I can help you, Durobe, if you help me. There will be no more fighting between my people and yours. You see we are great warriors, and what you have witnessed is only a fraction of what we're capable of. If you can lead us to the burning rock, we can make you stronger than any of the others. We can show you how to defeat the Chuiku. Of this you have my promise."

"You make a bold promise," Chuiku said. "How can you claim to tame a beast you have never seen?"

"Take me to your elders," Tanhk said. "I will go as your prisoner. If we agree to become allies, I will cross the river with your warriors. We will see these Chuiku are worthy of our respect."

Durobe grinned. "You certainly will."

THREE

Nandi was happy to spend the night in her bed. Though she enjoyed her time with Baba in the bush, she missed the comforts of home. She filled her stomach with mama's delicious lamb stew, and then sat on the wooden floor of their modest home as mama combed out her hair, removing the debris that accumulated in it during her walk with Baba. She loved them both without limit, and it bothered her that they could not all live together. She knew the reasons, and she respected the customs of her people, but it still annoyed her. Somehow, it didn't seem right.

She woke early before sunrise, nervous about the new day. She had been blooded, which meant this would be the day her life changed. A new person would become her mentor, a person she had admired all her life.

Nandi dressed as quietly as she could then crept for the door.

"Where are you going?"

She turned to see mama sitting on her bed, rubbing her eyes.

"Outside," Nandi replied.

"Why?"

"I wanted to walk through the city one more time before I go," she replied. "I wanted to see it as I am now, because when I return, I will be a different person."

Mama smiled at her as she stood. "The ancestors blessed me with a wise child. Amana will be pleased with you."

Nandi's skin tingled hearing the First Hunter's name. Like the marons, Amana did not reside in the city. She roamed the length and breadth of Chuikuland, enforcing its borders and keeping order among the marons. When the situation warranted, she would meet with the priestesses for advice and guidance. She was the only Chuiku allowed to do so; not even mama ranked high enough to commune with the Sacred Women. One day, if she passed Amana's scrutiny, it would be her duty as well.

"Go do what you must," mama said. "But hurry back. Breakfast will be ready soon."

Nandi nodded then rushed outside. The city was stirring, merchants setting up their carts for the morning business and farmers sauntering down the roads to their fields outside the walls. She could hear the singing of the elderly and the young as they prepared the morning meals, the smell of cooked meats and burning wood wafting in the air. As she followed the farmers the sun crept over the trees, its light rolling over the landscape with the morning mists. It was so beautiful. She would miss it so much.

People waved and called out her name as she ambled through the city. She was the head woman's daughter, so everyone knew her. It took most of the morning to walk the length of the city to its wooded borders. As she returned, she stopped by the market, which was now filled with hawking merchants and haggling customers.

"Nandi! Nandi!"

Nandi smiled. "Hasnaa!"

Hasnaa jogged up to Nandi and they hugged. She was a head shorter than Nandi, a stout girl with glittering light brown eyes and a dimpled smile. Nandi and Hasnaa had been friends for as long as she could remember; they were known as birth sisters, since they were born on the same day. Nandi had other birth sisters, but Hasnaa was the only one who she considered true.

"I heard the news," Hasnaa said. "Is it really true?"

"Yes," Nandi replied. "I go to live with the First Hunter."

"Are you afraid? I would be," Hasnaa said.

Nandi's smile faded. "A little. But I'm excited, too. It is an honor to be chosen."

"An honor for you. I would probably run away and hide in the bush like a rabbit."

The girls laughed, throwing their arms over each other's shoulders as they walked in step through the market. Hasnaa always pretended to be afraid of everything, but she was the bravest person Nandi knew. It was she who brought Nandi out of her shy ways when she was younger, and it was she who always got Nandi in all sorts of trouble. Nandi loved her for it.

Hasnaa stopped then gasped.

"Look! Do you see what I see?"

Nandi scanned the market. "See what? I don't . . ."

She grinned as she spotted the object of Hasnaa's attention

"Botberries!" Hasnaa exclaimed.

She let go of Nandi then ran to the cart. Nandi sauntered after her, laughing all the way.

Hasnaa loved botberries. She would eat them until they made her sick. Mama Tambika greeted the girls with a smile.

"Hasnaa, Nandi. What brings you to my cart?" she said in mock curiosity.

Hasnaa stepped forward, her eyes locked on the fat, ripe botberries.

"Mama Tambika, I would . . ."

"How many?" Mama Tambika asked.

"Three bunches!" Hasnaa replied.

"Three?" Mama Hasnaa frowned. "That will make you sick."

"There not all for me," Hasnaa said. "One bunch is a going away present for Nandi!"

Tambika cut her eyes at Nandi. "I hear you meet First Hunter soon."

Nandi smiled. "Yes. I can't wait!"

Tambika's expression became serious. "Why?"

"Because it is an honor to be chosen a First Hunter, that's why," Hasnaa replied.

"I'm not talking to you," Tambika said, never taking her eyes off Nandi. "Why are you happy to be chosen First Hunter?"

"Because like Hasnaa said, it is an honor," Nandi replied.

"Just because you are chosen does not mean you will become First Hunter," Tambika said. "The path is arduous, and can be fatal."

Nandi felt a chill. She had never considered that she could fail, or even more that she could die during her time with the First Hunter.

"You shouldn't talk about something you know nothing about," Hasnaa said to Tambika.

"And you should not sass your elders, girl," Tambika shot back. "Your mama will hear of this."

"It won't be the first time," Hasnaa said. "Come, First Hunter. Let's go somewhere nice and eat our berries."

Nandi felt Hasnaa grip her arm then pull her away from Tambika's cart. She walked backwards for a moment before turning to walk with her friend.

"Stupid sow!" Hasnaa said.

Hasnaa's insult snapped Nandi from her mood. She managed a giggle.

"You shouldn't insult an elder. She already promised to tell your mama about your smart mouth."

Hasnaa popped a botberry into her mouth. "It won't be the first beating I've received, nor the last I suspect. Some elders don't deserve respect."

Hasnaa broke off a bundle of berries and gave them to Nandi. Nandi picked a berry, rolling it between her fingers before eating it.

"She had no right talking to you as if you will fail," Hasnaa said. "She doesn't know you like I do."

Doubt came to Nandi as she ate her berry.

"But what if I do?"

Hasnaa made a rude sound with her mouth. "What if the sun does not shine again? What if water stops being wet? That will never happen, and you will never fail."

Nandi hugged Hasnaa then kissed her cheek.

"Hey!" Hasnaa shouted. "You almost made me drop my berries!"

They walked to the central courtyard of the city, sitting on a stone bench near the main well and finished their berries. Hasnaa rambled on and on about silly and serious things while Nandi listened and took in all the sights. The hours passed like minutes; dusk had come and it was time for her to go home and prepare. She stood, dusting off her skirt.

"I must go," she said.

Hasnaa looked at her, her eyes glistening. They hugged each other tight.

"Don't forget me, sister!" Hasnaa said.

"I won't be gone that long," Nandi replied.

Hasnaa squeezed her tighter. "I love you."

"I love you, too."

Nandi turned and walked away quickly. She didn't want Hasnaa to see her crying. By the time she reached home the tears had ceased and her face was dry, until she saw mama at the door. She ran to her and hugged her.

"I should have spent the day with you," she whispered.

Mama patted her head.

"You did the right thing. It's good to see the city. You'll remember what you are training to protect. Come, we must go. The others are waiting."

Nandi started for her room to gather her things but mama stopped her.

"No. You can bring nothing. Everything you need will be provided by Chui."

Nandi opened her mouth to protest but was silenced by mama's serious stare. Nandi's confidence drained as the reality of what she was about to do settled in. She followed mama through the city, the crowd gathering around them as they neared the central courtyard. The other elders waited for them dressed in ceremonial attire, long ivory robes resembling chui skin. The robes brushed their sandaled feet. Drummers flanked them, there calloused hands beating a steady solemn rhythm on the djembes.

"Go and show your respect," mama said.

Nandi approached the ring. She bowed before each elder and they touched her head. Once she was done, she returned to her mother. The drummers marched before them, leading them to the city gates. As they passed through the gates, Nandi's fear took hold. Her steps came haltingly; mama looked at her with worried eyes. Her mood was broken by the shrill shout of Hasnaa.

"Make us proud, Nandi!"

A cheer broke out among the onlookers and their energy swept the procession. The drummers pace quickened. They marched down the main road into the forest. After a time, they veered onto an unfamiliar path, following until it ended at a small clearing. A pedestal holding a torch sat in the center of the clearing; the drummers led them to it then ceased playing.

"Sit," mama said.

Nandi sat near the pedestal. Mama lit the torch then stepped away. She knelt next to Nandi, hugging her tight and kissing her.

"You will wait for the First Hunter," she said. "You are safe as long as you stay in the clearing."

"When will she come?" Nandi asked.

"When she is ready," mama replied. "Goodbye daughter. I love you."

"I love you too, mama!"

Nandi watched her escort leave the clearing. For a time, she could hear the drumming, but as darkness settled into the forest the sound faded, leaving the voice of the forest. Loneliness and fear slowly took hold of her the more time passed and dimness increased. The dark became so heavy she could no longer see the perimeter of the clearing.

"Where are you, First Hunter?" she whispered. "I am ready."

The night continued and First Hunter did not appear. Nandi's stomach growled from hunger. She had neglected to eat a good meal before leaving the city; the only thing she'd eaten was Hasnaa's botberries. She hoped the First Hunter had provisions with her, for Nandi had none. The fact that mama did not band anything for her meant that was how it was supposed to be.

More time passed and the First Hunter had not come. A worrying thought came to Nandi. What if something had happened to her? What if the First Hunter was dead? Would mama and the others return to retrieve her? Or would she be left alone in the woods? A part of that fear she pushed aside. Baba would find her. The marons constantly roamed the forests and a group would eventually come this way. Though encounters between marons could be violent, none would harm a woman from the village.

Nandi's musing was broken by the rustling of the bush before her. She stood on her feet, excitement pushing aside all her fears. The moment had finally come. The First Hunter had arrived. She expected the woman to step into the clearing; instead she found herself staring into the eyes of the largest chui she'd ever seen. Nandi stiffened as the spotted feline sauntered to her. Was this the First Hunter, or was this a chui coming to claim her as a meal?

"Why do you fear?" a female voice coming from behind her asked. "Is not the chui your totem? Is it not our protector?"

Nandi started to turn around.

"No!" the woman ordered. "Do not move. You are being judged. Look into the chui's eyes. Do not look away!"

Nandi stared at the chui as it edged closer and closer. When it reached her, it stood on its hind

legs, dropping its paws on her shoulders. Its breath
was wet and warm against her face as it sniffed. The
chui's touch darted from its mouth to brush her
cheek, rough against her skin. Then the chui fell
back to all fours, let out a low growl then sauntered
away, disappearing into the bush.

"You can turn around now," the woman said.

Nandi turned to look into the black eyes of
the First Hunter. She immediately prostrated before her.

"First Hunter!" she said. "I am honored to be
chosen by you . . . and the chui."

"Get up," the First Hunter said. "We must go.
You have one more test to pass."

"What is that?" Nandi asked.

"I will tell you when the time comes," the
First Hunter said. "Come. Your training begins
now."

The First Hunter walked away toward the
clearing's edge. Nandi followed, her hunger and
fear gone. Together they disappeared into the bush.

FOUR

Ahmo Se and his warriors trudged up the narrow road behind the birdman traitor. He stayed close to the solid rock wall on his right, afraid to get near the edge of the road. A few strides to his left the path ended abruptly in a sheer drop that disappeared into a thicket of clouds. He clutched the finely carved baton in his right hand more from fear than authority, praying that the gods of his homeland would protect him on this last part of their perilous journey.

Three months ago, Tahnk An chose him to subdue the bird folk, or Taiku as the called themselves. She gave to him the royal baton, a symbol of her authority which bestowed on him the right to represent her and the interest of Menu-Kash when dealing with the savages and their leaders. The baton also contained a tremendous amount of ashé, fueled by a nugget of kipande in its center. The symbolic weapon had more than proven itself early on when they were attacked by the bird-riding warriors. The kipande set the creatures ablaze, sending the fowl and their riders to a fiery death. After the first month the birdmen ceased their aerial attacks, preferring to fight on the ground rather than lose any more of their totems. The birdman foot soldiers were no match for the Kashite ranks, though Ahmo Se admired them for their ferocity and bravery.

The birdman raised his hand and the army halted.

"What is this?" Ahmo Se said to himself. He marched to the head of the column.

"Durobe, why are we stopping?" he said.

The birdman turned to him; his eyes despondent.

"I must rest," he answered. "It has been laborious climb."

"Liar," Ahmo Se retorted. "This is your homeland. You've walked these trails all your life."

"I can go no further," he said.

Ahmo Se pulled his sword free. "March forward now, or die here!"

A weak smile came to the birdman's face.

"I am already dead. And so are you."

The birdman ran to the edge of the road then jumped. Ahmo looked where the man had been, stunned by his actions. Durobe's last words echoed in his mind.

I am already dead and so are you.

"Run!" he shouted.

Ahmo began running just as rumbling shook the ground beneath his feet. He looked up to see boulders raining down the steep slopes. His warriors responded immediately to his command. They pressed against the stone wall, but it was too late for many. The rocks crashed into their ranks, smashing some and knocking others off the road and over the edge into oblivion. As the deluge ended the sound of chanting rose before them.

"Shields forward!" Ahmo shouted.

The warriors behind him worked around him then formed a shield barrier. Ahmo peered between the shields and saw an ominous sight. The birdman warriors advanced toward them, rolling a large boulder. They would push the Kashites from the road, killing those that managed to avoid the rock. Ahmo looked at the baton. He didn't know if what it possessed was strong enough, but he had no choice but to try.

"Step away," he ordered.

One of the warriors looked at him in concern.

"Commander, is this wise?"

"Step away!" he shouted.

The warriors opened the shield wall. Ahmo Se stepped forward, pointing the baton at the boulder. He squeezed the center as he was trained and a blue beam of light emerged. It struck the boulder, but to Ahmo's dismay it did not shatter it. Ahmo's hand shifted and the boulder moved with it. He grinned; he couldn't destroy the boulder but he could control it. He pulled his hand back then punched forward. The boulder smashed into the men pushing it, crushing them under its weight. He lifted the baton and the boulder lifted as well, exposing the fearful faces of the birdmen. Ahmo proceeded to wield the boulder like a club, smashing it down on his enemies as they fled in panic.

Ahmo dropped the boulder off the edge. He walked to the edge of the road, looking behind to the rest of his army. Those who had survived the boulder onslaught had reassembled. Such was the discipline of the Kashite army. He returned to the lead.

"Shields up!" he shouted.

Kashite shields clashing together echoed through the mountains."

"Forward!"

The Kashites advanced behind the protection of Ahmo Se. They met no resistance; no more boulders fell from above. The steep road gradually leveled off, an indication that they had reached the summit of the mountain. The mists broke before them, revealing a large stone city carved into the peaks. Before the city the bird man army waited. A lone man stood before them, dressed in a uniform of armor and feathers and wearing a helmet the resembled the head of their beloved bird of prey. Ahmo Se smiled. This was it, the final confrontation between the birdmen and Menu-Kash. They had chosen to make a stand on this mountain, led by this shaman. So be it.

Kashite warriors hurried to get in battle formation as the birdmen advanced. Ahmo Se stood ready, baton in his left hand, sword in his right. The birdmen did not expand their line to match the Kashites; they charged forward in a tight rank. They hoped to break the center and sent the Kashites running in panic. At least that is what Ahmo Se surmised. That would not happen.

The shaman let out a piercing scream then jumped into the air; his arms spread wide as if in flight. Ahmo Se was about to laugh until he saw the man expand and transform into the largest tai he'd seen since landing on the island. The Kashites gasped, some of the warriors stepping away. Ahmo Se was speechless for a moment, until he felt the baton in his hand.

"Keep formation!" he shouted.

This was the person the birdmen kept calling for, their 'First Hunter.' They had waited until the final moment in hopes that his ashé would finally crush the Kashites. Ahmo Se could not deny the fear running through him, but he would fight with his all and his baton. He raised the weapon and squeezed, releasing a blue beam at the tai. It veered away, the beam missing then striking one of the building behind them. The building exploded, its remains tumbling onto the hapless people in the city. The tai circled and attacked again. Ahmo So continued unleashing the energy, but the tai dodged each beam. Before he realized it, the giant bird was upon him and his warriors. Talons sharper than swords grazed his back as he dove, tearing his armor and chain mail like paper. The Kashite center broke and the birdman warriors poured through. The Kashite warriors responded immediately, shifting their formations so not to be outflanked. Ahmo Se scrambled to his feet to see the tai ravaging the rear of his warriors. Before he could aid them, the birdmen were upon them, spewing insults and swinging steel. Ahmo Se wielded his shotel in one hand, while keeping the baton in his other, waiting for a moment to use it against the Taiku First Hunter. His warriors attempted to keep formation, but the ravaging of the Tai on their ranks diminished their discipline. But these were well trained warriors, veterans of the constant wars between Menu-Kash and Haiset. They would not break; they would hold formation until the last warrior.

"High Guard! To me!" Ahmo shouted.

The High Guard, elite warriors of the Kashites, converged around Ahmo, giving him the respite he needed. He sheathed his shotel then pointed the baton at the tai. As he squeezed the center the tai looked in his direction. It moved quickly, but not quickly enough. The blue bolt struck one its

wings. It burst into blue flame and the tai tumbled
from the sky.

"Follow me!" Ahmo shouted. He sprinted to
where the First Hunter fell, the High Guard close
behind. A wall of birdman warriors formed around
the wounded Hunter. They were determined to protect him, but Ahmo was more determined to kill
him. He raised the baton and sent a bolt into the
warriors. The bolt struck them and exploded, sending birdman bodies flying in every direction. The
First Hunter knelt alone, holding his left shoulder
with his right hand, glaring at Ahmo and the High
Guard as they advanced on him. Birdman warriors
attempted to reach him, but the Kashite warriors
responded sooner, forming a shield barrier between
their fallen Hunter and them. Ahmo shoved the baton into his belt and unsheathed his shotel. He
stopped face to face with the warrior.

"Let them through," he shouted.

The Kashite warriors stepped aside. The
birdmen ignored them as they rushed to save their
Hunter. Ahmo waited until they were all in view
then with a quick stroke, cut off the Hunter's head.
The birdmen warriors paused, watching the Hunter
fall headless to the ground. Kashite warriors surrounded them, waiting for the signal to attack. The
birdmen fell to their knees, dropping their weapons.

"Take their arms," Ahmo ordered. "This war
is over."

* * *

By nightfall the battle scene had been
cleared. The bird folk had claimed their dead and
mourning fires burned throughout the city. The
Kashites established their camp outside the city

walls, not yet trusting the capitulation. A palisade served as a protective perimeter for the camp and guards were placed at close intervals, each within sight of each other. Ahmo Se's tent was set up in the center of the camp. He sat alone before a pedestal on which a fire blazed. Ahmo took a pouch from his war chest. He opened the pouch then sprinkled the contents into the fire. A thick smoke rose from the flames filling the tent. To Ahmo's surprise the smoke did not choke him; instead it filled him with a sense of calm. Light sparked within the smoke, bright flashes that coalesced into the image of the inside of Tahnk An's meeting room. Tahnk An stepped into view, draped in her night gown, a satisfied smile on her face.

"You have defeated them," she said.

Ahmo dropped to his knees, averting his eyes from Tahnk's image.

"Yes, Suti," he replied.

"Congratulations for your success. There will be a feast in your honor when you return. Have the elders come to you yet?"

"No, Suti. I have allowed them to bury their dead and given them a day of mourning."

"Excellent," Tahnk An replied. "You have good instincts. I want their First Hunter."

Ahmo hesitated before responding.

"What is it, Ahmo?" Tahnk An asked.

"I regret to inform you that their First Hunter is dead."

"I gave you instructions to capture the First Hunter. Was I not clear?"

Ahmo cleared his throat. "You were very clear, suti. However, their First Hunter was everything they claimed it to be. There was no way we could have defeated them without killing it."

"And what made it so powerful? From what we have gathered they are not fully aware of the power of kipande."

"I do not know what power they possess, but the person known as the First Hunter had the ability to transform into their totem."

"You lie," Tahnk Ah replied. "That is impossible."

"It is true, suti," Ahmo replied. "My warriors can attest to it. I was forced to use the baton against him."

"Fascinating," Tahnk An said. "I want the body. Wrap it well then bring it with you on your return."

"That won't be possible," Ahmo said. "We gave him to his people. They burned him this night."

"That's disappointing," Tahnk said. "But at least now we know these stories are true. We will have to be more careful when we confront the others."

Ahmo looked up, puzzled. "Others, Suti?"

"Yes, others," Tahnk An replied. "The Taiku are the first. There are other clans among these people. They are sure to hear of the Taiku defeat. We must plan to move against them quickly before they get the notion to unite against us. We would defeat them of course, but there is no need to allow them to make our victory more arduous than it needs to be."

"Will I have the honor to lead our armies against them?" Ahmo asked.

Tahnk An smiled. "We will see. For now, you must secure the Taiku. Offer them generous terms. We will need them to help us against the others."

"By your authority," Ahmo replied.

"Rest well, my warrior. You have long days ahead."

"Thank you, Suti."

The smoke slowly dissipated, Tahnk An's image with it. Ahmo was alone, a grin on his face. He would receive great honor when he returned to Menu-Kash, celebrated for defeating the inhabitants of this island and claiming the kipande hidden in its forests. A thought came to mind but he pushed it away. Ambition could be a dangerous thing, especially in the beginning. He would get his rest as the suti suggested. Tomorrow he would think on his idea again.

The morning was cold atop of the mountain. Ahmo woke shivering, his fire having expired during the night. He stirred from his bed to fetch wood and was greeted at his tent entrance by a warrior with an armful.

"For you, commander," the warrior said. "May I start your fire?"

Ahmo grinned. "Yes."

The warrior set about his duties as Ahmo dressed. By the time he finished a fire blazed in his tent. He was tempted to stay, but duty awaited.

"Thank you, warrior," he said.

"It is my honor, commander," the man said.

"What is your name?"

"Donk Or."

"Accompany me to the meeting," Ahmo said.

Donk Or's eyes widened.

"Me, sir?"

"Yes, you. I may need more assistance."

Donk Or smiled. "I'm honored, sir."

"Don't be so hasty," Ahmo said. "I can be quite demanding."

Ahmo left his tent, Donk Or close behind
him. His officers waited at their tents, a few of them
looking at the warrior with curious eyes. Ahmo ignored them, placing his attention on his second in
command, Heme Da.

"Heme," he said.

"Good morning, commander," Heme replied.

"Has the message been sent?"

"Yes commander. The Elders will meet us
outside the city gates."

"Are we ready?"

"Yes, we are, although I have a question."

"Ask," Ahmo said.

"Sir, these are a defeated people. I don't understand why we are meeting with them as if they
have won."

"The Suti has instructed me to handle the
Taiku gently," Ahmo replied. "We are to make them
allies."

"Why?" Heme asked.

"This war is most likely the first of many,"
Ahmo replied. "Across the river are many more
clans that we have no knowledge of. The Taiku do.
So, we will make them our friends and side with
them against their enemies. They will not know the
freedom of our own, but they will be treated better
than their own kind. By doing so, we insure the sub-
jugation of them all."

Heme smiled. "It is a good plan, commander."

"Our Suti is wise," Ahmo replied. "Now let's
meet our new friends."

Ahmo marched to the city gates, his commanders close behind. As they neared the gate
opened and the Taiku leaders streamed out. A
group of the birdmen carried a rectangular table

which they set a few strides from the city gates. Ahmo looked at the city ramparts; there were no warriors upon them. Still, he took precautions. His delegation halted outside of bow range. It took a moment for the birdman to realized why; their servants lifted the table then carried to the waiting Kashites. Ahmo observed the faces of the elders as they approached the table and sat. A myriad of emotions met his gaze; anger, resignation, hope, despair. He'd seen them all before in the faces of the people he had defeated in battle, except for the Haisetti. The farmer/warriors were a constant knife in the ribs of Menu-Kash, turning back their armies every war season. But that was a matter for another time.

Both parties sat, all except Ahmo. One of the Taiku elders returned to her feet to gaze at him defiantly.

"Thank you for agreeing to meet with us," Ahmo said in perfect Tai. The Elders seemed surprised that he knew their language. If Ahmo was anything else, he was always thorough.

"I am Ahmo Se, commander of the Kashites and representative of our most high suti, Tahnk An. Today is a sad day," he continued.

"Sad for whom?" the woman replied.

"I would like to know your name, if it is appropriate," Ahmo asked.

"Tet," the woman replied. "Eldest of the Old. What you have done cannot be forgiven."

Ahmo bowed his head. "I am not asking for your forgiveness. We understand that you are angry, as you have a right to be. You did not ask for us to be here. But we stand here because of actions from both our people. The blame must be shared."

"Why?" Tet shot back. "As you say yourself, we did not ask you to come here. You have violated our land, our sovereignty. There is no blame on our part, nor will we accept it. You have defeated us . . . for now."

"Do not take our kindness for weakness," Ahmo replied. "We meet with you because we do not want more bloodshed. Your First Hunter is dead. To continue to fight us would be fruitless."

The Tai elders shifted uncomfortable as Tet looked away. The death of the Hunter was a grievous loss for them. Ahmo suspected that they were strong enough to continue to fight for months, years even, but the superstitions tied to the single warrior broke their spirit.

"Again, why are we here?" Tet finally said.

"We are not interested in ruling your people," Ahmo said. "We wish merely to share in the bounty of your land. Our people will not venture beyond our city, except for in trade and by your permission. The cliffs are your home and so they shall remain. In return your warriors will no longer attack out towns and raid our homes. Our terms are simple."

"We do not want you here," Tet said.

"Yet here we are," Ahmo replied. "As I said, we do not seek to rule you. We see you as allies. Together we can strike against your true enemies, the nKus across the river."

Tet's eyebrows rose and Ahmo held back a grin. The other elders responded as well. The hate they bore for the Kashites dimmed compared to the enemies they knew.

"We will consider your offer," Tet said.

"This is not up for consideration," Ahmo said. "These are the only terms you will receive. If you refuse, the war will continue and you know what the outcome will be. Accept my terms today and we can both go back to our people and speak of peace. Refuse them, and the blood is on your hands."

Shock registered in Tet's eyes. She turned to the elders and they reflected the same emotion. When she turned to face Ahmo that emotion had turned to anger.

"As I said, we will consider your offer."

She spun about and stomped away; the other elders close behind. The servants picked up the table then scurried to catch up.

Ahmo clasped his hands behind his back as he watched them leave. The last part of his message was stern, but necessary. Heme stood beside him.

"Was that wise, commander?" he asked.

"I needed to know if they had any fight left in them," Ahmo said. "If so, we will settle things now. I have no wish to march back and have an uprising on my hands."

"Do you think they will fight?"

"I don't know," Ahmo admitted. "We will form ranks and advance to this spot. A show of force might calm them down."

Ahmo patted Heme's shoulder.

"If you need me, I'll be in my tent," he said.

"Yes, commander."

He turned to Donk Or.

"Fetch me breakfast," he said.

Donk bowed.

"Yes, commander."

The young warrior scampered away. As he ran to the commissary tent Ahmo spoke to Heme.

"What do you know of him?"

Heme frowned. "Nothing. A warrior from a minor family, I believe."

"Why would he come here?"

Heme shrugged. "Seeking honor in battle like the rest of us. Since the peace with Haiset such opportunity is hard to come by."

"The rewards may be better here as well," Ahmo replied. "And you're less likely to get a Haiset arrow in your eye."

The two laughed. 'Arrow blindness' was so common among Kashite warriors that Kashite merchants made a small fortune selling decorative eye patches. Both had avoided the dubious honor, at least for now.

Ahmo's breakfast was waiting when he entered his tent. Thankfully Donk Or was gone; Ahmo preferred to eat alone. As he ate, he thought of home. He took on the assignment with the promise of higher rank once he returned to Menu-Kash. So far, the Suti had fulfilled all her promises. He was commanding an army which was about to claim its first victory. If he could lead it across the river and defeat the remaining clans, his ascension to Elder would be assured. There would be no more fighting, just a life of contemplation, discussion and debauchery.

He was finishing his juice when his tent flap opened. Donk Or entered with a wide smile on his face.

"Commander, the birdmen elders have returned.

Ahmo wiped his mouth, grabbed his sword then followed Donk Or back to the meeting place. His other commanders were there, watching the Taiku elders approach. This time they came without their table. Tet walked up and stood before Ahmo.

"It is with a heavy heart that we accept your terms," she said. "We trust that you will honor them. If you do not, our vengeance will be swift."

Ahmo's commanders rustled at the threat, but he remained stoic. Instead he bowed to Tet then extended his hand. The elder took it cautiously. Ahmo pulled her into a hug.

"You have made a wise decision," he said.

He let the Elder go, savoring the shocked look on her face.

"Take care of your families," Ahmo said. "Mourn your dead and honor your warriors."

Tet still seemed skeptical.

"What will you do now? Occupy our city?"

"No," Ahmo replied. "My army will go back to our city. This is Taikuland. We will only return upon your permission . . . or your transgression."

Ahmo bowed deeply then walked away, his commanders following. Heme hurried to his side.

"We're leaving? Really?" he asked.

"Yes," Ahmo replied. "There is nothing left to do here."

"We can't give up ground, commander. If they decide to break their oath, we will have to fight all over again. This is not wise."

"Spare me your wisdom," Ahmo said. "The birdmen might break their oath, but they will not attack us. They were just a test. The real prize lies beyond the river. That is where the prize we seek is found."

"So, we will abandon all that we conquered?"

Ahmo grinned. "Of course not. The birdmen can have the highlands. We will establish a city at the base of the mountains. That way we will control all the resources that flow in and out of the hills. If they resist, we will starve them."

"What about the birds?"

Ahmo lifted his baton. "We have a weapon for them."

He patted Heme's back.

"Do not worry, my friend. This war is over. That, I can assure you."

FIVE

Nandi held her breath as the antelope walked below her. It stopped, looking side to side as if it sensed her presence. She watched, waiting for the right moment. After a few more minutes the beast relaxed. It lowered its head and grazed on the grass at the base of the tree in which Nandi perched. Nandi shifted as quiet as she could on the thick branch, making sure there were no obstacles between her and the antelope. She let go of the branch and fell toward the beast. Just as she thought she would claim her prey the antelope bolted. Nandi reached out, grabbing it by its long neck, her momentum helping her drag it to the ground. She locked her arms around its throat and her legs around its torso, careful to avoid its thrashing head. The creature stood and ran, Nandi clinging on as it dashed between trees. She bit the antelope's neck, cutting the main artery to its brain. The antelope bucked, throwing Nandi free. She crashed into a nearby tree, the impact stunning her. She lay still for a moment, letting the pain subside before standing. The antelope was gone.

Nandi looked about then finally found the spoor of the wounded beast. She searched about and found more fresh blood, giving her a sense of direction. She trotted through the brush, following the blood until she heard thrashing up ahead. Nandi ran to claim her prize. What she found instead halted her in her tracks.

The antelope lay dead before her. Standing over it was a black chui, the largest she'd ever seen. The cat glared at Nandi, its nostrils flaring as a growl escaped its mouth. Nandi crouched, releasing a similar sound from her throat. She would not claim this meal. The chui was too large and she had no weapons. Her display was to keep the feline from attacking her. She backed away until the chui focused its attention on its stolen meal. Nandi did not turn away until she was sure she was no longer the target. Fear became disappointment; she would go hungry tonight.

First Hunter Amana met her at the tree.

"You missed," she said.

"And now I'll go hungry," Nandi replied.

"Not tonight," Amana answered. "I did not miss."

Nandi's eyes widened. For weeks the rule had been if she did not kill, she did not eat.

"You are sharing?"

Amana turned and walked away. Nandi hurried to her side.

"You faced down the black chui," Amana said. "I thought it was the last time I would see you alive. You would not have been the first."

A chill ran through Nandi. She did not realize how dangerous that encounter had been.

"Your strength made it hesitate. That she allowed you to live means that she respects your territory. You will not see her again."

"Have you faced her?" Nandi asked.

"Yes," Amana replied. "It was not pleasant."

"She did not kill you."

Amana's expression became dour. "She almost did."

Nandi followed Amana to their camp. Her mentor had managed to find and kill her own antelope. The beast sprawled under the canopy. Amana gave her another surprise; a knife. Nandi's eyes widened like a child receiving a new toy.

"I passed!" she squealed.

Amana did well to hide her grin.

"Not quite," she said. You still must meet the priestesses."

Nandi and Amana dragged the antelope to a nearby low hanging branch. They set about butchering the beast. Blood covered Nandi's hands, but she was used to it. For the past three months she'd killed every animal she's eaten by hand, guided by Amana's instructions. In order to prepare for the chui's spirit, a First Hunter must live as one, Amana told her. It was the only way to earn chui's respect. In the beginning Nandi thought she was going to starve to death. She could never imagine being as stealthy and ferocious as her totem, but desperation and necessity were excellent teachers. Gradually she learned, finding herself eating most often than not, and becoming more agile than she thought possible.

Another surprise was revealed that day; Amana allowed her to build a fire. Not only would they have properly butchered meat, it would also be cooked. Together with fresh herbs and edible plants it was the best meal Nandi had since leaving the city. The greasy grin on her face said as much as she laid back against the ironwood tree, her stomach full.

"Was this my celebration meal?" she asked Amana.

The First Hunter sat beside her.

"Yes," she said. "We will smoke the remaining meat and gather more herbs and vegetables. Tomorrow we set out for the Mountain."

Nandi sat up.

"We go to see the priestesses?"

Amana nodded. "I have taught you all that I can. You have survived all your tests. All that stands between you and First Hunter is the priestesses' approval . . . and my death."

Nandi's joy was dashed by Amana's last words. The First Hunter had become like an aunt to her. To imagine her dead was appalling.

"Then I never wish to be First Hunter," Nandi stated.

"Don't be foolish," Amana replied. "Death comes to us all. It is the one hunter we can never defeat. Whether through battle or time I will join the ancestors. When that time comes, you will replace me. You know this. It is why you were chosen."

Nandi drew her legs up against her chest then wrapped her arms around them.

"I know this is true," she said. "I am not a child. Still, it is a reality I wish not to think about."

"Being a First Hunter means you must think about everything," Amana said. "The safety and existence of our people depends on it. You must enforce our boundaries. You will be responsible for our marons. You will lead us in times of war and you will administer the peace. To carry such responsibility means to think on things that most avoid."

Nandi was quiet. All her life she dreamed of being a First Hunter as did most Chuiku girls. She imagined herself roaming the forests free of responsibility, fighting the other First Hunters and honoring her people in victory. She never imagined the responsibilities that came with the position. Had she known, she may have had second thoughts. But she was here now, her training almost complete. She would not stop. She would never dishonor mama and baba.

It was as if Amana read her mind.

"It is not too late for you to go back to Mahalapi," she said. "It would not be the first time."

"No," Nandi answered. "I will be First Hunter if the priestesses decree it so. I will follow you, and when the ancestors call you to sit among them, I will protect our people as you have taught me."

Amana hugged her.

"I was hoping you would say that," she said. "In my entire life I have never met anyone more qualified to be First Hunter. I have trained many potential girls, but none of them have performed as well as you, not even myself."

"Do you think the priestesses will accept me?" Nandi asked.

"They would be foolish not to," Amana answered."

Nandi and Amana finished their meal. They cut up the rest of the animal then built a smoker to preserve the meat for the journey ahead. Nandi tingled with excitement. She was meeting the priestesses! Sleep was difficult; she kept trying to imagine what they looked like, how they would sound, what they would say. She fell asleep only to be awakened in what seemed to her moments later. Amana stood over her, a smile on her face.

"It is time," she said. "We must go."

Nandi jumped to her feet, eager for the journey. They banded their belongings then set out for
the Mountain. The trek took two weeks, during
which Amana continued to hone Nandi's skills.
They hunted, sparred and talked of the many secrets of the forest. Twice they encountered bands of
marons on their walkabouts, both bands showing
Amana the proper respect and deference. The first
encounter was brief; the warriors crossed a tembo
path Amana and Nandi followed. They nodded as
they passed, their eyes lingering on Nandi. The second encounter was much more involved.

It was dusk, the sun teasing the tops of the
trees before descending into the horizon. Amana
and Nandi had ended their walk for the day beside a
small pond surrounded by grasses and date trees, a
rare respite in the usually dense woods. Amana
heard the marons first; she lifted her head from
building the fire and looked into woods. Nandi
heard them moments later. The marons emerged
from the woods. There were six of them, and they
were in terrible shape. Each of them displayed fresh
wounds from recent battle, one wounded so badly
the others had to carry him. But there was one
maron that caught Nandi's eye. He walked behind
the others, a grim expression on his face. He bore
the chui marks on his shoulders and thighs like the
others with five black beaded necklaces around his
neck, acknowledging his kills. In that respect he was
no different than any other maron she'd encountered, except he looked to be no older than Nandi.
He was the youngest maron she'd encountered. He
looked up and their eyes met. A smirk came to his
lips; Nandi found herself smiling back before she
realized it.

"Marons, what is your trouble?" Amana asked, breaking Nandi's attention.

The eldest of the marons approached Amana. She extended her hand and he took it, bowing his head to kiss it. He honored Nandi with a slight nod. The others did the same, even the badly wounded maron. The young maron was the last to honor her. Unlike the others, he took Nandi's hand and kissed it as well.

"To the future Hunter," he said.

Nandi felt a warm rush as she nodded, fighting to keep a grin off her face.

"Set him down," Amana said, pointing at the wounded maron.

The marons set the man down and Amana examined him.

"These are Temboku wounds," Amana said. "They are far from their nKu."

"We said the same," the elder maron said. "We have fought other nKu warriors as well. This is not normal."

"Something is forcing them this way," Amana said as she opened her herb bag. "Nandi, help me."

Nandi took her eyes from the young maron and assisted Amana with preparing healing herbs for the wounded warrior. The other marons sat silent as they applied poultices to the man's wounds and gave him a purging tea to drink. The man took the gourd then nodded his head to Amana and Nandi.

"Thank you, First Hunter," he said. "We are lucky to have encountered you."

"Yes, you are," Amana replied with a smile. She patted the maron on his shoulder before standing.

"I will go to Tembokuland," she said.

The marons stood, ready to follow. Amana shook her head.

"No, you will not follow me. You are tired and wounded. I will find another band to come with me."

Disappointment showed on the marons faces. The elder maron nodded solemnly.

"We defer to your wisdom, although there is no band more formidable than ours."

Nandi shook with excitement as she gathered her items and began banding. She was going on the hunt with Amana!

"No, Nandi," Amana said. "You will not come with me."

Nandi was stunned. Her mouth fell open.

"But . . .but I am your protégé!"

Amana approached her then placed her hands on her shoulders.

"Yes, you are. But this is a dangerous journey. I cannot risk you. The day will come that we will fight together, but not now. I need you to stay with the marons until I return. They will honor you and protect you with their lives until I return."

"But Amana . . ."

Amana brought her finger to her lips, shushing Nandi.

"This is not a debate. You will stay. This will also give you time to bond with this band. Akida's words are true; this is a good band, almost as good as your baba's."

Nandi could say nothing more. The First Hunter had made her decision. Nandi watched her as she strode for the forest's edge.

"If I am not back in seven days gather the bands and come for me. Until I return you will treat

Nandi as you would treat me. If I hear otherwise I will kill you all."

Amana disappeared into the bush. Nandi's throat went dry as the marons turned their attention to her. Once again, her eyes drifted toward the young maron.

Akida knelt before her

"What do you wish, First Hunter?"

Akida's words caught her off guard. They were actually respecting her as First Hunter!

"Rest and heal as Amana . . . the First Hunter suggested. "That is all for the moment."

"Yes, First Hunter," he said. The marons placed down their weapons and sprawled out among the grasses. The young maron approached her. Nandi held her breath as he bowed.

"First Hunter, I am Etana," he said. "I would be honored if you would allow me to sit by you."

"Do what you wish," Nandi replied.

Etana bowed again. "Thank you, First Hunter."

Etana put down his weapons and gear then sat near Nandi. There was something comforting about him being so close; maybe it was that he looked to be close to her age. Most boys were taken into the bush and initiated by the time they reached Etana's age.

"Are you hungry?" he asked.

"No, but if I do get hungry, I can feed myself," Nandi answered. "You are not my servant."

"I'm sorry if I offended you," Etana said. "I will sit with the others."

"No," Nandi said. She cursed herself. She sounded too eager for him to stay.

"No, you did not offend me," she said. "As far as whether you stay or go, that is up to you."

Etana smiled, something she rarely saw a
maron do, even her baba. She couldn't help but
smile back.

"I have seen you before," Etana said.

Nandi jumped, her eyes wide.

"You have? Where? In the bush?"

"No. In Jikubwa."

Nandi Etana smiled searched her memory as
she studied his face. Nowhere could she find him.

"I don't remember you," she said. "I'm sorry."

"You don't need to apologize. I was not
memorable. I have changed since I have come to
the bush. The clan that took me in did not think I
would survive a season. I proved them wrong."

Nandi heard the bitterness in his voice.

"You don't like them, do you?"

Etana let his eyes answer him.

"You should go to another clan," she said.

Etana shook his head. "I will leave one day.
But when I do, I will join no other clan."

"You will hunt alone?"

Their eyes met. Nandi felt that rush again.

"Yes," Etana answered.

"You choose a harsh life. Maybe a short one."

"I will survive. I will have my skills and the
First Hunter to protect me."

Nandi knew when Etana said those last
words he did not mean Amana.

"We will see," she answered.

* * *

The days became weeks. Nandi and the
marons turned the area where they waited into a
camp, building sturdy huts from the nearby foliage.

They hunted during the day and trained during the night. Nandi had the chance to test her fighting skills against the marons and was pleasantly surprised by the outcome. Though the marons were more experienced fighters, her speed served her well. She enjoyed sparring against Etana most. He was very skilled for his age, like her, and he did not hold back. Akida admonished him the first time they fought but Nandi told him not to. She needed to be tested.

On the third week Nandi became concerned, as did the rest of the band. Akida sent out search groups, but none encountered the First Hunter. The mood of the camp became subdued as they waited. They were preparing to go on a morning hunt when Amana finally returned, striding into the camp as if she's only departed hours earlier. The look on her face was grim.

Akida was the first to speak to her. He bowed before speaking.

"First Hunter, where have . . ."

Amana stopped before him and said one word.

"Simbaku."

The marons took on the same demeanor and the First Hunter. Nandi had no idea what was going on.

"How many bands will we need?" Akida asked.

"Three," Amana replied. "Send for Kondo and Jabali. As soon as they arrive, we will depart."

Nandi was a mix of emotions when Amana said her baba's name. She would be happy to see him, but concerned that Amana had summoned his band for what would be a dangerous journey. She'd heard stories of the Simbaku. They were a powerful nKu, second only to the Chuiku, and very warlike. They were probably the reason the other nKus were encroaching on Chuiku grounds.

"Who else will fight with us?" Akida asked.

"The other nKus are too weary," Amana said. "This is a Chuiku matter. We can only expect help from the Dumaku."

"I will send runners now," Akida said. "Kondo and Jabali are near."

"Good."

Amana looked at Nandi.

"Come with me," she said.

Nandi ran to Amana then followed her to the waterhole. Amana squatted then took a handful of water. She washed her face before drinking. After a few more handfuls she looked at Nandi.

"I told you we would fight together. The time has come."

Nandi smiled at Amana; her emotion wasn't returned.

"I still have a mind to send you back to Jikubwa," she said.

"No!" Nandi blurted. "I must fight! The marons have sparred with me and they say I am good."

"The marons would not insult you and say otherwise. You are a future First Hunter and they do not wish to anger you. You have killed, but it was more by chance than intention."

"But will I actually have to fight?" Nandi asked. "Won't this be settled by you and the Simbaku First Hunter?"

"Normally yes," Amana replied. "But the Simbaku are not known to follow custom. They see themselves above the whims of the ancestors. They think they are the true rulers of all nKus."

"Why would they believe such a thing?"

"Because they once were," Amana said. "The Simbaku once controlled all within the Circle. Their rule was harsh and angered many, but none would face their First Hunter. Until our ancestor."

"I have not heard this story," Nandi said.

"That is because it is my story to tell," Amana replied. "The First Hunter came to take a wife among our people. The woman he chose defied him. They fought, and before all that witnessed a chui came from the forest and aided her, killing the Simbaku First Hunter. The woman, her family and others fled, eventually coming to where we stand today. They adopted the chui as their totem, and the woman became our first Hunter."

"What is her name?" Nandi asked.

"Hediye," Amana answered. "She was Mwindaji wa kwanza, The First Hunter. You and I follow in her shadow. There will never be a Hunter greater than her."

"I will be greater than her," Nandi said.

Amana laughed. "You cannot go back in time and take her place. That is the only way you could surpass her."

Nandi laughed with Amana, but inside she promised to herself that she would make her words truth.

* * *

The marons bands arrived two days after the summons was sent. Kondo's band arrived with the morning sun, singing loudly. Theband entered the clearing in a joyful mood; apparently they were on good terms with Akida's marons. After paying respect to Amana and Nandi they mingled with the other marons sharing stories and boasts. The arrival of Jabili's band was much more subdued. There was no warning of their coming; they appeared from the woods suddenly, weapons in hand and suspicion on their serious faces. The other marons fell silent, there eyes narrowed. Nandi saw her father and called out his name.

"Baba!"

Jabili, her father, smiled when he saw her. The other marons of his band relaxed, lowereing their weapons. Amana walked with Nandi then stood back as Nandi and her father embraced.

"Hello, Little Hunter," he said.

"Hi, baba," she said. No matter how old she became she still felt like a girl in her baba's arms.

"That is not the way to greet a First Hunter," Amana said.

Baba released Nandi then greeted them both with a bow and a kiss on the hand.

"Forgive me, First Hunter," he said. "It has been a long time since I have seen my daughter. Although she is destined to be First Hunter, she is still my little flower."

Their reunion was interupted by Kondo and Akili. Jabili shook their hands, though his demeanor shifted.

"You come as if you did not believe us," Kondo said.

"We have been decieved before," Jabili replied.

"We would not use the First Hunter's summons in such a way," Akili retorted.

Jabili answered with narrow eyes and a smirk.

"We are not here to fight each other," Amana said. "Gather your men. We leave immediately."

The Chuiku war party gathered their weapons and set out for Simbakuland. Amana kept the pace rapid and the rests short to avoid the tensions between the bands. Everyone was too tired to squabble by sundown, grabbing what little rest allowed. As they neared Simbakuland Amana slowed the pace, allowing the bands to rest more and gather their strength. Their energy was refocused on the Simbaku, their boasts targeted toward the warriors of the othe clan if they violated the rules of challenge. Amana had warned of their crossing into othe nKulands and of their intent, so they met no opposition.

The forests of Tembokuland dwindled, giving way to the grasses of Simbakuland. The Chuiku strode across the land with no fear. Tradition required them to approach the challenge grounds unmolested, but the bands kept a wary eye. They were dealing with the Simbaku, and they were not known to follow tradition.

As the day drew to a close they reached the challenge grounds. The land rose slowly into a plateau that bristled with acacias. The trees had been planted to form a natural ring around the bare ground used for challenges. The Chuiku reached the summit and immediately saw the fires of the Simbaku on the opposite side. Amana raised her hand and the band stood still.

"We will camp here," she said. "Akili, send a runner to the Simbaku to let them know we are here."

"I will go," Etana said before Akili could assign the task. The maron leader looked at the young Chui and smiled.

"Go then," he said. "And try not to pick a fight. The ancestors are not prepared for you yet."

Etana smiled at Akili and then at Nandi. Nandi's face flushed as she looked away.

"I will return," he said before sprinting across the grounds.

Amana stood beside Akili and they watched Etana.

"He is an eager one," Amana commented.

"Yes," Akili replied. "And a good fighter for his age. He will take my place if he decides to stay."

"There are tensions?" Amana asked.

"Etana is one who keeps to himself," Akili replied. "I think he will become bandless."

"That is a rare thing," Amana said. "Yet is is how our totem lives."

"It's not life for a maron," Akili said. "But it's not my place to stop him."

"No, it's not," Amana agreed.

Nandi stood close by, listening to their conversation. Once a maron chose to live alone, they were never seen again. The thought of never seeing Etana again made Nandi sad. She frowned, then pulled herself from such thoughts. She was a future First Hunter. She would live a similar life, but at least she served the nKu.

The Chuiku waited for Etana's return. He arrived moments later, trotting toward them with a grin on his face.

"This is not good," Akili commented.

"What do you mean?" Amana asked.

"If Etana has a grin on his face he's been up to mischief," Akili answered. "I think when we meet the Simbaku their mood will be sour."

"It doesn't matter," Amana said. "We are not here to make friends."

Etana bowed before Amana and Akili.

"The Simbaku are many," he said. "And they are angry."

"What did you say to them?" Akili asked.

"I told them we had come to leave them on the ground like tembo dung."

Nandi covered her mouth so no one would hear her laughter. Etana glanced at her and winked. Amana did not hide her amusement. She laughed loudly.

"I like you, young maron," she said. "You will make a nice companion for Nandi when she is ready."

Nandi and Etana eyes widened in surprise. She liked Etana, but the notion of a companion had not crossed her mind. She looked at Etana, who seemed just as shocked.

Amana strode away and everyone followed. Nandi grew more nervous with each step; by the time the Simbaku came into veiw her hands were shaking. An arm draped her shoulders and she looked to her right to see her baba's smiling face.

"Do not worry," he said. "The First Hunter and I will watch over you."

Nandi's fear faded.

"I am not worried, baba," she said. "Just anxious."

Baba laughed. "As you say."

The Simbaku were close enough to see their faces and they were enraged. Nandi had the feeling that Etana had not shared everything he said to them. The Simbaku warriors halted as their First Hunter contined to advance. He was an imposing figure, tall and broad with skin the color of his totem. His light brown hair formed an intimidating mane about his head. It seemed he has already taken his totem form. His face twisted with anger as he eyes went to Etana.

"Did you send that fool to insult me?" he shouted.

Amana stepped forward, her demeanor casual.

"I did not," she replied. "I sent him to tell you of our arrival. How he chose to tell you was his own doing."

The Simbaku First Hunter's eyes bore into Amana.

"And you did not admonish him?"

"What difference does it make?" Amana said. "Your challenge is against me."

"When I finish with you, I will deal with him."

"When I crush you," Amana replied, "you will return to your homes and contemplate your bad choices."

The Simbaku First Hunter replied with a roar that shook Nandi. He transformed into the simba, pounced at Amana while she was still in her mortal shell. It was a violation of a challenge. The marons and Simbaku warrrors surged forward. Amana dodged the simba as she transformed.

"Stay back!" Amana yelled before she took full form. Nandi had never seen her as totem and she was mesmerised. As the Chui she deftly avoided the Simba's attacks, jumping toward him to deliver a scratch or a bite. With every landed blow the simba roared in frustration.

"You can give up now," Amana said. "There would be no shame in it. You lose nothing except the right to intrude on the others land."

The Simbaku First Hunter answer with a roar and leap that seemed to catch Amana offguard.

Nandi gasped as the simba crashed into the Chui, wrapping its powerful forelimbs around her.

"No!" Nandi screamed.

Amana did not attempt to break away. Instead she gripped the Simba with her paws, ducking her head under its massive jaws and clamping down with her fangs on his throat. The simba froze as it rolled on his back.

"Will the Simbaku have to look for a new First Hunter, or are we done here?" Amana said between her teeth.

The Simbaku First Hunter said nothing. Amana closed her jaw tighter.

"Answer me or I'll rip out your throat!"

The Simba First Hunter moaned before answering.

"We are done," he said.

Amana released the First Hunter then leaped away. She tranformed, standing naked and wounded before the marons. Nandi ran to her with her clothes and Amana dressed, her eyes on the Simbaku First Hunter. The man transformed. He lay naked on his stomach, his right hand reaching for his throat as he pushed himself up from the ground.

"Will you honor what has happened here?" Amana asked.

"Of course," he said. "But know this. When we meet again, I will not be as generous as you were."

"We will not meet again," Amana replied. "Twice I have spared your life. Do not try my patience."

The Simbaku First Hunter looked away. Amana turned and walked away.

"Come," she said to the others. "This is over."

The Chuiku returned the way they came, the marons in the rear keeping a wary eye on the Simbaku warriors. Akili and Jabili walked close to Amana.

"Will they attack us?" Jabili asked.

"Most likely," Amana replied. "The Simbaku don't take defeat well."

"And they brought an army with them," Akili added.

"Keep walking,"Amana said. "We will need our strength."

As if reading her mind, an angry roar ripped the tense silence. It was answered by a chorus of roars from the throats of the Simbaku warriors. Nandi turned to look. The Simabuku warriors ran for them, shields and spears raised high. She looked ahead to the bush. They were too far.

"First Hunter," she said. "We should . . ."

"Keep walking," Amana said. "We are safe. The marons are not the only ones I summoned."

The Simbaku closed the ground quickly but still had not reached them.

"Listen for my signal," Amana said loud enough for everyone to hear. "Do exactly what I say. If you hesitate, you will die."

Nandi shook. She peered over her shoulder again and nervousness coursed through her body. She would fight, but there were too many. They could not stop them in the open.

The Simbaku stopped then threw their spears. The marons dodged them then yelled taunts.

"Do we run now?" Nandi asked Amana.

Amana patted her shoulder then smiled.

"We will not run from the Simbaku."

The Simbaku continued their pursuit. Nandi watch Amana as she finally turned to look at the Simbaku then gaze at the bush. It was then that Nandi saw them, dozens of warriors emerging from the forest armed with bows.

"Down!" Amana shouted.

The marons flattened on the ground. Nandi was still standing, watching the new warriors load their bows then pull back their bowstrings. Someone grabbed her hand, yanking her to the ground as the warrior released. The silence was broken again, this time by the painful cries of the Simbaku warriors. Nandi looked to her side. Etana looked back at her smiling.

"Who are they?" she asked.

"Paaku," Etana replied. "They are our allies. First Hunter must have contacted them as well. She planned well."

The Paaku warriors fired another round of arrows then disappeared into the bush. First Hunter sprang to her feet and Nandi and the marons followed, ready for battle. But the Simbaku had had enough. They gathered their dead and wounded then retreated to their homeland. The Simbaku First Hunter lingered, glaring at Amana. He spat, then stomped away.

"It's not over," Akili said.

"It never will be," Amana replied. "But that one will not try us again."

Nandi heard Amana's and Akili's words, but her attention was captured by the Paaku. She'd never met people from another nKu except the Taiku. This days she's met two; one as an enemy, the other as a friend. A tall woman with skin like midnight, long braids and a painted face approached Amana. The First Hunter greeted her with a smile and a warm hug.

"Makena, it is good to see you," Amana said.

"It is good to see you too, sister," Makena replied.

"You will feast with us?" Amana asked.

"Of course," Makena replied. "Killing Simbaku always makes us hungry."

The women laughed and Nandi joined them. Makena turned to Nandi.

"Who are you?" she asked.

Nandi stood taller as she answered.

"I am Nandi, protege' of The First Hunter."

"She is a proud one," Makena commented to Amana.

"She deserves to be," Amana replied. "I see great promise in her."

Makena nodded to Nandi. "That is a great compliment coming from your First Hunter. Make sure it is not in vain."

"I won't," Nandi answered.

"Come," Makena said. "I have someone you should meet."

Nandi looked to Amana for permission.

"Go," she said. "Makena is to be trusted above all others."

Nandi followed the Paaku warrior to a group of warriors standing together chatting. The warriors' conversation diminished as they approached. One warrior, a girl no older than Nandi approached, a smile on her face.

"Hello, sister," the girl said.

"I know that smile Siza," Makena replied. "How many?"

"Three," Siza answered.

Makena shook her head.

"Nandi, this is my sister Siza. Siza, this is Nandi. She is the protegé of First Hunter Amana. Unlike the other nKus, we do not have a First Hunter. We do have warriors and commanders. I'm commander; my sister Siza wants to take my place one day. She is well on her way. It is good that you two know each other."

Nandi bowed to Siza, which seemed to surprise the girl.

"It is an honor to meet you Siza," she said.

"The honor is mine," Siza replied.

"You two should get to know each other," Makena said.

She shared a smile then walked away. Nandi and Siza shifted about, unsure what to say.to each other.

"I am glad you came to help us," Nandi said. "The Simbaku are fearsome warriors."

Siza nodded. "I was nervous when Makena said we were coming to fight them. This is my first battle."

Nandi's eyes lit up with excitement.

"Mine, too!"

They laughed then walked off together to sit under a large tree.

"My hands shook as I drew my bowstring," Siza continued. "My first arrow missed, but not my second. I killed three of them! How many did you kill?"

"None," Nandi said. "We were there to witness the challenge between Amana and the Simbaku First Hunter. But I have killed someone."

The image of the fight with the Taiku warrior flashed into her head and her excitement was dampened.

"You do not seem proud," Siza said.

"I was afraid when it happened," she said. "His blood was on my hands."

Siza's smile faded.

"I don't know if I could do that."

"You already have," Nandi said. "Three times!"

"It is different I would think," Siza said. "I am far away. I do not kill a warrior. My arrow does. You were fighting with a warrior and defeated him."

"Your arrow finds its mark because of you. You load the bow; you pull the bowstring, you aim and you release. The arrow finds its mark because of you."

Siza's smile disappeared. She stared at her hands for a moment then looked up at Nandi. They hugged.

"We are killers, we two," Siza said.

"Yes we are," Nandi replied.

The girls let go of each other. Nandi knew that from this moment on she and Siza would be friends.

S I X

The Kashite caravan took itstime traveling up the winding road leading to the Taiku capital. They were wary, for they carried precious cargo. Tahnk An rode in her gilded carriage, swaying with the rhythm of the beasts pulling her and the others up the steep road. Six months had passed since Ahmo Se subdued the birdfolk and forced them to terms. During that time Awere had become somewhat peaceful. There were flare ups here and there, but for the most part the birdfolk were settling into their yoke. But with peace came other concerns.

Leadership was a fickle thing. People tend to follow those that show strength and resolve. They admire those whose actions are bold and visible. It was for these reasons that Ahmo Se had become popular among the common folk. It was he that defeated the Taiku, and it was he who had negotiated the peace between them and the Kashites. The Taiku accepted him as well, despite the fact that he killed their supreme warrior, their 'First Hunter.' It did not matter that Tahnk An planned the campaign and gave Ahmo Se the baton which he used to turn the war to their favor. Ahmo Se had become a threat.

Ahmo Se's new status was the reason for her journey. It was time the Taiku knew their true ruler. For his part Ahmo has shown no ambition to usurp her, but Tahnk knew better than to drop her guard. Many a ruler had been replaced by an ambition general, and those who controlled the army were powerful players. Her visit was to re-establish her reputation not only to the birdfolk, but to her own as well.

Once the climb to the center of Taiku had begun, there was no stopping. The narrow road afforded no rest sites, so the trek continued through darkness, the way lit by torchbearers. Taiku guides met them halfway to the city and assisted the procession to the top of the plateau. It was still dark when they arrived, so Tahnk could not see the city profile, with the exception of the torchlight flickering in the distance. She gazed upon the silhouette of the city from her coach as her servants set up her tent. Once they were done she entered and inspected.

"Draw me a bath," she ordered.

Her servants scurried away in search of water to fill her porcelian tub. As she waited Commander Se entered the hut.

"You were not summoned," Tahnk said.

The commander bowed before speaking.

"I know, but I thought it prudent to brief you before we met with the Taiku elders."

"I have been studying the birdfolk since we breached the mountains," Tahnk replied. "I doubt there is anything you can share with me that I don't already know. Besides, you forget that it was my plan that secured the victory for you. It seems everyone has forgotten."

"I will be forever grateful for your council," Ahmo Se replied. "No one appreciates your wisdom more than I. However, wrongly or rightly, the Taiku consider me their conqueror."

"Then we must change this perception, don't you think?"

"Yes, we must," the commander replied.

Tanhk clasped her hands behind her back. "Since you created this situation, how to you propose we repair it?"

"You must fight me," Ahmo Se replied.

"What?" Tanhk's shock caused her mouth to drop open.

"You must fight me," Ahmo repeated. "These people follow champions. The First Hunter was theirs. Since I defeated him, they see me as their new champion. Well, not exactly. They have made it clear that I am not and never will be considered Taiku, but they will respect my word and wishes because I killed their First Hunter. If you defeat me, they will do the same for you."

"If?" Tanhk's eyes narrowed.

"When you defeat me," Ahmo said, correcting himself.

"I see."

Tahnk's eyes drifted to the tent entrance as her servants arrived with her tub.

"Leave us," she ordered. "I will send for you when I am ready."

Ahmo bowed. "As you wish."

Ahmo left her tent. Tanhk lounged as her servants prepared her bath, contemplating Ahmo's words. Would he actually challenge her? No, he knew better. The ashé she shared with him through the baton was only a fraction of what she possessed. Surely he did not think she would give him enough power to challenge her. She laughed. Of course he didn't.

"Suti, your bath is ready," her servant said.

Tanhk stood from the lounge and strolled to the tub, taking off her clothes along the way. Her servants helped her into the steaming scented water. The dust and stress of the journey left her body as she descended to the elixer. She lay her head on the cushioned head rest and closed her eyes, images of Menu-Kash filling her thoughts. It had been months since she left and she missed it sorely. She knew her duty, but it did not curb her longing. The reward was she would climb in ranking when she returned, her ashé bolstered by the source of kipande on this island. If she could find it.

Tanhk sat up suddenly,splashing water from the tub. Her servants came immediately to cleaning up the spill, concern in their eyes.

Tama, her most attentive servant, sent the others away.

"My Suti, you are trembling. Is something wrong?"Are you cold? We can have a fire built."

"No, Tama. I am not cold," Tahnk replied. "I am furious."

Tama helped her climb from the tub then followed her to her closet. When she stopped before her garments he stood before her and began to undress.

"Would you like me to pleasure you?"

Tahnk shook her head. "There is no time. Fetch my guards."

Tama nodded then left the room. The other servants returned to dry her then dress her.

The servants brought Tanhk's mirror. She barely looked at herself, so deep was her anger.

"Send word to Ahmo that I am ready," she said.

Tahnk sat on her lounge, scolding herself for her foolishness. She had been jealous because Ahmo had endeared himself to the Taiku. But that was trivial compared to what she suspected he had done.

Tama returned with one of Tahnk's warriors. The man prostrated before her. At least his warriors still respected her.

"Suti, we are ready," he said.

Tahnk stood.

"Lead us," she said.

The Medji exited the tent, followed by Tanhk and her servants. A contingent of warriors waited outside; they prostrated as Tanhk emerged. They rose on her command then formed around the Suti and her entourage. Normally such a gesture would go unnoticed, but Tanhk's suspisions made her wary of the attention. She reached into her robes, wrapping her fingers around her baton. The warmth of the weapon comforted her and she smiled.

Ahmo and the Taiku elders waited for them before the walls of the birdfolk's city. It was an impressive sight; towering stone walls surrounding structures built to resemble the mountains. There were birds everywhere, their flying giving the city a sense of movement. The people sat on the walls and looked from there windows. They were expecting a show, and Tanhk would give it to them.

As they neared Ahmo the Medji broke rank and filed away. Tahnk and her people continued to walk until they stood before Ahmo, the commander flanked by two of his senior officers. They prostrated before her.

"I am sorry that this is necessary," Ahmo said.

"I am, too," Tahnk replied.

"I promise that it will not take long."

"I'm sure of it," Tanhk replied.

"Please follow me," Ahmo said.

Tanhk followed the commander to the area where the Taiku elders sat. An elder woman stood, looking at Tanhk with narrow eyes.

"This is the one who is your leader?" the woman said.

"Yes," Ahmo replied.

"I can see why you will challenge her. See is weak."

Tanhk anger burned inside her, but she did not show it. Instead she smiled at the woman and nodded.

"I am disappointed that my appearance does not please you," Tahnk said. "I have worked hard among my people to gain the position I now hold. I hope and can pursuade you it is deserved."

The woman smirked. "We shall see."

Two Medji warriors approached, one joining Tahnk.

"The warriors will take us to opposite sides of the field," Ahmo whispered. When the elder raises her hand, we fight. There are no rules, whomever remains standing is the victor. I must resist in order for the Taiku to believe this is a true battle. Are you ready, Pharsa?"

"I am," Tanhk replied.

The warrior escorted Tahnk to her place. Tanhk faced Ahmo then looked to the elder. The elder gazed at her then to Ahmo. She raised her hand.

Ahmo snatched out his baton and Tahnk did not move. He sent a blue bolt streaking toward her but Tahnk remained still. She closed her eyes as the bolt struck her chest. Tahnk felt the powers disperse through her body then gather into the baton at her waist. This was a killing strike. Ahmo was truly attempting to defeat her before these birdfolk.

Tahnk took her baton from her waist sash. She looked at the commander, savoring the stunned look on his face. She raised her baton, feeling the pressure fighting for release. Her bolt burned a path to the commander and he raised his baton to protect himself. The bolt hesitated and Tahnk was surprised. Apparently the commander had gained some form of ashé from the birdfolk he thought would help him win. He was wrong. Tahnk tighten her grip on her baton and sent another bolt. It merged into the first bolt and consumed Ahmo, the man screaming as he was cremated. Tahnk threw her baton at the Taiku elders. It fell among them then exploded, blinding the onlookers. When the light cleared, the elders were ashes. Tahnk opened her hand and the baton appeared. Onlookers wailed, screamed and fled from the scene. Ahmo's Medji looked dumbfounded for a moment then quickly prostrated before their Pharsa. Tahnk smiles as her anger ebbed. This foolishness was over. She tilted her head and a servant appeared at her side.

"Send word to the Medji to enter the birdfolk city and find the kipande inside," she said. "Kill everyone who tries to resist you. Do not leave the city until you have it. I am returning to Awere."

SEVEN

Nandi and the First Hunter gazed at the blue monolith jutting out of the surrounding forest. If there was any place in nKuland that deserved to be the dwelling of priestesses, this towering massive stone was surely it. She felt the energy emanating from it even though they still have miles to go before reaching the base. Amana told her they would not be able to see the summit. She believed her.

"Enough gawking," Amana said, breaking her trance. "The priestesses are waiting."

"How do they know we are coming?" Nandi asked.

"They always know," Amana replied.

Amana pushed her way through the dense foliage, Nandi close behind. She warned Nandi not to harm any of the plants, nor would they hunt. This forest belonged to the priestesses, and any violation of their creatures would lessen her chances. Chances for what, the First Hunter did not say.

For two days they traversed the forest, walking during the sunlight and camping at night. They burned no fires, eating the fruits, grain and dried meat they prepared before the journey. At night they rested, exhausted from the day's trek. On the third day the forest thinned, the trees replaced by tall grasses and scattered shrubs. Animals of all types wandered about, some Nandi recognized and others she did not. This was truly a wonderous place.

Nandi's awe was dampened when she noticed a pride of simbas keeping pace with them. She took her spear from her back.

"No," Amana said.

"But those are simbas," Nandi replied. "And they are following us."

"They will not attack," Amana said. "They are the eyes of the priestesses."

Nandi wasn't convinced. She held on to her spear.

"They sense your fear," Amana said. "Put your spear back in its sheath and they will go away."

Nandi looked at Amana, still unconvinced.

"Do it now Nandi, or we will have come all this way for nothing."

Nandi let out a frustrated sigh then put the spear away, keeping her eyes on the pride. The simbas relaxed, playing among themselves before sauntering away. Amana grasped Nandi's shoulder, then squeezed it hard.

"Never doubt my word again," she said. "I have been here before for. You have not. The rules of the woods do not apply here. All is controlled by the priestesses."

"I did not doubt you, First Hunter," Nandi said. "I . . ."

The wind fled Nandi's body as a sudden pressure clutched her. Her arms were pinned to her sides as she was lifted off the ground. Nandi tried to scream, but she had no voice. The voice that lifted her dragged her through the forest.

"Nandi!" Amana shouted. "Nandi!"

Amana pursued her, but she was not fast enough. Branches and limbs broke against her body, pummeling her as she sped through the bush. Was this the priestesses' punishment for threatening their own?

She slowed and the grip about her loosened. Nandi thought her punishment was over until she saw what lay ahead. It was the land that Amana told her was forbidden, the circle void of life which she was not to enter. Nandi struggled against the force but couldn't free herself. The priestesses had decided to kill her for her insolence.

Nandi burst from the bush into the wasteland. The force released her and she fell onto the ground. Her breath came back to her, but she realized this was only a respite. They would kill her soon, she thought. Nandi stood then stared into the bright void. If she was to die, she would not die on her knees. She dared to glance behind her. Amana stood at the edge of the boundary. Her mouth moved, but Nandi could not hear her. Tears flowed down her face. Nandi was about to call out to her when she felt a presence. She turned to face the void again. The light dimmed, revealing the base of the towering monolith. But that was not all. Three figures approached her; as they neared their details became clear. They were women, their hair rising over their heads like crowns, their voluptuous bodies covered by shimmering blue fabrics of a like Nandi had never seen. Each woman glittered with bands of precious gems surrounding their necks, biceps, wrists and ankles. These were the priestesses; of this Nandi had no doubt. The force reappeared, pushing her gently to her knees and bending her head. When the priestesses reached her, all she could see was their jeweled bare feet.

They touched her and she was consumed by unimaginable heat. Yet she did not cry out. Her body welcomed it and the pleasure she felt was beyond anything she'd experienced. When they took their hands away the force released her. Nandi looked into the eyes of the priestesses and was spellbound.

"Our world is changing," they said in unison, their voices harmonizing like a beautiful song. "Many will die . . . even us. But you will protect those that remain. Rise, First Hunter. There is much for you to do."

Nandi stood.

"Priestesses, I . . ."

Darkness enveloped her; when it was gone, she stood beside Amana. The First Hunter hugged her tight and cried.

"They spared you!" she said.

Nandi held Amana apprehensively. Something had changed. She did not feel as if Amana was her elder any longer. She felt as if they were equal. When they let each other go, she could tell that Amana sensed it, too.

"They called me First Hunter," Nandi said.

Amana nodded, her face solemn. "So be it. Come, I have much to show you and I don't have much time."

Amana grasped her hand then lead her away. Nandi looked over her shoulder into the barren land. She could not see the priestesses, but she could feel them. They had changed her; into what, she did not know. Something told her she would find out soon.

EIGHT

Tahnk An sat at her desk reviewing the most recent reports from the Taiku cities when the acolyte burst into her room. She looked up from her work, an angry expression on her stern face.

"Are you mad?" she snapped. "Who allowed you here?"

Her guards entered moments later, their swords drawn.

"We are sorry, Suti," one of them said. "He used ashé to evade us."

Tahnk came her feet, her hands at her side.

"You used ashé against my Medji?"

She was raising her hand to kill the acolyte when he fell to his knees and prostrated before her.

"My Suti, please forgive me!" he pleaded. "I have come to take you to the temple. The Na-Set summons you."

Tahnk's anger transformed to dread. She steadied herself before responding.

"Leave me," she said. "Meet me at my compound entrance."

The acolyte stood then backed out of the room. The Medji followed him as he hurried away. Tahnk made sure they were gone before slumping into her chair and trembling. The Na-Set summoned her indirectly, which meant she was not pleased. The operations had gone on longer than planned, but there had been unforeseen obstacles, such as the Taiku resistance. She was making progress despite everything. Her army was almost ready to move into the interior to find and claim the kipande source.

There was another reason the Na-Set could be reaching out to her. The situation in Menu-Kash may have become unstable, and the Na-Set was marshalling her resources. Kipande would be vital to such a move, which would give Tahnk some advantage. Though she did not wish ill will on her homeland, a tenuous situation would work to her advantage.

Tahnk took her time dressing, making sure her appearance would not offend the Na-Set. This land was lacking in the proper ingredients for her make-up; what she used would have to do. She inspected herself in the mirror and was not pleased. If she was lucky, the Na-Set's concerns would not include her appearance.

She met the acolyte and her guards at the compound entrance. Together they made their way to the temple, their stern faces and purposeful gait conveying their urgency. The timid crowds parted like the sea to a ship's bow. The temple occupied the center of Awere, the rectangular structure covering several blocks. A single narrow spire rose from the center, the stone pulled from the nearby mountains. It was the first permanent structure built in the city; the other buildings were built around it, with all roads leading to the roundabout ringing it. The chariots circled the temple three times as was customary before stopping before the entrance. The temple priest had gathered before the entrance door, their solemn faces hiding their true emotions. Tahnk Ah could feel their disquiet. A direct summons from the Na-Set was a serious matter for all involved.

Amoses, the senior priest, greeted her with a slight bow. Tahnk An and the priest were equals, though once inside the temple Tahnk An differed to her. Amoses nodded.

"Welcome, Suti," she said.

"Thank you, Amoses."

"The Na-Set waits. Follow me."

Tahnk An joined Amoses and they led the entourage to the central worship room.

"I knew this would happen," Amoses said. "You waste too much time with these savages."

"Do not question how I run Awere, I will not criticize how you run the temple. I see your attendance is lower than the last time I visited."

"The situation is being addressed," Amoses replied. "Without the Na-Set's intervention."

Tahnk An had no retort. They entered the central sanctuary. Talisman and incense covered the dais, a dense smoke rising from burning fragrant wood.

The high priest ambled out of the room, the entourage following. The Medji closed the doors, leaving Tahnk An in darkness save for the wavering light from the dais flames.

Tahnk prostrated before the pedestal, awaiting the Na-Set's arrival. The smoke thickened as it rose higher, churning like a storm despite the stillness of the chamber. After a few moments the smoke coalesced into a female form. The facial features became distinct; a smooth handsome face marred by a frown.

"Rise, Tahnk An," the Na-Set said.

Tahnk An raised her head to look upon the stern gaze of the Na-Set. Long ago they had been friends, growing up together in the gardens of Kash. They were separated as they reached initiation age, sent south to Napat for administrative training Tahnk An; the Na-Set to Daarset to train in the mysteries of the sonchais. Tahnk An had become the servant, her childhood friend the master. Tahnk An pushed back the memories as she stood.

"I live to serve, Na-Set," she said.

"Apparently not well," the Na-Set replied. Her sharp tone cut Tahnk An like a blade. "Three years ago, you promised me we would have the bounty of this island, yet today you stand before me with your hands empty."

"There were unexpected challenges," Tahnk An replied. "We expected the island to be uninhabited. It's not. The savages have put up a formidable resistance. Their ashé is strong."

"It is because of the kipande, no doubt," the Na-Set replied. "Which makes it even more important that we claim it. I'm sure you have surmised that our situation at home has become more unstable."

"Yes, I have," Tahnk An replied. "I'm am organizing an expedition to the source as we speak. We will claim it and begin mining immediately."

"Do you have the resources?" the Na-Set asked. "The cost will be heavy."

Tahnk dared to smile. "The savages are plentiful. Once we subdue the rest of them, we will have all the labor we need."

"Take care," the Na-Set cautioned. "To have thrived being so close to such a large source of kipande is unusual. They may be stronger than you think. Do not underestimate them."

"I will not, Na-Set."

The smoke began to disperse.

"Do not fail me," the Na-Set warned.

"I will not," Tahnk An replied. "I look forward to your next visit."

The Na-Set smiled as her face faded.

"No, you do not," she said.

Tahnk An lingered in the chamber until she stopped trembling. She stood then marched from the room. Amoses and the acolytes were waiting, their faces anxious. Amoses stepped forward.

"What did the Na... "

"Shut up!" Tahnk barked. "If the Na-Set meant for you to know she would have summoned you."

Her warriors surrounded her at the temple entrance and they returned to her palace. Tahnk stepped out of her chariot, her face a reflection of her foul mood.

"Go to my commanders and tell them to meet here within the hour," she said. "Anyone who is not in attendance will be executed."

The Medji hurried away. Tahnk continued to her large conference room, her servants following.

"Get the map," she ordered. Tahnk did not know which servants received her order, but she knew they would follow her demand without haste. They knew her moods and knew not to hesitate. She went to her room and changed clothes, using the time to marshal her fear. Time had run out; the mountain had to be taken.

The map was in place and her commanders present when she entered the council room. The commanders looked upon her with curious eyes.

"I have received word from the Na-Set," she said. "We must take the mountain as soon as possible."

The commanders looked at each other. Their discomfort was obvious.

"Speak," Tahnk said. "This is no time for reluctance."

The commanders' eyes settled on Aharon, her new senior commander. She was capable and knew her place, unlike her predecessor. She was also rather cautious, not a good trait for a general.

"Suti," she said. "We are not ready. The Taiku are still resistant. To launch a campaign into the interior would stretch our forces."

"Then include the Taiku," Tahnk said.

Aharon blinked with confusion.

"Suti, beg my pardon, but I do not think the Taiku will fight with us as allies."

"They won't," Tahnk said. "But they will fight against whomever we encounter. They hate the other inhabitants of this island as much as they hate us. This campaign will give them the opportunity to kill their traditional enemies and gain honor as well. And maybe it will quell their anger against us, at least for a time."

"It is a good plan," Aharon agreed.

As if she would disagree, Tahnk An thought. She despised warriors like Aharon. She preferred generals that challenged her ideas and pushed her to greater ideas.

"Send word to the Taiku elders of our plan. If they are agreeable, we will meet within the week."

Aharon bowed. "Yes, Pharsa."

Tahnk An turned her back on them. "Leave me."

The commanders bowed in unison then exited the council room.

NINE

Nandi searched the foliage near the shallow stream for spoor. Siza stood nearby, her bow loaded. Nandi's actions were fueled more by smell than sight; since she began her training her senses were heightened, especially her sense of smell. It was this ability that led her to the blood-stained leaves of a small bush near the stream edge.

She stood then looked to her new friend.

"It crossed here," she said.

Siza left out a breath. "We'll eat well tonight."

Nandi stood then turned to Siza with a smile.

"We haven't found it yet."

"It's my fault," Siza said. "I did not strike its heart."

"It jumped the string," Nandi said. "It happens."

"Not for me," Siza said. "I'm to be First Hunter. I cannot miss."

Nandi sauntered to her friend and gave her a hug.

"We are both still in training," she said. "We're allowed a miss or two."

She waded into the stream.

"Come on. We need to find it before the scavengers do."

They crossed the stream. Nandi picked up the trail and they followed it into the bush. A few minutes later they came upon the bush deer's body next to a large ironwood tree. Luckily the fisi had not found it. Together they set about dressing their kill. Nandi watched Siza hang the bush deer from a low hanging branch and proceed to cut away the skin. She was much better at such things than Nandi, especially since Nandi had taken to her training. She glanced at her nails, sharpened and toughening to kill with her bare hands. Sometimes her training worried her. To be Chiu First Hunter meant transforming, unlike Siza's nKu. What if the transformation did not reverse? What if she was killed in the form of a chui? What would happen to her ashé?

"I could use some help," Siza said, breaking her thoughts.

Nandi unsheathed her knife and joined Siza dressing their kill. They built two fires; one for cooking their meal and the other for smoking the meat they would not eat. Nandi went back to the stream for water and they cooked a savory stew from the deer meat, local vegetables and spices they carried with them. It was a filling meal, the best they'd had in a few days. Afterwards they lay on their backs under the forest canopy.

"One more week," Siza said. "Then we return to our training."

"I'm ready," Nandi said.

"I'm not," Siza replied.

Nandi sat up, surprised at Siza's comment. "Why not?"

Siza sat up, leaning on her left elbow to face Nandi. She plucked a blade of grass and chewed on it.

"I did not ask to be chosen, nor did I want to be," she said.

"So why are you here?"

"Because my family's blood line is that of the First Hunter. The eldest daughter is destined. There is no choice."

Nandi sat up. "That doesn't seem fair. Among the Chui the choice must be accepted."

"I wish I was Chui," Siza said.

"Don't let Makenda hear you say that."

Siza shrugged. "Makenda knows my feelings. She also knows that it doesn't make a difference. She didn't have a choice, nor do I. It is our way."

Nandi was about to answer when she heard an odd sound. She froze, concentration on the source.

"Nandi? What are you . . . "?

Nandi held up her hand to silence her friend.

"Something is flying toward us. Something large."

Siza grabbed her bow and arrow quiver then jumped to her feet. Nandi strained her ears and heard the rhythmic beating coming closer. She signaled Siza to hide as she pressed against a nearby iron wood. A dark shape flashed by overheard. Nandi grabbed her spear then ran toward the sound of the flying being. Siza followed.

Nandi and Siza maneuvered through the foliage as they followed the sound, running. until they reached a breach in the forest. Before them was an expanse of grass teeming with the local wildlife. If she ran out into the savannah she would be seen; she stopped at the forest edge and watched the flying creature cross and then disappear over the horizon.

"What was that?" Siza asked.

"Taiku," Nandi, replied. "Two of them. They're flying in the direction of the Blue Mound."

"Why would they come so far into your Chuikuland?"

"I sure it's something to do with the Bindamu," Nandi replied. "We must go back now."

They returned to their camp, gathered their things then set out for Jikubwa. It took them three days of hard travelling to reach the city. Her mother and the others were surprised to see her, her mother greeting her with a warm hug. If not for the circumstances, Nandi would have been happy to see her, too.

"Mama," she said. "We saw Taiku flying over our land. I think they were headed for the Blue Mound. We must call First Hunter and the marons."

"Where is First Hunter? She was not with you?"

"No. Siza and I were together. That is when we saw the tai."

"We will send the signal," Mama said. Her stern face softened as she embraced Nandi again. They had not seen each other since she left with Amana over a year ago.

"Come," Mama said. "You must eat and then you must rest."

Nandi and Siza followed Mama to their home. The signal drums rumbled while the women walked. Nandi almost forgot their current crisis as the smell of Mama's stew reached her. She went to the table and sat, her mouth watering. Siza sat beside her.

"Whatever it is, it smells delicious," she said.

"It is," Nandi replied. "It's goat stew."

Mama filled their bowls then sat them on the table. They waited until Mama joined them with her own bowl before filling their mouths. Nandi closed her eyes as she savored the spicy concoction.

"This is so good, Mama!" she exclaimed.

"You've been away too long," Mama replied. "It's the same as it was when you left."

"Well, I've never tasted it before, and I think it's wonderful!" Siza said.

Mama smiled. "It seems I've acquired a new daughter. What is your name?"

"Siza. Excuse my manners. I should have told you before I sat down to share food with you."

"It's not your error," Mama said. "That belongs to the person who brought you here."

Nandi peek up from her bowl.

"I'm sorry."

"You came for a serious reason, so I understand," Mama said. She turned her attention back to Siza.

"You are Paaku?" she asked.

"Yes," Siza replied. "My sister is Makenda, our First Hunter."

The signal drums were answered by drumming from the distance.

"The marons have answered," Mama said. "Now we wait for the First Hunter. Until then, we rest and prepare."

The marons arrived a day later. Nandi was happy to see Baba again; she was also surprised when Abasi arrived. His maron band was the furthest away from the city and were rarely encountered. Though he left after his initiation rites like all boys, they had been very close as siblings. He caught her unaware, lifting her in the air and spinning her around before dropping her on her feet.

"Abasi!" she said, half laughing. "You can't do that. I'm to be First Hunter one day."

"One day, but not today." His smile was infectious. It didn't take him long to notice Siza. He brushed by Nandi and bowed.

"Habarigani," he said. "I am Abasi, Nandi's handsome brother."

Siza laughed. "I would not call you handsome, Nandi's brother."

Abasi smiled wider. "You can call me beautiful then. I don't mind."

Nandi shoved Abasi away.

"Go on now," she said. "We are here for serious matters. This is not the Planting Festival."

Abasi hugged Nandi then bowed to Siza.

"Whatever it is, we are ready," he said. He sauntered away to join the other marons.

"Your brother looks strong," Siza said. "And he is charming."

Nandi rolled her eyes. "You will be a First Hunter. You'll have no time for men."

"That is the Chuiku way, not the Paaku. We are allowed a husband and family if we choose."

"Why would you want one?" Nandi shrugged. "Besides, you just met Abasi. Eventually he'll wear on you like a rough stone."

"You're his sister," Siza replied. "You don't know him the way I wish to."

Nandi was saved by the arrival drums.

"The First Hunter is here!"

The Chuiku gathered at the enclosure entrance. Amana strode into the city with her usual serious face, her expression shifting slightly when she saw Nandi. Amana nodded to her protégé then continued to Mama.

"Great Mother," Amana said. "It is always to see you, but I am surprised it is so soon."

"Nandi arrived a few day ago with serious news," Mama replied. We will hold council so that everyone can hear her words."

Nandi, Siza, Mama, Amana and the others met at the meeting tree. Mama took her place among the matriarchs, while the elder marons sat opposite them. Amana and Nandi stood between them.

"We have call you together for this serious matter," Mama said. "The Taiku have breached our borders, violating our peace. Nandi?"

Nandi stepped away from Amana before speaking. "Today I saw two tais flying overhead. They were heading to the Blue Mound."

"How do you know this?" Mama Kesi asked. Mama Kesi was second only to Nandi's mama in rank. She was a thin woman with white braided white hair and a skeptical personality

"A flying tai does not always carry an nKu. It could have been a wild pair. And how do you know they were heading to Blue Mound? Did you follow them? And how could they approach the Mound? The priestesses would not allow it."

The other matriarchs and elder marons nodded in agreement to the matriarch's questions.

Nandi bowed to Mama Kesi. "Honored Mother, I saw the riders on the tais back, so I am sure they were not wild. As for them approaching the Mound, we did not follow them there. They traveled too fast."

Mama Kesi frowned. "So, I asked again, how did you know their destination was the Blue Mound?"

Nandi hesitated to answer, knowing that she would sound foolish.

"Tell them the truth," Amana said.

Nandi cut her eyes at the First Hunter then took a deep breath.

"Because I felt it."

The matriarchs murmured, sharing doubtful glances. The marons remained quiet, but their skeptical expressions spoke the word they did not utter.

"Hear me," Amana said. The others fell quiet. "I took Nandi to the Blue Mound."

Mama and Baba jumped to their feet.

"What?" Mama exclaimed.

"I did was I am expected to do," Amana said. "All potential First Hunters must be presented to the priestesses."

"But she is too young," Baba said. Mama Kesi glared him into silence. Marons were observers and followers, nothing more.

"I believed she was ready," Amana said. "The fact that she stands here should tell you enough. But for those who are skeptical, I will tell you that she passed beyond the barrier and was not harmed."

The Chuiku fell silent. Nandi looked for Mama and found her with a stunned expression on her face. Baba looked the same way. Everyone's attentions shifted to Mama.

"If the priestesses have accepted her, then her word is true," Mama said. "Now we must ask ourselves why the Taiku threaten us."

"It is not them," a male voice said.

Etana stood among the marons.

"You have not been given permission to speak," Mama Kesi said.

"I'll allow it," Mama replied. "Come forward, Etana.

Etana made his way to the edge of the circle.

"The Taiku do not think for themselves anymore," he said. "They are pets to the Bindamu. Their First Hunter was killed by a Bindamu warrior, and he was killed by his leader in a duel for power."

"How do you know this?" Mama asked.

"Because I have been among them," Etana answered.

A buzz of disapproval swept the gathering. The maron elders stood, waving their clubs in anger.

"This is your fault, Akili," one of the maron elders said. "He is of your band."

"I answer to no band," Etana said. "I go where I please."

"So, you provoked them!" another elder accused.

"The Taiku are so defeated they never noticed me," Etana said. "If they did, they would have challenged me and I would have died with honor. But what Nandi says is true. They are gathering their army. I believe they plan to cross the river and march to the Blue Mound."

Mama looked to the First Hunter.

"It seems we are at war," she said. "The Chuiku are in your hands."

Amana nodded. She faced the marons.

"Marons!"

The marons sprang to their feet, their eyes on her.

"We need to know more of the Bindamu's intentions. I believe Etana can show us the way."

Etana smirked. He looked at Nandi and she smiled.

"The Bindamu will not cross the river," Amana said. "Sisters!"

The woman of Chuiku stood.

"We must prepare as well. Together our people will meet the invaders at the Hagosa. It will be their burial ground!"

The Chuiku ululated as one. Nandi felt a rush through her body. The Chuiku were going to war.

TEN

Tahnk An studied the forest beyond the river from atop Awere's ramparts. Below, the streets teemed with her warriors; armed, armored and ready. She glanced toward the hills and frowned. The Taiku pledged their support, but she was still skeptical. They used their birds to survey the Chuiku territory and attended discussions planning the most direct route to the mountain of kipande. Tahnk knew preparing for a battle and fighting a battle were two separate things. She would march, no matter what the bird folk decided to do. She had no choice.

Aharon appeared at her left shoulder.

"Suti," she said. "We are ready."

Tahnk nodded, her attention still focused on the riverbank.

"It seems they are unaware of our intentions," Aharon said.

"Don't be foolish," Tahnk replied. "The Chuiku know we are coming. You can be sure of that. You can't assemble an army this large in secret. They are waiting on the opposite bank, deep enough not to expose their ranks yet close enough to see us. They hope to use the river's advantage to defeat us, attacking as we cross."

She looked to Taharka, her lead engineer. "Are the bridges ready?"

Taharka, a dark brown man with head ringed with gray hair bowed.

"They are ready, Suti. We have delivered them to the Taiku, and they have fitted the harnesses to their birds."

Tahnk nodded her approval. She wished she had more time to draw up a better plan, but the visit from the Na-Set let her know that time had run out. She had no idea what she was up against; the Chuiku were experts at keeping their numbers secret. Their main fighting force, the marons, were constantly on the move. Only the women occupied their cities and villages, and they kept their military capacity hidden. None of the scouts she sent, Medji or Taiku, had returned. So, her plan was simple; strike hard, strike fast, and hope for victory. Normally she would send her regular army to take the brunt of the battle, saving the Medji for the final devastating blow. But she did not have such luxury. Instead the Medji would lead the attack. They would punch a hole in the Chuiku center, allowing her warriors to flank both wings.

Tahnk surveyed the scene one last time before leaving the ramparts. She hurried down the steep steps then climbed into her awaiting chariot. The Medji stood in double file behind her; the remaining warriors in rank behind them. She had no words of encouragement; either they would win, or they would lose. She looked at the trumpeters standing before her chariot, awaiting her command.

"Give the signal," she said.

The trumpeters bowed then raised their horns to their lips. Their cheeks tightened as they played short shrill bursts. The city gates creaked loudly as they were raised. Tahnk An jerked the reins of her chariots and cracked her whip. Her horses reared then galloped forward at full speed. The Medji slammed their swords against their shield and followed, running at a pace that matched Tahnk An's chariot. They emerged from the city, spreading out in a line even with their Suti. Tahnk looked to either side of her as she placed down her whip then took her baton from her sash.

* * *

Nandi's sweaty palms made gripping her spear difficult. She cursed herself for her uneasiness as she stood behind the marons. Their demeanor was much different. They paced and shook their weapons, anxious for the battle about to take place. Flanking them were the Paaku archers, led by their first hunter and Siza. Amana paced at the edge of the woods just beyond the riverbank. Nandi could take it no longer; he pushed her way through the marons and joined Amana.

"I told you to stay behind the marons," Amana said without looking at her. "You must be protected.

"I'm a warrior," Nandi replied. "I'll protect myself."

"If I die you must be ready to take my place," Amana said. "This is not time for stubbornness. This is not about you; it is about our people.

"I can . . ."

The sound of trumpets rose over the Bindamu city walls. Moments later the gates opened and a chariot charged into the open, followed by a group of warriors that stretched out to both sides of the chariot.

"They are coming!" Amana shouted. "Prepare!"

The Paaku loaded their bows while the marons surged forward. Amana raised her hand, stopping their advance.

"Stay within the trees," she said. "Let them come to us."

The Bindamu rushed up to the river, stopping just out of arrow range. Nandi could see the chariot rider clearly. The woman looked majestic, her armor shimmering in the sunlight. Her face was attractive yet stern, her dark eyes sweeping the forest perimeter. The woman reached for the sash around her waist, extracted a short ebony baton. The sight of the object struck Nandi like a physical blow; she stumbled away holding her head.

"Get back!" Amana shouted. She turned to the others; her face marred with fear. "Get back now!"

Most of the marons heeded the First Hunter's warning. They fell back deeper into the woods, following the women who had come to fight. Nandi walked backwards slowly, still trying to understand what was about to happen. Amana grabbed her arm and began dragging her away.

"Didn't you hear me?" she scolded. "We must . . ."

A searing blue light burst from the Bindamu woman's baton. Amana shoved Nandi to the ground then shielded her as a blast of heat washed over them like a fiery wave. The heat sucked away the air; Nandi and Amana gasped as they attempted to breath. Nandi felt Amana roll from atop her and she sat up, trying to catch her breath. She opened her eyes to horror. Trees had been burned like spent torches; the ground scoured by the fire. Charred bodies of the marons that lingered littered the scorched earth. Terror hit her as she wondered if Baba or Etana was among those dead. A familiar shriek snatched her attention to the sky. Tai flew toward the river, carrying large platforms between them. They placed the objects across the river and the Bindamu rushed across. The tai shrieked again, but this time the cries were those of pain. The Paaku had recovered. They shot arrows into the birds and their riders, driving them back. As the bird warriors retreated, the archers turned their barrage on the Bindamu warriors crossing the bridges.

Nandi scrambled to her feet when she heard the marons regrouping. They rushed by her and surged by the First Hunter, smashing into the Bindamu warriors crossing the platforms. Amana ran toward the melee, transforming into the totem but instead joining the battle she jumped high, soaring over the fight and disappearing into haze left by the blast. Nandi's shock dissipated, replaced by fury. She plunged into the fight, stabbing a Bindamu warrior in the throat before melding into the battle.

* * *

Tahnk An looked on the battle scene slightly shocked. Her baton had done much more damage than she expected, a testimony to the kipande source nearby. If she had known of its proximity she could have taken on these savages on her own, or at least with minimum support. To her relief the Taiku kept their word. The birdmen arrived with the bridges, dropping them into place. As they positioned the final bridges a shower arrows rose from the woods, driving the birdmen away. The arrows then fell on the Medji, who raised their shield for protection. Then the savages appeared, covered in leather armor and brandishing swords and spears. The met the Medji with skilled fury, stopping their advance. These were fearless, seasoned fighters; rarely had she seen warriors stand up to the Medji so fiercely. They would need her help.

The beast came out of the mist, mouth agape and claws spread wide. Tahnk jumped from her chariot and grimaced as the claws ripped her shoulder. She rolled to her feet and turned in time to meet the leopard's second attack. She pointed the baton at it and released its energy, the blue fire engulfing the beast. But instead of burning the beast into ashes, the creature transformed into a woman. The woman looked at her, just as stunned as Tahnk.

The woman's confusion was brief. She jumped into the chariot and attacked Tahnk, landing blows to her face and chest before she was able fight back. They struggled bare-handed; whoever this woman was, she was skilled. Tahnk had achieved the rank of master among the Medji, yet it was taking her all her skills to keep this woman at bay. It was the same with her warriors, these savages, despite being outnumbered, were driving the Medji out of the forest, off the platforms and into the river. The tide of the battle was turning; defeat had become a possibility. If she could use the baton one more time, she could kill this woman and join her warriors. She needed a distraction . . ."

It was a Taiku that save her. The bird hit the woman with its talons, knocking her to the ground. The woman stumbled then rolled onto her knees. She jumped, wrapping her arms around the bird's sharp beak then jerking it to the ground. The rider fell as the woman twisted and broke the bird's neck. She pounced at the rider, driving her fingers into his chest as she bit into his neck and ripped away his flesh. Then she was the leopard again. She faced Tahnk who now held her baton, grinning as the cat woman growled.

"Let's try this again," Tahnk An said as she pointed the baton at the woman.

* * *

They were winning. Nandi sensed it despite the fighting swirling around her. She spun, stabbed, clubbed and dodged by instinct, taking on every Medji that managed to attack. The Paaku abandoned their bows, jumping into the fray with daggers and swords. But these warriors would not surrender. This was a fight to the death for both sides.

The Chuiku forced the Medji into the river and to their bridges. Nandi led a group of marons across one of the bridges, jabbing faces, and legs with her spear. As she reached the opposite side of the bridge, she saw Amana in chui form charging the chariot woman. The chariot woman held the baton in her hand.

"No!" Nandi screamed.

She knocked a Medji off the bridge then sprinted toward the women. Amana leaped; the woman squeezed the baton. Blue flames roared, consuming Amana. When they cleared, the First Hunter lay on the ground badly burned. The scream in Nandi's throat became a roar as she pounced the distance between her and the chariot woman. The woman spun toward Nandi and her eyes widened.

She attempted to point the baton at Nandi, but Nandi swiped it away with her paw. Nandi landed on the woman chest, biting into her throat as they both slammed into the dirt. Nandi bit deeper, wrapping her forelimbs around the woman's body and crushing her against her. The woman attempted to wriggle free but Nandi bit harder, clutching the woman until her life flowed from her body with the blood running from Nandi's mouth. Nandi tossed the woman's body aside then rushed to Amana. When she reached her side, she was in human form again, tears running down her cheeks. The First Hunter shifted; Nandi cradled her burned upper body.

"You are First Hunter now," Amana said, her voice a whisper.

Nandi shook her head. "No. Mama will heal you."

"There is no healing for this," Amana said. "The blue flame was like that of the mountain. If I did not die now, I would die later. It would be slow and painful. I'm happy the priestesses have favored me."

A hand touched her shoulder; Nandi looked up to see Etana.

"The Bindamu warriors are defeated," he said. "Those we did not kill flee to their city. What should we do?"

Nandi and Etana looked to Amana. The First Hunter managed to smile.

"It is not my place to say," she said. "Nandi is First Hunter now."

Amana closed her eyes, then died.

ELEVEN

The ceremony began at daybreak. The bodies of those lost were carried by wagons to the burial site where the graves had been dug. The families that lost loved ones trailed the wagons in silence, their white robes and purple headwraps joining them together as one. Almost every clan suffered. The true extent of the cost was not revealed until long after the battle was over. The Chuiku had won, but paid a bitter price. Almost half of the marons were killed, and a third of the women warriors. If not for Nandi slaying the Bindamu leader, it would have been much worse.

Nandi led the procession to the mound. Although Baba, mama, and Abasi had survived, she mourned for Amana and the others. She was First Hunter now and all of Chuikuland was her family. It was a burden laid upon her too soon, but one she had to accept, especially now.

The procession reached the mound. The wagons circled the rim of the burial pit and the families removed their loved ones from the wagons. They carried them like newborns, which in a sense they were. Although their lives had ended in Chuikuland, their new lives had just begun among the ancestors. Care had to be taken, less their spirits became frightened and remained among the living to cause havoc. After the bodies had been placed, Nandi visited each one, whispering the words that Mama taught her, words that would have been shared with her by Amana had she survived.

"Farewell, chui," she said. "We will dance together soon."

Though her words were meant for everyone, for Nandi they resonated for Amana. She knelt by the woman's body wrapped tight in burial cloth, her face exposed. Nandi kissed her cold cheek then brushed her hand across her forehead. Nandi had received her calling too soon, but she would do her best to be the First Hunter Amana taught her to be.

When she was done, she climbed from the tomb, her face wet with tears. She joined the circle, holding hands with Abasa and Etana while Mama took her place before them. The drummers played; their rhythm energetic yet respectful. Mama raised her hands then looked into the heavens.

"Priestesses! Our loved ones stand at your door awaiting their new lives. Only you can show the way. Will you accept them?"

The Chuiku looked to the sky for the answer. For a moment there was nothing, then Nandi noticed a cloud forming over the burial site. The cloud expanded, blocking the sun and casting a cooling shadow over everyone. A light drizzle fell and the Chuiku danced. The priestesses were present; they were opening the way. Nandi saw them among the clouds, their eyes on her, their solemn faces almost identical.

"This is only the beginning," they said to her. "You will be tested."

The drizzle continued until the ground was soaked. The cloud dissipated, releasing the sun from its internment. The mourners, satisfied their loved ones were among their ancestors, trailed off, talking among themselves.

Mama found her way to Nandi.

"You have done well," she said.

Nandi wrapped her arms around Mama's waist.

"I'm not ready," she said.

"No one is ever ready to accept great responsibility. You will figure things out on your own," Mama said. "And you have us to help you. For now, you must rest. Things are not settled."

Nandi knew what Mama meant.

The next few weeks were uneventful. Everyone went about their daily tasks, the heaviness of the battle slowly dissipating. Nandi spent her time at home with Mama. As First Hunter she should have been patrolling Chuikuland, but there were more important issues to deal with. Those issues presented themselves at daybreak. Warning drums sounded in the city and the women armed themselves. Nandi and Mama rushed to the city center to see an expected sight. A Taiku messenger climbed down from his mount, a peace baton in his hand.

"I bring word from the Kashites," he said. "They wish to meet at the river to discuss terms."

"Terms for what?" Mama asked.

"Terms for peace," the messenger replied.

"We will meet them in three days," Mama said.

The Taiku nodded. He climbed on his mount and flew away.

* * *

Three days later Nandi stood alone at the banks of the Hagosa, watching the Kashite approach. There were ten total; seven Bindamu and three Taiku. The Bindamu were warriors, yet they carried no weapons. As they neared the river Nandi stepped into the cool waters and crossed onto the bank. The Kashites approached her warily, their eyes trained on the woods behind her.

"Don't concern yourself," Nandi said. "I came alone."

A woman stepped forward and bowed. Her eyes strayed to the forest before she spoke.

"Honored First Hunter," she began, "I am Senior Commander Aharon. I have been chosen by my people to negotiate terms of peace."

"There will be no negotiations," Nandi replied. "This river is the border. You will not cross it."

"I understand your concerns," the commander said. "We were hoping to establish relations that would benefit both our people."

"Like it has benefited the Taiku?" Nandi stared at the Taiku and they looked away. She pointed at the river again.

"This is the border. If your people cross it, they will be killed. We want nothing from you, nor do we wish to share anything with you."

The commander opened her hands and smiled.

"First Hunter, if only we could . . ."

Nandi transformed into the chui. The Taiku fled; the Bindamu stood frozen in fear. Nandi paced before leaping over the river. She glared at the commander before slipping into the forest. Mama waited for her as she transformed.

"There will be peace for a time," she said.

Nandi dressed.

"When they come, we will be ready," she replied.

They watched the Bindamu hurry back to
their city, then began their journey home.

PART TWO:

HUNTED

TWELVE

They were trespassing.

For fifteen years the Hagosa River stood as the border, separating the natives of nKuland from the invaders from Menu-Kash. Much blood had been shed to establish the watery boundary, but neither side believed it would stand forever. The merchant caravan crossing at the fording point knew what they perpetrated could be the cause of war, but greed overruled fear of death and common sense. They had items to sell and wealth to gain and nothing would quench their hunger. Their guards had been paid three times their worth in hopes that if danger came, they would defend the caravan with their lives. Most were natives themselves; they accompanied their conquerors not for wealth but for a chance to kill their traditional enemies and regain some dignity. They too, were naïve. They knew not what trouble they stirred.

Nandi, Siza and Abasi observed the Bindamu as they crossed the river separating Chuikuland from Bindamuland. Nandi counted twenty of them, twelve Bindamu men and six women. The breach of their territory angered her, but what angered her most was the nKu leading the foreigners. The claw tattoos on their shoulders revealed them as Taiku, only nKu to fall to the invaders thus far.

"What do we do?" Abasi asked.

"We kill them all," Siza answered.

"No," Nandi said. "Only seven of them carry weapons, nine including the Taiku."

Nandi folded her arms across her chest. "Siza, stay here and cover us with your bow. Abasi and I will deal with this."

Siza nodded then loaded her bow.

Nandi looked at her brother then grinned.

"Come Abasi. Let's hunt."

Abasi grinned. "Yes sister, let's."

Sister and brother ran down the steep slope, weaving through the dense foliage with speed and stealth. As they neared the caravan they separated, Abasi working his way toward the center of the group while Nandi continued to the road ahead. The Taiku became aware of her presence before the others, raising their heads then looking about with concern. Nandi burst from the bush before the Taiku could warn the others. She threw her spear into the chest of the first Tiaku before he could draw his sword; she ducked the swing of the other Taiku as she jerked her spear from his dead cohort's body. She spun about, slamming the blunt end of her spear into the Taiku's ribs then chopped into his head with the knife-like spear head.

She glimpsed Abasi attacking the Bindamu warriors in the midst of the wagons as the others ran toward her. Three Bindamu lay dead with arrows protruding from their necks. Nandi dealt with the two Bindamu quickly but the last one possessed skill. They sparred, spear against swords, Nandi grinning with respect of the foreigner's talent. She saw Abasi creeping up from behind then shook her head; this was her kill.

The Bindamu faltered, his endurance far short of his skill. Nandi swept him off his feet with her spear. The man fell on his back, his swords knocked from his hands. Nandi planted her foot on his chest as she placed her spearhead against his throat.

"Ask for quarter and I will give it for you were a worthy opponent," she said.

The man spat at her instead.

"You get no begging from me, crut!" he said.

Nandi pushed the spear into his throat. She kept her foot on his chest until he stopped thrashing.

She looked up into the angry face of a short, round Bindamu draped in a dingy robe and jangling with jewels.

"What is the meaning of this?" he whined. "We are not an army! We are merely traders seeking barter."

Nandi cracked the man across the mouth with her spear butt. He fell on his haunches as he covered his bleeding mouth.

"You crossed the river. You broke the treaty. No one asked you to come, nor were you invited. Leave now before we kill the rest of you."

The others needed no prompting; they scurried to turn the wagons about. The pompous one stood on his feet then lowered his hands, blood running down his chin then dripping onto his robe.

"I will remember you," he said.

"And I will remember you," Nandi answered. "If I see you here again, I will kill you."

The merchant walked backwards, stabbing a finger at Nandi.

"My name is Thutmos," he said. "Remember it, savage. You will not see me again, but you will see my vengeance!"

Nandi raised her spear as if to throw it; the Bindamu Thutmos yelped, turned then ran. Abasi glared at the fleeing man as he came to Nandi's side.

"They are poor fighters," he said. "I still wonder how they defeated the Tai."

"Don't underestimate them," Nandi replied. "This was a merchant train. The guards were hired, although that one' - she pointed at the man she'd stabbed in the throat- 'displayed some skill.'

Siza emerged from the bush. She strolled to the Bindamu she killed then jerked her arrows from their corpses.

"We should follow them to make sure they don't double back," she said. Her eyes were on Abasi.

Nandi grinned. "You two follow them. I'll head back to Jikubwa. The Matrons must be informed."

Abasi and Siza sprinted down the road. Nandi watched them and her mind drifted to Etana. It had been three years since she'd seen him, three years since she journeyed east for his company. She looked around her and was reminded why. Serious times were ahead for the Chuiku and as First Hunter it was her responsibility to protect the people. Etana would have to wait.

Nandi set off at a hunter's pace down the trail leading to Jikubwa. She was three days from the city; with good weather she would reach it a day sooner without Siza to slow her down. She ran until dusk overtook her then receded into the bush to make camp. The first night she slept soundly, comforted by the dreams of her childhood in these woods. She remembered chasing game with her small bow and the proud look on mama and baba's face when she came home with a full game bag. Those were pleasant easy days, long before the Bindamu. The next night she was haunted by the spirits of the men she killed. She prayed, asking the Priestess to accept their spirits so they would leave her in peace.

On the morning of the third day the walls of Jikubwa rose over the horizon. He took the small horn from her hip then trumpeted her arrival. The rampart guards responded. Nandi placed her spear against a nearby tree then sat to tie her loose braids into a tight bundle that fell below her buttocks. She wrapped the braids carefully then took her bracelets and other baubles from her pouch. By the time the city guards arrived on stag back she had transformed from Nandi First Hunter to Nandi, *Bintifalme* of the Chuiku.

Bishara, the garrison captain, was the first to reach her. A riderless stag was tethered to her mount. She dismounted her stag then bowed.

"Welcome home, Bintifalme," she said. "The Malkia has been worried about you. You have been hunting a long time."

Bishara looked about. "Where is Siza?"

"She is with Abasi, following Bindamu."

Bishara's eyes went wide. "Bindamu?"

Nandi nodded. "They crossed the Hagosa. I must meet with the Matrons immediately."

She mounted her stag then rode into the city with the guard through the wide gates and down the paved avenue leading to the city center. The guards turned away as she approached the palace. The palace servants greeted her at the gilded doors, taking her stag after she dismounted.

Nandi entered the palace alone. She strode down the elongated foyer, passing through a gauntlet of images of her ancestors. She glanced at them, each a woman of strong features. She was a continuation of their lineage, but she was not sure she deserved to be.

"Where were you?" her mother shouted, her voice echoing across the atrium. The elegant elderly woman sauntered to Nandi with her arms folded across her chest, her long skirt swishing against the granite floor.

"There are rumors that the Bindamu are about and you ride off as if nothing is the matter."

"They are no longer rumors," Nandi said. "Abasi, Siza and I came across a merchant train crossing the Hagosa. We killed the guards then sent them back."

The Malkia's eyes narrowed. "You fought them?"

Nandi looked puzzled. "Of course. I'm First Hunter."

"You are Bintifalme! You are my heir! You could have been killed!"

"What was I to do? Let them reach the city?"

"You could have sent word back to us! We have marons to deal with such emergencies."

"Siza and Abasi were with me. We dealt with it," Nandi said.

The women glared at each other for a moment before her mother relented.

"I will summon the Matrons," her mother said. "Be kind enough to do your duty and send word to the marons. Maybe Etana will come. It's been years since you've seen him."

Nandi said nothing as she walked away. Much had changed among the Chuiku since she became First Hunter. They once were a simple people, now they took on the ways of the invaders. Mama was more concerned with decorum than action, more occupied with her bearing a child than protecting their nKu. But Nandi had not changed. She would do her duty. She hoped Etana would stay away as he always did. Now was not the time.

THIRTEEN

Thutmos barged into the officers meeting, drawing the glares from the persons seated around the oblong mahogany table. He wore a silken robe festooned with jewels with sleeves that ended just shy of his fingers. Each digit of his hand displayed a golden ring representing the ten provinces of Menu-Kash, a deliberate display of his relation to the Na-Set. A royal purple turban sat on his head, held together by a jeweled broach. Dendera Cheops, the garrison commander, a tall, umber skinned man with clan scars proudly displayed on his cheeks, stood then leaned on the table with both hands.

"You have your duties," he said to his subordinates. "We will meet tomorrow at the same time."

The officers stood in unison, saluted then marched from the room single file. Thutmos waited until the last man was gone before plopping down in the nearest chair. Dendera folded his thick arms across his chest.

"It couldn't wait, Thutmos?" he said.

"No, it couldn't. Look at me. What do you see?"

It had taken Thutmos three weeks of healing and attention before he deemed himself suitable for public viewing. Despite that his disfigurement was still prominent and possibly permanent according to his personal surgeon.

"A pompous, overweight merchant who constantly wastes my time," the commander said.

"You wouldn't take that tone with me if we were in Menu-Kash proper," Thutmos said.

"No, I wouldn't. But we are not across the sea, are we? I have authority here."

Thutmos intertwined his fingers under his chin.

"Yes, you do, but I have the Na-Set's blood. A certain word to a certain person and you'll end up in the Rains."

Dendera sat hard opposite the merchant as Thutmos smiled.

"Now commander, look at me again. What do you see?"

"It seems you've been in a brawl," Dendera said. "One of your brethren catch you cheating him? Or did you try to shortchange a courtesan?"

"No! My train was ambushed by Chuiku!"

The commander sat at attention. "Where? When?"

Thutmos looked away. "We crossed the Hagosa . . ."

Dendera slumped in his chair. "You entered Chuikuland?"

"Yes, but . . ."

"You know Chuikuland is off limits," the commander said.

"You don't need to remind me," Thutmos replied. "I'm well aware of that."

"Then whatever happened to you has nothing to do with me or my warriors."

Thutmos jumped to his feet. "I was attacked! My guards were killed. We are lucky they didn't steal my goods!"

"You have nothing the Chuiku want," Dendera said. "And you violated the treaty. We have nothing else to discuss."

"You've become too close to them!" Thutmos said. "You depend on their council. Half your ranks are Bodantu. I wouldn't be surprised if I found one of them in your bed!"

"Watch yourself, da-Menu," Dendera said. "Your insults are coming close to creating consequences."

"People were killed; our people," Thutmos said. "This was a direct attack on Menu-Kash sovereignty! There must be some sort of retaliation."

"Menu-Kash will move on Chuikuland in its own time. Until I receive orders to do so my army will stay on this side of the river. I suggest you do the same."

"Nandi will pay for this!"

Dendera sat up; his eyes wide.

"Did you say Nandi?"

"Yes."

"Then thank Edu you live. She is First Hunter of the Chuiku. She is also the reason we stay on this side of the river."

I don't care who she is!" Thutmos shouted. "She insulted me and Menu-Kash. She must pay! This affront can't go unavenged!"

Dendera rubbed his stubbly chin. "There is a way."

Thutmos stood. "I'm listening."

"There is a man who might exact your revenge for the right price."

"He's not one of your Bodantu, is he?"

Dendera laughed. "No. He is from Menu-Kash proper."

"Who is he?"

"Sinzabak."

Thutmos gasped. "A Wandau sonchai? Here?"

The commander nodded.

"Where can I find him?" Thutmos asked anxiously.

"In the transient district. He arrived two weeks ago."

Thutmos's eyes narrowed as he stood.

"Why are y ou helping me?"

"Because I didn't come here to babysit," Dendera answered. "There is no honor this duty, no way to claim prestige. With this cat woman dead maybe the Na-Set will allow us to do what we came here to do."

Thutmos came to his feet. "Thank you, commander."

Dendera shook his head then grinned.

"I'm surprised you're taking my advice. I thought bloodlines didn't believe in sorcery."

Thutmos returned his smile.

"I believe in whatever serves my purpose, commander. Good day."

FOURTEEN

Nandi stood before the Matrons dressed in a white halter, her hair twisted in a single braid wrapped in white cotton cloth. A white linen skirt rested low on her hips, the side slits revealing her toned thighs and Chui tattoos. The markings matched the tattoos on her shoulders, the symbols of their clan. The matrons sat before her, eleven women clothed in brightly covered dresses, their heads covered with matching colored turbans. Behind the Matrons sat the Elder marons, each summoned from their sojourns to attend this important meeting. They were present out of respect of their age, but they would have no say on the matter of the day. Nandi's eyes wandered to her father and she shared a brief smile with him. It had been ten seasons since she'd seen him; his hair was nearly gone and that which remained was gray. Sadness touched her; his sojourn would end soon.

She saw Siza as well. Her best friend was Paaku, not Chuiku, but her nKu had been allies so long many thought of them as one. Thick black stripes adorned her shoulders and thighs. She returned two days ago wearing the silly smile most hunters displayed after sojourning with their consort. Nandi was sure Abasi shared the same face. She frowned; if her friend wasn't careful, she would find herself with child, making her useless in the coming storm.

Mama stood then turned to face the Matrons. She was dressed similar to the Matrons with the exception of the Chui cloak hanging from her shoulders, held together about her neck by a single gold cord. She took her time studying those in attendance, nodding her head as she smiled.

"It has been a long time since we all sat together," she said. "The young marons come for the festivals, but the elder chui stay on sojourn. I guess we old ones are not as interesting as we used to be."

A ripple of laughter filled the meeting chamber. Even baba smiled, which was something he rarely did. Mama would be angry if she knew how much time she spent him. He was a good teacher and a master hunter. Amana was better of course, but she'd learned much from baba as well. It was her secret as well as her strength.

"But such gathering never come in good times," her mother continued. "The Bindamu violated the treaty. Two weeks ago, they crossed the Hagosa. Nandi, Abasi and Siza attacked then sent them back. But more will come as they did before. We know it."

"They have been here long before."

Nandi tensed upon hearing the familiar voice. Etana stepped forward, his spear across his back, his bow, arrows and sword bouncing off his hip. Sweat still glistened on his bare chest; apparently, he'd just arrived. Other young men followed him and none of them were smiling.

"What are you doing here?" Mama asked. "You were summoned, but not to this meeting."

Etana stepped forward.

"I'm sure this meeting is about war," Etana said. "Giving honor to you, Malkia, we are not here to be rude. If we are to be asked to fight, then we should be here. Besides, we have been fighting the Bindamu for months."

Nandi's eyes went wide.

"For months?" she said.

Etana's eyes fell on her, a slight smile coming to his face.

"Our borders are long," he said. "Some Bindamu have come alone, some in small groups. All have died."

"We are already at war, it seems," the Malkia said.

"May I continue to speak, Malkia?" Etana asked.

Mama nodded.

"We have crossed the river, too. The Bindamu have built towns not far from the river. Their army gathers in a town they call Accru. The Taiku gather there as well. The Bindamu say it is to protect their people, but the Taiku are anxious for Chuiku trophies."

Mama's eyes finally fell on Nandi's. "What say you, Hunter?"

"Another war is coming, there is no doubt of this," she said. "The question is how do we fight it? I know every hunter in this room. I know their strength and their heart. But if we fight the Bindamu alone, we will lose. It has been many seasons since the last war and we still haven't recovered. We are too few."

Chaos erupted. The males yelled at her in protest, the Matrons wailed in anger. Nandi stood still, her eyes focused on her mama who looked back at her with respect. She waited until the mael-strom subsided before speaking again.

"Hear me out. No one can defeat us in clan war. Our warriors are skilled and our tambiko is strong. But the Bindamu have something we don't; they have discipline and they have numbers. The only way we can stop them is to join with the other nKu."

The silence was as deafening as the previous outburst.

"That has never happened," a Matron said.

"It has, once," mama said. "The legends say that long ago, when our people first came to this land, we were one people. Our tambikos were one, so the geseres sing. But we grew apart then became enemies. But now we have a greater enemy, one that threatens to destroy us all. Either we come to-gether and live, or we fight separately and die."

Etana tilted his head. "So how do you plan on bringing the nKu together? We can't fight one war in order to win another."

"I will summon the Priestess and ask for challenge rites," Nandi said.

Etana laughed. "No one will fight you. They know they will lose."

"I'm not challenging their Hunters," Nandi said. "I'm challenging their tambikos."

FIFTEEN

Awere's transient district was the home for new arrivals to the city. It was also the most orderly of its districts due to the overbearing presence of warriors, constables and others paid to enforce the Empire's edicts. Thutmos felt perfectly safe walking its wide, clean paver brick streets covered in his black hooded robe. He was making an obvious statement of hiding his identity, which attracted the attention of many, a few who attempted to look under his hood. He shooed them away with his walking stick and continued down the street, the directions to his destination memorized.

Thutmos hesitated when reached the steep hill leading to the lodges. He took a deep breath then attacked the hill like a mountain climber. When he reached his destination at the middle of the hill, he was totally exhausted. He leaned against the battered wooden lodge door waiting to catch his breath before knocking. The person inside was less patient; the door swung open and Thutmos tumbled inside.

His nose was assailed by bitter smells and pungent concoctions. He scrambled to his feet, immersing his head into a cloudy mix that made him sneeze and stung his eyes. Through the haze he saw tables covered with glassware of all kinds, each containing liquids of various colors. The room reminded him of the alchemist labs of Menu-Kash proper, those valued vaults that created the wonders which made Menu-Kash supreme over all the nations of Ki Khanga. The man scurrying between the tables was unlike any of Menu-Kash. Although his purple robe resembled that of Menu-Kash lineage, he was not of the blood. His was an ancient order, one of the last cultures to succumb to Menu-Kash's might. Though the last to submit, they were the first to accept the name 'da-Menu.

"Sinzabak?" Thutmos said.

The sonchai turned toward Thutmos.

"Who calls my name?" he said in a raspy voice. "Who enters my home?"

"Thutmos of Menu-Kash."

Sinzabak wiped his hands on his robe as he approached Thutmos.

"The highborn," he said. "I think you are lost. I have nothing that would interest you."

"But you do," Thutmos said. "The commander said you would be of use if I needed someone killed."

Sinzabak moved closer to Thutmos, their noses almost touching. His breath made the nobleman's nose crinkle.

"I might, but it will not be cheap," he whispered. "My methods are unique."

"I'm sure," Thutmos said.

"What do you wish?"

"I need a certain Bodantu killed, a Chuiku to be exact."

"The Chuiku are beyond the river," the sonchai said. "It is forbidden."

"I'm told you can circumvent that."

"I can," Sinzabak said. "But that will cost more."

"How can I be sure you can accomplish this task?"

Sinzabak held out his open hand.

"Do you know why I came here, High Born? I am here because the spirits are dead in Menu-Kash. The da-Menu put their faith in our Pharsa and they worship that which they make with their own hands. They ignore the spirits, and the spirits ignore them."

Smoke gathered over his palm, forming a ragged sphere.

But here, the spirits are alive!"

Sinzabak blinked his eyes and the sphere became a cloud, flashing lightning then raining into his palm.

Thutmos stepped away from the sonchai. This was real conjuring, not the performances the imperial priest displayed for the masses.

"I need this done as soon as possible," he said.

"Then let us see who we are dealing with," Sinzabak replied.

The cloud over his hand expanded, engulfing them both. Thutmos stiffened as he felt tendrils searching his mind. The encounter between him and the Chuiku woman appeared in such detail that he felt the blow to his mouth as if it just occurred. When the cloud dissipated, he reached for his mouth expecting to feel blood. To his relief there was none.

"I will do it," Sinzabak said as he hurried back to his table. "Deliver two thousand cowries to me by morning. I will contact you when the deed is done."

"So be it," Thutmos said. He hurried from the house, happy to be back in fresh air. Sinzabak

was a dangerous man, he concluded. He would have
to make other arrangements for the sonchai once
the Chuiku was dealt with.

* * *

Sinzabak hands quaked as he poured the red
liquid into an empty container. The Menu-Kash
High Blood was a fool. He had no idea who he had
stumbled upon. He would kill the woman, but not
for Thutmos' reasons. The spirits favored this woman. If he did not stop her now, it would be the end
of his own plans. He took the container to his fire
and began his work.

SIXTEEN

Nandi sat on a smooth chunk of granite, watching the narrow trail that led from the city. Two weeks had passed, and everyone was still in an uproar about her decision to challenge the tambikos. Some thought her crazy; others thought it was impossible. The only Chuiku that seemed to agree with were mama, Siza, Abasi and Etana. Since mama was Malkia permission was granted. But she had caused a rift between the Malkia and the Matrons, a situation that would spell problems in the near future.

Laughter broke her musing. She looked up to see Abasi and Siza walking hand in hand down the trail. They saw her then released each other, their smiles fading. Nandi scolded herself; it wasn't that she didn't like seeing them happy; it wasn't the time for such things. She needed them both, and an expectant child would make them less reliable.

"You shouldn't be so distracted. It could cost you your life."

She jerked about to see Etana emerging from the woods behind her. It angered her that he surprised her; it angered her more when he smiled.

"This is not the time for games," she said.

"Who said I was playing," Etana replied. "If you plan to challenge tambikos, you need to be diligent. Who knows when they will strike?"

Abasi and Siza had reached her. They nodded to Etana's wisdom.

"I didn't ask you here for criticism," she said. "I asked you here to help me."

"How can we help?" Abasi said.

"I plan to travel to the mountain and asked for the Priestess' assistance."

"That's a long journey which passes through other nKu land. You will be challenged at every turn," Siza said.

"This is why I asked that you come with me."

"You know I will," Siza said.

"I will, too," Abasi said. "We are family."

Everyone looked at Etana.

"I have no wish to travel with you, Nandi."

He turned then walked away.

"You should follow him," Siza said. Abasi nodded his agreement.

Nandi sighed then went after Etana.

"Etana, wait," she said.

He stopped then looked back at her.

"All I have done is wait for you, Nandi. It's been five years since we sojourned. Now you want me to trek with you to see the Priestess so you can risk your life fighting tambikos."

"You forget who I am," she said. "I'm First Hunter. I'm responsible for our nKu."

"That doesn't prevent you from being with me."

"It does," Nandi said. "You remember the last war. We suffered too much and lost too many. You know what's about to befall us. You've crossed the river and seen it. I won't say it in front of the others but challenging the tambikos is a desperate act. There is so many Bindamu now. Many more than before. It's true I might die challenging the tambikos. But I'd rather die doing so than to see our people crushed by the Bindamu."

"This is why we should be with each other," Etana replied. "I don't want my last memories of you to be in anger."

Nandi said nothing. The emotions roiling inside took her voice.

"I will come," he said. "But this must be a sojourn as well."

Nandi's eyes narrowed. "No."

"Then I wish you well, and I pray for your safe return."

Nandi watched him walk away until she could no longer see him. Why didn't he understand? All he could think about was being with her when their entire existence was at stake. When she returned to the rock where Siza and Abasi waited her mood had soured.

"He's not coming?" Abasi asked.

Nandi shook her head.

Siza touched her shoulder. "Nandi, maybe if you . . ."

Nandi knocked Siza's hand away.

"Go back to the city and gather your things. We leave tonight."

Siza placed her hands on her hips.

"Nandi, we must talk about this! Etana is a valuable ally."

"Do as I say, Siza!" Gone was Nandi the friend; in her place was First Hunter.

Siza bowed. "Yes, First Hunter. Come Abasi."

The two walked away. Nandi sat, watching the water churn over the rocks below.

SEVENTEEN

Sinzabak sat naked in the center of the blood drawn circle. Beside him lay a chui carcass. He paid the Taiku hunter who killed it well, for he risked his life crossing the Hagosa to obtain it. The hunter took to the task eagerly; it was chance for him to shame his hated enemies. Sinzabak grinned; in the end it was their differences that would doom them, their inability to overcome their hatreds and petty conflicts and unite against an enemy determined to consume them all. As it was for the world that once was, it would be for the nKu.

Three clay bowls sat before him. One contained the fluids of the Chui, its blood, urine, saliva, its essence. The second held a concoction that took weeks to make, a potion containing ancient alchemy enhanced by new science from Menu-Kash. The third bowl was empty. Sinzabak waved his hands over it, invoking the spirits he served, asking them to fly from beyond the angry Sea and over the Ur mountains to settle before him in this land that promised so much. Sweat ran from his body in rivulets, dripping into the bowl as he chanted. He opened his eyes and was pleased with what he saw. A storm swirled in the once empty cup, the presence of the sacred spirits answering his call. He was right in believing this land was held what had been lost in Menu-Kash.

He picked up the other bowls then poured their contents into the third. The fluids churned as they mixed like a tiny tempest, shaking the third bowl to the point the sonchai feared it would spill. He reached out toward it then pulled his hand back; he could do nothing until the solution was complete.

The bowl ceased shuddering. The fluid cleared, a sign that his efforts were successful. Sinzabak grasped it with both hands then raised it over his head.

"Rainmakers! I humble myself before you. It is said the Chuiku are invincible. Their First Hunter is unmatched, they say. The Chuiku fight without mercy and kill with no remorse, they say. But will the Chuiku kill that which they honor?"

Sinzabak drank the potion. His body trembled as he swallowed it, the fluid leaking out the corners of his mouth and staining his skin. He finished the last drop and he stiffened, the bowl falling from his hands. He collapsed onto his side, convulsions wracking his thin frame as he crawled to the Chui carcass. With his last effort he lifted himself up then collapsed upon the feline body. Both bodies melded as the potion seeped from the sonchai's pores, dissolving them like acid. Then the fluids reformed into a different Chui, a large hulking beast with eyes filled with reason.

"Beware, Nandi of the Chuiku!" Sinzabak the Chui growled. "Your tambiko is coming for you!

EIGHTEEN

Nandi, Siza, and Abasi beheld the mountain which the Priestess claimed as home. A dense forest blanketed the steep slopes, a wall of green so thick they could not find a way through. But that was only the first challenge. The second was the sheer granite walls rising from the forest. From a distance there seemed no way the stone walls could be scaled. The three sat beside the stream surrounding the peak, sharing despondent stares.

"There must be a way up," Nandi said.

"It's been many years since anyone visited the Priestess," Siza said. "Maybe she's dead and the pathway is blocked."

"No," Nandi said. Although Siza could be right, something told Nandi otherwise.

Abasi shrugged then stood. "Let's see if there's a way."

He ambled to the woods. As he entered a thorn laced vine struck his face like a whip. He yelled then fell back, blood seeping through his fingers on his cheek.

"I think she's still alive," he said. "At least her defenses are."

Siza rushed to his side to tend his wound. Nandi walked cautiously to the forest edge.

"What are you doing?" Siza called out. "You saw what just happened to Abasi!"

Nandi tensed; her sharp eyes focused on the foliage. The trees and shrubs rustled as she neared; to her surprise they opened a path to her.

"Come, sister," a familiar voice said in her head.

Nandi stepped into the forest. The foliage closed immediately behind her, cutting off Abasi and Siza's protests. She followed the emerging path for what seemed like hours, stopping only to rest or relieve herself. Fruits appeared whenever she hungered, and water gathered wherever she thirsted. The forest gradually cleared, giving way to the stony peak of the mountain. Nandi studied the smooth rock face for handholds but saw none. Then the ground shook and the mountain rumbled. Nandi fled toward the forest, anticipating a stone avalanche. Instead an opening appeared before her, a gap barely wide enough for one person. Nandi treaded toward it then peered inside. A light flickered in the distance, growing brighter and steadier with every second. Nandi backed away as the light grew so intense, she had to shield her eyes.

"Welcome, Nandi of the Chuiku."

The voice that rang in her head now resonated before her. She uncovered her eyes to see a beautiful umber woman standing before her, her scant blue clothing accented by bracelets and jewels. The woman held a carved staff which emitted a pulsing light. Nandi fell to her knees.

"Priestess," she said.

"Stand, my sister," the Priestess commanded. "In times such as these, you and I are equal."

Nandi came to her feet unable to hide the puzzlement on her face.

"I know why you are here," the priestess said. "The Chuiku are not the only ones under siege. The Bindamu seek not only our land and our people, they also seek our soul. They have brought powerful spirits with them, spirits that wish to claim here what they have lost in their own realms. So, we must fight on different planes, my sister. You must fight for our people and I must fight for our gods."

"Must I claim the tambikos?" Nandi asked.

"Yes," the Priestess answered. "The nKu grow weak. Many have lost their faith. Those who have not, fear they are next. They call for tambikos that do not respond for deep inside the other nKu don't believe in them. But the Chuiku tambiko and the others persist because of you and the other Hunters."

The priestess touched her own chest. Her hand glowed as she pulled it away. A ball of light hovered over her palm."

"Come closer, sister."

Nandi hesitated, not sure what the light would do to her.

"Do not fear, First Hunter."

The priestess extended her hand holding the light. Nandi felt its heat but did not move. The Priestess pressed the light against Nandi's chest. Energy coursed through Nandi, renewing her body and spirit.

"I share my essence with you," the priestess said. "It is all I have to give. I wish you well in your struggle."

"Will we win?"

The priestess looked away. "I do not know."

When she looked back there was a hopeful smile on her face.

"Go back to your people, Nandi. Your first task will soon be upon you."

Nandi bowed then ran for the forest. She stopped then turned back. The Priestess was gone, the fissure in the stone sealed.

"Thank you, Priestess," she said. "I will not fail you."

She faded into the trees.

NINETEEN

Sinzabak peered at the city with feline eyes under the cover of darkness, his nostrils flaring as he searched for the one he came to kill. It took two weeks for him to reach the Chuiku city, more than enough time to become accustomed to his new form. It was a strong, vital body, one that would serve his purpose well. The flesh of two nKu unfortunate enough to cross his path filled his stomach. The Chuiku would be helpless before him.

Nandi's scent broke his musing. It was strong and acrid, filled with the sweat of exertion. It would make her that much easier to kill. He climbed down from his perch then proceeded to the city.

Nandi blew her horn as the city came into view. She was exhausted, but the sight of home gave energy to her legs. Abasi and Siza ran behind her, their heavy breathing conveying their fatigue as well. They were home; now the real work would begin.

They entered the clearing surrounding the city. An odd sensation gripped Nandi's and she slowed her pace. Her eyes were drawn to the western woods; there was movement among the trees. Nandi took her spear from her back. The tension in her gut increased.

"Something is coming," she said.

No sooner had the words left her lips did that something emerge into the moonlight. Nandi's mouth went dry as the pain inside pushed her to her knees.

"Chui!" Abasi said.

Siza and Abasi knelt before their tambiko. Nandi could barely see; the pain in her so great.

"Nandi," Chui said. "First Hunter of the Chuiku. Submit to me."

Nandi dropped her weapons. Chui raised its mighty head.

"The time of the nKu is done," it said. "The tambikos must step aside for greater gods, as must its people. They must sacrifice those that would fight against the change."

Nandi raised her head, her mind reeling in confusion.

"Great Chui, the Priestess told us we must fight. She said those across the sea have come to steal our land and our spirits."

Chui pounced, landing inches away from Nandi.

"The Priestess lies! She seeks to save herself. She cares nothing for you."

Nandi's pain subsided, replaced by familiar warmth.

"No." she said. "The Priestess does not lie. It is you who lies."

"Nandi!" Abasi said. "Do not question the wisdom of Chui."

Nandi stood, her fists clenched. "This is not Chui."

The beast roared then struck at her with its paw. Nandi bent backwards, grabbing her spear as she brought her legs over her head then crouched into a fighting stance.

"What are you doing?" Siza shouted. "This is Chui!"

"No, it's not!" Nandi dodged another paw then plunged her spear into the beast's side. It howled then backed away.

Nandi charged after it. The spear fell from her hands as they transformed into furred paws. Her body changed as well, the spots on her shoulders and hips spreading throughout her skin. By the time she reached the beast she resembled it in every way.

"No!" the beast cried out.

Nandi unleashed her full fury, slashing and biting the beast. They clinched each other, rolling around the clearing fighting for advantage. Nandi found the beast's throat then bit hard. She felt its blood flood her mouth as it struggled to free itself. The beast ripped her body with its hind legs but Nandi would not let go. The beast shuddered. It let out a man-like cry as it went limp in her grip.

Nandi stepped away then watched as the beast transformed into the body of a small naked man. She transformed as well, standing bloodied before him. A wave of pain and fatigue passed over her; she was about to collapse when Siza caught her. She looked into her friend's eyes then managed to smile.

"I told you it was not Chui," she said.

"He wasn't," Siza replied. "But you are."

TWENTY

Nandi and Etana sat beside the stream holding hands as they watched the water tumble over
the smooth stones. Three weeks had passed since
she killed the Bindamu sorcerer. Her wounds were
healed, but her soul was a different matter. As soon
as she recovered, she sent for Etana. They met at
the stream and made it their home for a time,
spending their days and nights making love, eating
and sleeping. For a week they did so, but on this
particular morning Nandi sensed it time to bring an
end to their paradise.

Etana looked into her eyes.

"Why?" he said. "When you became Chui, I
knew I had lost you. I never expected you to contact
me again. But here we are and I don't understand
why."

"Because being with you makes this all real,"
she said. "I always knew I had a duty to fulfill, but
never like this. My own mother bows to me. But you
haven't changed. You still see me as I was, as I am."

Etana shifted then looked away.

"Etana?"

"It's difficult to see you the same way," Etana
confessed "You are more than I imagined, yet I still
see inside you the woman I love. I pray that once
this is over you will return to who you once were."

Etana's words stung, but at least they were honest. If honesty was all he could offer it was enough.

"The Priestess says I must challenge the other tambikos. Will you come?"

"I will, but I will not travel in your camp," Etana said.

Nandi pulled away, her eyes wide. "Why not?"

"I believe distance between us would be best."

Nandi didn't answer. Another feeling was rising in her.

"Leave me," she said.

Etana stood, pulling her up as well. They kissed for a long moment before she let him go. Etana walked away, glancing back at her until the woods blocked her view. No sooner had he disappeared did a pulsing brightness descend from above. The light coalesced before her into the Priestess.

"Hello, sister," the Priestess said.

Nandi tried to kneel but the Priestess grasped her wrist then tugged her up.

"You have slain the imposter," the Priestess said.

"Yes, sister. With your help."

The Priestess smiled. "The tambikos are safe inside those who believe in them."

"But what if the sorcerer had killed me?"

"The tambiko would have returned to me," the Priestess said. "You are not the first that has come to me, Nandi. All the tambikos reside in warriors such as you."

"So why do you come to me?" she asked.

"Because I favor you, Nandi. You are the strongest of the Hunters. If you cannot bring the nKus together then our cause is lost."

"It is a heavy burden," Nandi said with a worried smile.

"Yet it is one you must bear," the Priestess replied.

"I will do my best," Nandi said.

"That is all I can ask. And I will do mine."

The Priestess hugged Nandi, startling her. The embrace was warm and comforting like a mother's hug. Then she released her and faded into light once more, rising over the stream and leaving Nandi alone.

* * *

The day of departure had come. Everyone in Jikubwa gathered in the clearing to wish them well. Nandi, Siza and Abasi hugged everyone, accepting their blessings and prayers with sincerity. Even men had come, giving their blessings as well. Nandi adjusted her back pack, inspected her sword, her knives and her spear. She looked at her brother and best friend then shared a smile.

"Where to first?" Siza asked.

"The Temboku," Nandi replied.

Abasi whistled. "Are you sure? Their First Hunter is formidable."

"If I defeat her, the rest should be easy," Nandi said.

Siza nodded. "Then the Temboku it is.

Nandi blew her horn and the others responded. A familiar reply caught Nandi's ear; she looked to the woods and saw Etana standing just within the trees, smiling at her.

"You are with me," she whispered.

Together they ran down the trail. The Chuiku remained in the clearing, blowing their horns until the trio disappeared over the horizon.

Nandi and Siza

Nandi as Priestess

Siza

Abasi

Etana

Aziza the Priestess

PART THREE:

A GATHERING OF SPIRITS

TWENTY-ONE

They arrived with the pilgrims from Menu-Kash, surviving the year long journey across the volatile Kudisan Sea. When their ship moored on the coastline shadowed by the towering Ur Mountains, they disembarked with the others. Heavy hooded cloaks protected them from the harsh cold, garments that would be discarded once they reached the land beyond the mountains. They bore large bands on their backs, carrying the weight effortlessly as they joined the long line of new arrivals give their reason for coming to the new land. They spoke rarely, and when did it was to each other. The first of them to reach the immigration officer had to bend deeply to scribble his name on the census sheet.

"State your skill," the bored officer said.

"Carpenter," the man replied.

The officer looked up to the man.

"That's a strange accent you have," he said. "From where do you hail?"

"The Rains," the man replied.

A fearful look gripped the census taker's face. He stamped the man's papers with a shaky hand.

"Welcome to Botanduland," he said.

The others were granted entry. They took no rest, bypassing the rest facilities and joining those waiting for the next wagon to the interior. The mule drawn coaches crept into the massive tunnel which cut through the mountains separating the frigid barren coastline from the warm verdant interior. A week-long journey in darkness interrupted by rock slides and other mishaps did not stir their emotions. They had a sure destination and an unwavering purpose.

When they arrived in Awere they made their way to Sinzabak's home. The door was unlocked so they entered. One of them, the shortest of the three, stopped in the center of the room. He took off his cloak then revealed a face that confirmed his Rains origin, grey skin and large eyes with slit pupils.

"Our brother is dead," he said.

"Does he linger?" the tall one asked.

"Barely. His death was long ago and far from here."

The third one removed her robe. She walked along the bench tops, passing her hands along the stained wood.

"A transformation elixir," she said. "Animal spirit."

The tall one closed his eyes. He reached out his hands and the others grasped them. They stood rigid as they shared minds, searching for the reason of their brother's death. When they opened their eyes, they knew.

"A bold plan, but Sinzabak was always one for boldness."

"The Chuiku are responsible," the woman said.

The tall man nodded. "The woman Nandi and the one who is called Priestess."

They let go each other's hands.

"This land is rich in spirit," the short stout one said. "Our gods will thrive here."

"The ones called Taiku are broken. Their spirit has abandoned them," the tall man said.

The woman nodded. "They seek new faith. We will provide it."

"But the others are defiant," the stout man said. "We must finish what our brother began."

"First the Priestess," the woman said.

"Then Nandi," the stout one replied.

TWENTY-TWO

The Priestess stood at the entrance to her temple, chilled by the foul wind blowing from the east. They had come at last to claim her realm. She pulled her hood tight against her head then sighed. Years ago, there would have a host of spirits surrounding her, but the others transcended, no longer compelled to watch over beings that barely remembered them. The tambikos still thrived, but since she placed them in the hearts of the various First Hunters, they were no longer companions. She was alone in this fight, at least almost alone.

"Aziza," she said. "I am Aziza!" she shouted out loud to keep from forgetting her name. It had been so long since it had been spoken. It echoed among the peaks, her only audience.

The wind bit into her skin and she retreated into the temple. A fire blazed in the center of the cavernous structure, giving movement to the various statues pressed against the circular walls. She walked the perimeter, touching each sculpture as she passed, gathering confidence with every caress. She then approached the fire then knelt before it.

"Tell me what to do," she said. "Guide me with your wisdom."

"The Others have come," the fire replied. *"You cannot face them until the tambikos are united."*

"But they may come for me first," she replied.

"Then you must come to us. Nkuland is no longer our home."

"No," the Priestess said. "I promised Nandi I would help her."

"It was a foolish promise. She is nKu. She will fail."

"You underestimate her."

"And you believe in those with mortal weakness. Look what they have done to us. Their minds are fleeting. You'll be a memory soon, nothing more."

The Priestess did not answer.

"Join us," the fire said. *"Join us, Aziza."*

The mention of her name almost broke her resolve. She so wanted to be among them. But when she thought of Nandi and how the Chui woman believed in her the weakness abated.

"I leave the temple," the Priestess said. "But I will not come to you. I'll face the Others."

"You will perish."

Aziza turned her back to the flames then walked away.

"So be it."

She trudged to the edge of the precipice.

"It's up to us, Nandi," she whispered.

Aziza spread her arms then leapt from the mountain, hovered in the air for a moment, then plunged toward to her fate.

* * *

Nandi ambled through the short grass toward the Temboku city, her arms extended to her sides and her hands open. Her spear was secured to her back, her swords and knives resting at her waist. Siza walked beside her in the same pose, her bow and arrows snug in her hip quivers. Abasi was not with them. He hid in the tree line, ready to act if the meeting did not go well. And somewhere, Etana lurked. Nandi had not seen him since they set out but she knew he followed. She could sense him and his presence gave her confidence. Most of all she could sense the Priestess. She was not present, but knowing her powers rested inside her gave Nandi the courage to do what she must do.

Nandi noticed the tembo herd lingering between the city and the woods. Unlike the Chuiku the Temboku had a close relationship with the animals their tambiko represented. It was the herd that warned of their arrival, the matriarch looking their way then trumpeting her agitation. The rest of the herd answered; moment later the Temboku emerged from their city. It was a large group of warriors and all of them were armed.

"This doesn't look good," Siza said.

"We must trust the Priestess," Nandi replied.

"I'd rather trust my bow, your spear and our feet," Siza said.

"Don't show fear, no matter what they do," Nandi said.

"I'm not afraid," Siza replied, "just prudent."

The Temboku surrounded them, keeping just out of bow range. Three warriors continued to approach, two men wearing long grey robes and a towering woman garbed in leather armor and carrying an enormous axe. They halted before Nandi and Siza.

"I am Nandi, First Hunter," Nandi said.

The woman stepped forward.

"We know who you are," she said. "I am Winda. The Priestess said you would come."

Nandi hid her surprise. She was under the assumption the Priestess had only spoken to her. Apparently, she was wrong.

Winda possessed a warm, motherly countenance. She smiled and dimples pitted her plump cheeks, her expression odd to Nandi considering the situation.

"Then you know why I am here," Nandi said.

The three Temboku nodded in unison.

"You can tell the other Chuiku he can come forward," the other man said.

"What are speaking of?" Siza said.

They heard a yelp from behind them. Nandi and Siza turned to see Abasi fleeing the woods pursued by two young tembos. Under any other circumstances they would have laughed.

"Let's be about this then," Winda said. "The sooner I claim your tambiko the sooner I can be about gathering the others."

The Priestess had told them all the same thing, Nandi surmised. She jerked her spear off her back, feeling betrayed.

No sooner had the others backed away did Winda attack. She was much faster than her bulk suggested. Nandi raised her spear, blocking Winda's blow just below the axe head, the blade stopping inches from Nandi's forehead. She shook from her arms to her feet, stumbling away from the impact. Had her arms been shorter the blow would have split her skull. She dodged the second swing then managed to prick Winda's arm with her spear tip. Winda winced then backed away.

Winda was much stronger than Nandi, but Nandi's speed allowed her to keep the woman at bay. Still, it was becoming more obvious that the two were equal in skill.

Winda swung her axe down at Nandi. Nandi sprinted forward then jabbed her spear into Winda's thigh. Instead of collapsing to her knee, the woman let out a shrill cry then grasp Nandi's spear with both hands. She transformed, her bulk increasing, her skin becoming gray like the tembos of her city. Her face changed as well, her nose elongating into a trunk, her canine teeth emerging from her mouth to become two metal clad tusks. Winda became the Temboku tambiko while Nandi struggled in her nKu form. Winda yanked the spear from her thigh with her trunk then threw it far, Nandi flying away with it. Nandi yelled and her voice became a growl. She landed on four paws.

As Chui she returned to the fight. She was much stronger and swifter, dodging Winda's tusks, leaping in to strike with her claws. She roared as Winda tired, the Temboku's attacks becoming less focus as she lost energy and blood. Winda collapsed to her knees, her breathing shallow and rapid. Nandi leaped into her chest, knocking her onto her back. She gripped Winda's neck in her mouth but did not bite. Winda turned her massive head to the side, closing her eyes in concession. Both women transformed back to their nKu forms.

The stunned Temboku wrapped Winda in robes, cutting their eyes at Nandi as she dressed alone. Siza had her bow out notched with an arrow; Abasi's sword was half out his sheath.

"The fighting is done," Winda said.

She stumbled to Nandi.

"The Priestess favors you," Winda said. "Still it will not go easy for you. None of us will concede."

"I understand," Nandi said. "Neither would I."

"My axe and my people are yours," Winda said. "What do you wish of us?"

"Wait for my return, or whomever defeats the tambikos," Nandi said. "We have a greater enemy and we must be prepared. Will the Temboku be ready?"

Winda nodded. "We will. Where will you go next?"

"To the Simbaku," Nandi said.

Winda whistled. "The Priestess be with you, Nandi."

"I hope she is," Nandi replied.

TWENTY-THREE

The Taiku district of Awere occupied the northernmost section of the city, nestled against the cliffs that once served as their home. They were the first to encounter the Menu-Kash as they breached the Ur Mountains, the first to draw Menu-Kash blood, and the first to fall to the Menu-Kash war machine. There were some that speculated if the first encounter between nKu and Bindamu had been peaceful the cultures would exist in harmony. That, of course, was a lie. Menu-Kash tolerated no equals or rivals.

The Taiku that called Awere home were far from those earlier folks. Humbled and humiliated by Menu-Kash, they existed under the invaders' rule for a generation. Many among them never knew of life in the peaks; others wished to forget. And then there were the elders who would some-times stare above at odd moments, remembering their former glory then pray for a tambiko which seemed to have forgotten them.

When the strange woman appeared in the district at the onset of the rainy season her presence did not go unnoticed. The Taiku numbers were small enough where everyone knew each other, and if they did not it was easy to find someone who did. But no one recognized this woman. She owned no home in the district, nor did she reside in any of the guest homes provided for Menu-Kash officials. Most disconcerting was her odd skin color and cat-like eyes. When she attended the communal meals on Third days no one refused her, yet she spoke to no one in return. She smiled, ate, and then disappeared into the dark streets when the meal was done.

Finally, on her third appearance during the communal meal, the elders approached her.

"Who are you?" they asked.

The woman seemed to grow taller as she answered.

"I am Tai," she said.

The elders looked at each other They were not amused.

"If this is a joke, it is not a very good one," Cazembe, the youngest elder said. "Are you a *makaapweke* from the cliffs? Some say a few of us still live in the rocks."

The woman smiled. "No. I bring you a message. Your tambiko lives. It waits for you."

A gruff looking man by the name of Mani stepped forward from the elders, anger radiating from his scarred face.

"Leave us!" he shouted. "It is bad enough that you take advantage of our charity. Now you insult us? You go too far, Bindamu!"

The woman threw off her hooded robe then spread her long arms. Feathers emerged from her skin as her body transformed. The people gathered around the woman as her face melded into beak and crown.

Cazembe and the others staggered back, their faces filled with awe.

"Tai!" Cazembe exclaimed.

The bird woman sprang into the air. She circled over the astonished throng then ascended into the dark sky, disappearing from the Taiku's view and leaving them all babbling in wonder. The bird woman soared over the city for a brief moment then descended on a small home perched on a steep hill in the foreigner's district. As her feet touched the ground the woman no longer resembled the Tai or their tambiko. She was a woman of The Rains.

Her companions waited for her as entered the house.

"Do they believe?" the tall one asked.

"They will soon," the woman said. "Their tambiko has returned to them. They will do as it asks."

"It is good," the stout one said. "Our time goes short. Nandi subdued the Temboku and now she travels to Simbakuland."

"And the Priestess draws near," the tall one said.

The woman nodded. "We will be ready. The Tai will be our disciples. Those who have lost faith will believe again, but they will believe in our gods."

The tall one grinned. "First the nKu, then the Menu-Kash. Thus, it shall be."

"Thus, it shall be," the others repeated.

TWENTY-FOUR

Aziza soared over the perimeter of nKuland, verdant forests and grasslands streaking under her in a blur of green. The forests gave way when she crossed the Hagosa into Menu-Kash territory. Wide roads scarred the open ground, clumps of trees held captive by a brown void. In the distance she saw Awere, a gray sore pressed against the Ur Mountains, a foreign malignance sucking the life from her homeland. She veered her course away from the city to the eastern mountains then flew upward, the air losing its heat as she climbed higher and higher. Frigid air enveloped her as she surpassed the highest peak. What she saw startled her and gave her pause. She was familiar with the height of the Ur, but never had she seen the breath of it. She was astounded. The mountains spanned further than she could see even at her altitude. The thought that the Menu-Kash bored through them to reach nKuland raised fear in her heart. What type of people were that determined? She would soon find out.

She glided over the mountain range. The gray jagged peaks revealed no sign of life, only bitter snow-capped rock. For three days she flew before the horizon changed. Instead of gray rock, there was gray sky.

"What are you doing?"

"I need to know from where these people come."
"You will not like what you discover."
"We'll see."

The mountains dwindled into a black rocky shore. Docks peppered the beach head for miles filled with large ships depositing countless numbers of people. The Menu-Kash were like a disease overwhelming its host. The people filed into odd wagons that emitted a coughing sound as they rolled on thin metal rails then disappeared into the solitary tunnel. Aziza surmised the wagons were headed to Awere.

The voice of the ocean commanded Aziza's attention. She gazed into the stormy sea and the dour horizon. She flew into the tempest, fighting the violent winds churning the waters below into deadly storms. She weakened and lost altitude but was determined not to turn back.

"Why must you persist?".
"If you are not here to help me then leave me be!"

Warm energy encased her; lifting her fatigue. She felt as if she was cradled in her mother's arms, and in a sense she was.

"So, you will know and give up this foolishness."

She flew faster now, the surrounding storms deflected by her spiritual shield. The storms finally abated, the sea calm and beautiful. Land appeared over the horizon, another shoreline crammed with docks, buildings and ships.

"Menu-Kash."

Aziza soared over the land of her enemies for days. Every part of Menu-Kash writhed with people, so much so the landscape seemed in constant motion. Though the sheer number of people fascinated her, it was the lack of something else that caused her the most discomfort. The land was vacant of spirits except in a few distant places where the rain fell constantly. The energy emanating from the cloud covered regions was similar to that she felt in Awere.

"Do you see now? They will consume us."
"Why must it be?"

She was pulled in a direction against her will. She fought to no avail. Her protector was now her captor, taking her to a remote mountain range bordering Menu-Kash's polar regions. She descended into a rock formation that seemed too angular to be natural. The force placed her on cold rock, and then illuminated the cave with light. Aziza gasped at what she saw.

"Now do you understand?"

Aziza nodded as tears streamed down her cheeks.

"Come to us, sister. You'll be safe."

Aziza shook her head. "No. I will fight with the nKu. Either help me or leave me be."

The cave fell silent.

"You have made your decision," Aziza said. "And I have made mine."

She lifted from the cave floor then flew into the open, her strength revitalized. She knew the truth now. She would find Nandi and share it with her. Together they would fight.

TWENTY-FIVE

The Temboku shared one of their sprawling
lodges with Nandi and the others so they could rest
before traveling to Simbakuland. They provided the
Chuiku with fresh food and water and their healers
tended to Nandi's wounds. Siza stayed by her side,
watching the Temboku healers with suspicion.
Abasi stood guard outside the lodge, accompanied
by the two tembo that chased him from the woods.
His former adversaries had become friendly companions, pulling at him playfully with their trunks
attempting to distract him from his duty.

A healer massaged a pungent ointment into
Nandi's wounds which deadened the pain and set
the cuts healing before her eyes. Another healer
rubbed a different ointment into her weary muscles
which eased their tightness. As she succumbed to
their attentions Winda strode into the lodge.

"How do you feel, sister?" she asked.

"Like a goddess," Nandi said. "Your healers
are wonderful."

"They are my personal healers," Winda said.
"You earned them."

"With this attention I'm surprised I defeated
you,"

Winda let loose a hearty laugh that filled the
lodge.

"There is no attention better than that of a Priestess."

"She favored us both," Nandi said.

"No, she favored you. We Temboku can sense such things. I knew I was defeated before we fought. Still I hoped for better."

"I see," Nandi said.

"The Simbaku won't be as sensitive."

Nandi frowned. "I know."

Winda sat on the ground. "Their First Hunter. You have history with him."

"Yes," Nandi said. "When he attained the position, he came to Chuikuland with a proposition. He suggested an alliance with us, one sealed by marriage."

"It was before she was joined with Etana," Siza added.

Nandi nodded. "When I refused, he attacked me."

Winda's eyes went wide. "Did he hurt you?"

"Yes," Nandi said as her eyes narrowed. "And I almost killed him."

Winda smirked. "Almost?"

"The elders intervened," Nandi said. "His death would have meant *vita* between our nKu and the elders did not wish it."

Winda nodded. "And now you will fight him again."

Nandi didn't answer.

Winda stood. "You know how it must end between the two of you. If I could go with you I would. A swollen river rages between the Temboku and the Simbaku. But this is your task. Rest well, and may the Priestess be with you."

Later that night, as Abasi and Siza enjoyed each other's company in the lodge, Nandi slipped into the woods. She was deep into the darkness when she felt Etana's approach. He prided himself as a man of stealth, but Nandi always sensed him. She pretended not to, wandering in the darkness until she felt his arms slip around her waist from behind.

"If I was a Simbaku you'd be dead," he said.

"Good thing you're not," she replied.

She turned in his arms to face him then pulled him into a kiss. Their bodies pressed hard together; Nandi thought of ending the distance between them that moment. But reminders of her duty and the upcoming confrontation quelled her feelings. She ended the kiss then gently pushed Etana away.

"We leave for Simbakuland tomorrow," she said.

Etana hesitated before replying. "I know."

"Will you be with us?" she asked.

"Of course, I will.'

"No. I mean close with us."

"I can't do that. Abasi and I are *chuiwanuame*. We won't stand each other's company long."

"Then stay as close as you can," she said. "We may need you."

"I'll try," he said.

She kissed him lightly, and they gazed at each other, their eyes doing Nandi wouldn't allow. Etana grinned then trotted away; Nandi watched him go then returned to the Temboku lodge.

* * *

Simbakuland was a three-day trek over the rolling hills of Tembokuland. Unlike Winda's land there we no forests, only grasses and scattered shrubs. The open range made it impossible to approach in stealth, so Nandi, Siza and Abasi strode across the flat expanse making no attempt at disguise. Nandi held her spear in guard position as did Abasi with his sword. Siza walked with an arrow notched in her bow, her eyes scanning the horizon. She stopped then raised her bow, aiming ahead of them.

"They are coming," she said.

Nandi strained her eyes, barely made out the rising dust cloud. Moments later she heard the roars of the advancing party. Siza slowed her pace, taking position behind Nandi and Siza. Abasi walked faster, acting as vanguard. The Simbaku came into view. There were fifteen, all armed with Simbaku short swords, heavy shields and throwing spears. Niko, the Simbaku First Hunter, led them. All were running. This was not to be a formal challenge. The Simbaku were coming to kill them.

"Siza!" Nandi shouted.

Siza loosed and arrow, spearing the Simbaku running alongside Niko through the throat. Niko immediately took refuge behind the others. Two more Simbaku went down, Siza's arrows protruding from their heads. Three Simbaku ran toward her and were cut off by Abasi and his whirling sword. He held the Simbaku long enough for Siza to shoot another down before she dropped her bow and joined Abasi with her machetes.

Nandi faced off against the other six. She glimpsed Niko sitting cross-legged behind them, a wide grin on his face. They would wear her down then he would finish her. That was his plan.

Nandi swung her spear wide, holding her attackers at bay. Once came too close; Nandi cracked his skull with the blunt end of her spear. Another Simbaku attacked with more bravery than skill; Nandi speared the man in his chest, lifted him over her head then dumped his limp body behind her. A third Simbaku slammed into her before she could bring her spear to bear, tackling her. He straddled her then raised his head to release a triumphant roar when familiar hands slammed his mouth shut then twisted his head, breaking his neck. Etana kicked the man away.

"Stay behind me," he said. "Save your energy for Niko."

Etana attacked the Simbaku with ferocity and skill almost equal to Nandi. As he drove the Simbaku away with his sword and dagger Niko waited, his eyes locked on Nandi. He threw his head back then roared, transforming into the Simbaku tambiko. Nandi dropped her weapons then sprinted toward him. This time her transformation was immediate. Niko and Nandi slammed together, rolling as they bit and clawed each other. Though Nandi matched Niko attacks, she knew she couldn't keep up this pace. Niko was bigger and stronger; he would eventually wear her down. She tried to break free but Niko held fast.

"I should have killed you long ago," he said, his nKu voice in her head.

"You couldn't then. You won't now," she said.

Nandi couldn't break free, so she did the only thing she could do. She pressed her head against Niko's neck until she felt the pulsing vein running to his head. She gripped him tight then bit down with all her might. It was the same technique Amana used long ago, and it was just as effective. Niko roared in pain, ripping at her torso and back with his forelegs and hind legs. Nandi felt her flesh tear and blood flow from her but she refused to let go. Niko rolled and clawed, battering her against the ground but she held firm. Finally, her mouth filled with his blood, the warm bitter fluid almost forcing her to gag and let go. Niko shuddered; he roared again then collapse on her. Nandi's head fell to the side, her blood and Niko's blood trickling from her open mouth. She was too weak to free herself. Pain consumed her as she struggled to stay conscious. The pressure eased as Siza, Abasi and Etana pushed Niko's body away.

"Nandi? Nandi!" Etana said.

But Nandi did not hear him. Her eyes were transfixed on the sky as peace settled upon her. She reached out with her arms.

"Priestess," she whispered.

Her arms fell to her side as she closed her eyes.

TWENTY-SIX

The Taiku hurried through their communal evening meal as they had for the past weeks then looked into the sky. Their elders wore tattered Tai robes, remnants of a faith lost long ago. The woman had not been seen since she revealed herself and her purpose, yet they prayed she would return. They were tired of being servants to the Bindamu.

It was a young girl who saw it first. She jumped from her mother's lap, stabbing her finger toward the sky.

"Look! Look!"

The giant tai circled the city, spiraling tighter and tighter as it descended into the Taiku courtyard. The people parted as the bird landed then transformed to the woman, her bare feet touching worn stone. The Taiku dropped to their knees then placed their faces onto the stone, covering their heads with their hands. The woman was pleased. This was not respect; this was worship.

"Rise," she said. "We are all equal under the Rains."

The Taiku came to their feet. The Elders approached, their hunched shoulders and furtive looks a sign of their fear and reverence.

"Tai, what are these Rains you speak of?" the Cazembe asked.

"The Rains bring life," she answered. "The Rains mute the harshness of the sun, the Rains cleanse the land. The Rains revive and renew."

She raised her hands over her head then chanted. A small cloud formed above her fingers then ascended, expanding to cover the entire city section. A light mist fell upon the Taiku, an energizing liquid that tingled on their skin. Children pranced and giggled, filled with energy from the gentle downpour. Men and women grinned and embraced, some with friendship, others with amorous intentions. The elders smiled as well; their wrinkles less prominent.

"You feel it," she said. "You understand now. I was broken in the mountains, deserted by you, ignored by the ancestors. The Rains came from across the sea and healed me as I have come to heal you. I have returned to make you strong and break the Menu-Kash chains that bind your bodies and minds."

She transformed into the tai then sprang into the air, her massive beating wings stirring a tempest.

"Will you follow me?" she shouted. "Will the Taiku rise?"

"Yes!" they shouted. "Yes!"

*   *   *

Aziza flew low over the Ur Mountains, weighed down by the knowledge of the hidden temple. The ancestors beckoned her, granting her a place among them, a place where she could free herself from the nKu and their burden. Their time was over, they said. But she had promised Nandi she would help her. Could she desert the Chuiku woman to deal with this alone?

Pain broke her musing as something hard slammed into her. She spun, flailing her arms and legs. She rocked as she was struck again. This time the blow had the opposite effect, clearing her head and steadying her flight. She blinked her eyes then saw her attacker speeding toward her, a bearded man draped in a gray robe that fluttered about him, his features blurred by a buffet of clouds surrounding him. Aziza remained motionless until the man was almost upon her and then dodged to her right. She glimpsed the man's shocked face as he sped by then slammed into a nearby peak. She followed, her staff glowing bright in her angry hands.

"You cannot defeat them!" the ancestors said.

"Either help me or leave me be!" Aziza shouted. "I will not abandon the nKu!"

The man was climbing out of the rubble of his impact when Aziza struck him on the head with her staff. The misty barrier slowed her blow, but still the man was stunned. She spun around, hitting the man in the abdomen with the back of her staff. He doubled over as she brought the staff down on his head again. Strength surged in her arms; she heard a cracking sound as her staff struck home. The man slumped to the ground.

"We are with you," the ancestors said.

Aziza smiled. "Then let's finish this!"

TWENTY-SEVEN

Nandi awoke to a familiar face. Winda and her healers smiled as Nandi sat up and her stomach rumbled.

"I'm hungry," she said.

"And you're alive," Winda said. "We weren't sure you'd live."

"The Priestess protects me," Nandi said. "I can't fail."

"You almost did."

Siza and Abasi entered the room.

"The Simbaku continued fighting despite your victory," Siza said. "Abasi, Etana and I held them off best we could but they almost overwhelmed us. Then the Temboku came."

Winda turned away, a blushing smile on her face.

"I thought you weren't coming," Nandi said.

"I changed my mind," Winda said.

Nandi wanted to ask for Etana but she knew that would not be appropriate. There was something more; she could see it in Winda's eyes.

"Now that you are recovered there are those who wish to meet you."

Winda went to the door. "Let them enter."

Nandi sat up in the bed as Abasi and Siza took up position on either side of her. Hunters entered the room and Nandi's heart thumped against her chest with joy. Vifaruku, Nguruweku, Mambaku, Kibokoku, and Nyaniku stood before her bed, all with smiles.

"What is this, Winda?" she said.

"When you returned from your victory against the Simbaku I sent the word to the other nKu. I told them that the Temboku would stand with you. I told them you had the blessing of the Priestess. The others decided to do so as well."

Nandi looked at the Hunters, noting a significant absence.

"What of the Nyatiku?"

Winda frowned. "The Nyatiku are . . . stubborn."

Nandi's fists clenched.

"Then I must convince them otherwise."

* * *

Nandi marched across the shallow marshland but she was not alone. Siza and Abasi flanked her as always; Siza with her bow loaded, Abasi with swords drawn. Behind her the other Hunters followed. They would all be needed. The Nyatiku possessed no single Hunter. Like their tambiko, they protected each other as a group, which made them the most formidable. They yielded to no one, not even the Simbaku. If the Bindamu managed to cross the river and defeat each nKu, the Nyatiku would be their last and most difficult challenge.

Despite their herd defense, there was still one Nyatiku Nandi would have to confront. Like the Temboku, the Nyatiku lived beside their tambiko. Their cities consisted of clusters of homes resting on stilts which protected them from the marsh and frequent flooding. Narrow towers crowned with flat observation platforms rose over the buildings. There was no doubt they'd been seen; Nandi knew they were expected.

A deep moan-like sound emerged from the city. It was answered, the crooning resonating in Nandi's gut. The crooning subsided; moments later the ground trembled beneath Nandi's feet.

"They're coming!" Abasi said.

Nandi looked to Winda then nodded. The Temboku hunters unwrapped the bundles they carried, revealing long sturdy spears with broad leaf spearheads. The Hunters formed a circle around Nandi, Abasi and Siza.

"Are you sure this will work?" Siza asked.

"Against a stampede? No," Nandi confessed. "But the Nyatiku will not deliberately hurt the Temboku. The true battle is between me and their Hunter. If she is honorable, this should only be a display."

"And if she is not?" Siza asked.

Nandi answered her friend with a smile. "We'll be trampled to death."

The Nyatiku galloped into view, broad warriors wearing bovine masks and riding their heavy horned tambikos. It was a frightening image, one that would break the spirits of lesser warriors.

"Stand firm!" Nandi shouted. "If you don't yield, they will!"

Her warriors tightened their circle then lowered their spears. Siza raised her bow then took aim.

"No, sister," Nandi said. "We will give them the chance."

The drumming hooves and bellowing voices drowned out all other sounds. Nandi began to doubt her strategy as the herd closed. The warriors braced; just beyond spear range the herd veered left and right, encircling the Temboku and Chuiku.

Winda came to her side.

"I saw her" the Temboku warrior said. "She waits for you beyond the circle."

Winda crouched then linked her fingers together. Nandi took a few steps back, and then ran at her friend as fast as she could. She stepped into Winda's hands and Winda sprang upward, heaving Nandi into the air.

"Up you go!"

Winda flung Nandi high and far. Nandi somersaulted, increasing her distance. She landed on her feet before the startled Nyatiku Hunter, the broad woman's eyes wide with surprise. Neither had time to transform into their tambikos so they fought as Hunters. Nandi attacked her immediately, slashing the Hunter with her swords. The Hunter recovered, blocking the swords with her horn-shield with a force that shook Nandi's wrist. Nandi circled and struck, the Hunter turning with her as she blocked each blow. A commotion from her right distracted her; one of the Nyatiku managed to return. He was almost upon Nandi when Etana tackled him.

The distraction was enough. Nandi turned into the Hunter's shield. The shield smashed her face and she blacked out; when her senses returned the Hunter towered over her, shield raised for a killing blow. Nandi twisted, sweeping the Hunter's feet from under her. The Hunter crashed onto her side and Nandi scrambled atop then pummeled her with her sword hilt. She could have killed her, but that was not her aim. When she saw the Hunter was almost unconscious, she relented.

"What is your name?" she asked.

"Orma," the Hunter said.

Nandi pressed her blade against Orma's neck.

"Do you submit your tambiko?"

Orma grimaced. "Yes."

Nandi eased off the woman, her sword still pressed against the Nyatiku's neck. When she looked up, she was surrounded by Nyatiku and the others. The Nyatiku looked solemn, her friends and allies triumphant. Nandi was overwhelmed with relief. Her task was complete; she had united the remaining tambikos. Winda strode to her, smiling like a proud parent.

"You have succeeded, my sister. What do we do now?"

Nandi's eyes narrowed. "We go to war."

TWENTY-EIGHT

The nKu were one. Nandi led the warriors to Jikubwa and was greeted by the cheers and accolades of her people. The other warriors responded not in shame, but with pride. Though each had been defeated, they fell to a worthy opponent, a woman who more than lived up to her reputation. Most of all, she was blessed by the Priestess.

Ten thousand warriors gathered at the city, straining supplies and hospitality. Nandi knew they had to move soon, but she hesitated. She fulfilled her task; now she waited for word from the Priestess. Without her they could not march on the Bindamu.

She rested in her mother's home, reveling the cooking she'd been away from for so long. She also enjoyed in the silence. All her life her mother constantly critiqued, admonished and lectured her about her duty. But after her return her mother barely said a word. Nandi finally asked her the looming question.

"Mama, why are you so quiet?"

Mama looked at her, her face bright with pride.

"Because I have nothing left to say."

The Priestess arrived a week after Nandi's return. She appeared during the night, resembling a falling star that became as bright as the rising sun.

The city emptied upon her arrival, everyone following Nandi as she ran to the field the Priestess chose as her landfall. Nandi shielded her eyes until the brightness subsided into a gentle glow emanating from the Priestess's white garments and her staff. She raised her head then shared a solemn smile with Nandi.

"Hello, sister," she said.

Nandi walked to her and they hugged. They were sisters, bound by a fate neither of them could determine. The Priestess pushed her to arm's length.

"You've changed," she said.

"So have you," Nandi replied.

The Priestess looked over her shoulder.

"They have come," she said. "The tambikos are yours. I can feel them inside you."

"Yes, they are," Nandi replied.

"Good. We will need them sooner than expected. Another enemy has emerged, one as dangerous as the Bindamu."

"Who?"

"They call themselves Watoto Dhoruba," the Priestess answered. "They have come from across the sea to claim our land and our souls. The Bindamu fear them but have controlled them because their numbers are few. But now they claim the Taiku and they mean to claim us all."

Nandi eyes narrowed. "The Taiku follow them?"

"Yes," the Priestess answered. "We must strike now before they steal our souls as well."

Nandi took her horn from her waist then blew. The Chuiku responded then gathered about her and the Priestess. Horns in the distance signaled the men were coming as well. She waited until all had gathered and settled before speaking.

"You all know we have gathered to fight the Bindamu."

A cheer rose among the warriors; Nandi waited for it to subside.

"It is a war long coming, but before we fight them, we must fight our own. The Taiku have been corrupted by others from across the sea. These new strangers will lead our own against us."

"Our Priestess won't allow it!" someone shouted.

The Priestess stepped forward.

"These others are strong," the Priestess said. "It will take all of us to resist them."

Siza emerged from the crowd.

"Won't the Bindamu use this as an advantage?"

"The Bindamu cower in their homes," the Priestess said.

Siza frowned. "So, if we defeat these others and the Taiku we save the Bindamu? I say let them finish their work before we march."

The Priestess approached Siza. Nandi's friend stepped away, her face fearful. The Priestess smiled then touched Siza's cheek.

"I know your people have suffered greatly from the Bindamu," she said. "These others will only grow stronger. I traveled across the sea. More of them wait to come. We must stop them now. So, we will spare the Bindamu . . . for now."

Siza nodded. "I am with Nandi, which means I am with you, Priestess."

The Priestess turned to Nandi, nodding for her to continue.

"Gather your weapons and possessions," Nandi said. "We march today!"

* * *

Black clouds roiled over Awere, the lightning and thunder a continuous barrage on the hapless citizens. People cowered in their homes, fearing the source of the violent storm that produced no rain yet showered fear and hopelessness upon them. But the streets were not empty. The Taiku raced about, waving spears, swords and bows and answering the clouds with their traditional war cry.

The Watoto walked together, surrounded by those pledged to give their lives for them. They looked up to the clouds and smiled. At least one had come. There would be others.

"They are together," he said.

"I feel them," she answered. "It makes our task easier."

"Both are stronger than before," he said.

She looked again to the storm. "Dhoruba is here."

The clouds rumbled with a force that shook the surrounding buildings. The Watoto looked at each other and smiled.

"Dhoruba calls," he said.

"And I will answer," she replied.

He stepped away as she raised her arms. Taiku guards gathered around her then knelt. Her body shuddered as she transformed into the tambiko. The guards unsheathed their knives then plunged them into their stomachs, releasing their souls for her use. She absorbed them as she leaped into the air then flapped her huge wings. Higher and higher she flew until she touched the clouds and felt the coolness of Dhoruba's embrace.

"I am yours to use," she said.

Her form faded as she became one with the cloud. A new form replaced her, a human figure with arms of lightning and a head and torso of clouds. Tornadoes spun down from its mid-section to the city below, destroying buildings and scattering the inhabitants. Dhoruba strode toward the walls, sensing its purpose. She was near.

* * *

The Priestess, Nandi and the others watched in awe from the banks of the Hagosa as the storm spirit strode toward them. Nandi looked to her spiritual sister; the question obvious in her fearful eyes.

"I don't know," the Priestess said. "But I will try. Give me the tambikos."

"I don't know how," Nandi said.

"Clear you mind, and then open your heart."

Nandi shut her eyes. A storm stronger than the one approaching raged in her head.

"I can't!" she shouted.

Dhoruba's voice grew louder as it came closer. A vanguard of Taiku warriors appeared on the horizon; the sight of the crazed warriors sparked the feeling of old rivalries in Nandi's mind. But still she couldn't clear her head.

"Take my hands," the Priestess said. "Quickly now!"

Nandi grasped the Priestess's hands. Aziza's touch calmed the tempest in her mind. The tambikos took shape, each beast majestic and powerful. She staggered as the tambikos transferred from her body to the Priestess. Nandi let go of her hands and fell back into Abasi's arms. Abasi held her tight until her strength returned.

She looked at the Priestess with new understanding.

"Go, my sister," she said. "If we survive this day, we have much to discuss."

The Priestess smiled then raised her staff over her head. It glowed, pushing back the encroaching darkness. She rose into the sky then streaked toward the storm giant.

Nandi's attention turned to the advancing Taiku.

"Hunters!" she shouted.

The hunters converged around her, their faces stern.

"We will deal with these lost ones," she said. "The others will stay behind. We must conserve our strength for the Bindamu. But this should be easy. We are Hunters, no?"

Confident laughter passed among them. Nandi felt the tambikos' strength despite passing them to Priestess. She would be strong as long as her sister was strong. They would support each other.

Winda pushed her bulk through the other Hunters.

"Enough of this talk! Let's kill some bird folk!"

She trumpeted like her tambiko then charged ahead, spinning her massive war axe over her head. Nandi and the others ran after her.

Aziza glanced at the Hunters advancing to meet the Taiku. She hoped the battle would be brief; the Taiku were misguided, and they would need the nKu to face the threat to come. Her staff

grew brighter as she neared Dhoruba, her power
building with every moment.

"*You persist,*" they said in her head.

"Look what the Watoto have brought to our
world," she said. "Once they kill our people, they
will come for us. I won't let that happen. As I said
before, either help me or leave me be."

Aziza felt their power envelope her.

"This is all we have," they said. "You have
one chance. You must choose the perfect time to
strike. Do not fail us."

The fireball that was the Priestess streaked
toward Dhoruba. The storm god clasped its electric
hands then struck the Priestess, deflecting her attack. Aziza smashed into the mountains, sparking
an avalanche which tumbled down into Awere. The
Priestess recovered then resumed her attack.
Dhoruba turned to meet her. It opened its mouth,
releasing a vertical whirlwind. Aziza dodged the ne-
farious blast. She raised her staff then brought it
down hard on Dhoruba's head. The storm god collapsed to its knees, crying out in pain and anger.
She hit Dhoruba over and over, feeling it weaken
with each strike.

* * *

The Watoto watched in shock as the nKu
priestess struck Dhoruba. He was about to come to
its aid when the storm god's voice filled his head.

"Kill the Chuiku Hunter! Break the bond!"

He opened his hands and swords material-
ized in his palms. With a cry like thunder he
charged, rapidly closing the gap between him and
his new followers. He leaped high; the swords
raised over his head. Below him the Hunters fought,

cutting down the Taiku despite their crazed fury. He
saw her, flanked by her cohorts, fighting with grace
and skill. For a brief moment he admired her. She
would have made a great follower.

"Nandi!"

Winda's deep voice caught Nandi's attention,
breaking her battle trance. She looked to the right
from where the call came and saw the Temboku
Hunter pointing upward. Nandi looked up; a man
wrapped in grey robes wielding two massive curved
swords descended toward her. She blocked the stab
of a Taiku warrior attempting to take advantage of
the distraction then rolled away. Her airborne attacker landed on the hapless Taiku, crushing him.
The man attacked, slashing and hacking at Nandi
with both blades. Each block shook her arms and
drained her strength. Her spear flew from her grip,
her hands too weak to hold it. She pulled her sword;
no sooner did she have it in her grasp did the man
knock it free. He moved in for a killing blow when
Winda barreled into him, knocking him off balance.

She turned toward Nandi.

"Run," she shouted. "He's too strong for you.
I'll . . ."

A sword point emerged from Winda's chest,
stifling her words as she fell to her knees. The man
loomed over Winda from behind, his other sword
raised. A quick swipe and Winda's head toppled
from her body.

The Watoto attacked. Nandi did not back
away; instead she ducked under the man's swords
then slammed her right fist into his stomach. The
man bent slightly, air whooshing from his mouth.
Nandi twisted her hips, driving her left fist into his
abdomen again. She hit him again and again until
the man almost doubled over. Nandi delivered a vi-

cious uppercut to the man's chin, knocking him
backwards. She followed him until he fell onto his
back then she pounced him, pummeling his face
until her knuckles bled. She stopped; the man lay
still but he still breathed. Nandi ripped the scarf
from his face, revealing a visage belonging to nothing she'd experienced on man or beast. She shook
off her horror, stood then staggered to its swords.
She lifted the large blade, stumbled back to the
Watoto then hacked at its head and neck until his
head fell free.

*   *   *

High above Aziza and the storm god traded
blows, each exchange like thunder. Aziza weakened
with each clash but refused to relent. Then the
storm god shuddered. It looked to the ground then
emitted a cry that deafened the Priestess. Aziza recovered, taking advantage of the distraction. She
gripped her staff with both hands then drove it into
the storm god's forehead. The storm guard trapped
Aziza in its hands, electric currents stunning her. It
opened its mouth revealing a cavern of churning
rocks, trees and other debris. Aziza reached out,
concentrating what power she possessed on her
staff. She looked to the heavens.
"Help me!" she shouted.
Aziza jolted as the ancestors answered her
call. Bolts streaked from her hands to her staff then
ran down into the storm god's head. The storm god
quaked and its grip loosened. Then it burst into a
swirling torrent, pouring down rain onto the nKu
and the city. Aziza spied a large bird tumbling from
the clouds. She watched it transform as it plummet-
ed; as it struck the ground it had returned to its

human form. Aziza followed, catching her staff as she descended. She landed beside the broken form of the Watoto woman. Aziza placed her hand on the woman's head and then closed her eyes.

"Go to your gods," she whispered.

She raised her head. The Hunters stood victorious, the Taiku kneeling before them in submission. Nandi stood between them, supported by her brother and her Siza. Aziza ambled to them, her strength growing with each step. Their eyes met and she felt Nandi's sadness.

"It is done," Aziza said.

"Winda is dead," Nandi answered. "As are so many others. This was not a victory. We cannot fight the Bindamu now. We are too weak."

"You are right," Aziza said. "But the Bindamu are weak as well. Take the Taiku with you."

Nandi nodded. The other Hunters heard Aziza's words and set about rounding up the Taiku and their wounded. They did not resist.

"There are other matters we must speak of, Nandi," Aziza said.

"Now?" Nandi's voice betrayed her annoyance.

"Not now, but soon," Aziza said. "I must thank the ancestors."

Nandi and the others watched the Priestess rise into the sky then disappear into the clouds. Nandi looked to her friends.

"Let's go home," she said. "We are done here."

* * *

The Temboku buried Winda and their dead in the sacred grove bordering the powerful Milele River. Nandi attended the ceremony, as she did the ceremonies of all the nKu who fought and died with them that day. The journey left her weak, exhausted and irritable but she felt obligated. They rallied to her expecting victory against the Bindamu but instead fought a battle against their own which may have meant ruin for them if the Bindamu had not been weakened as well by the Watoto's thwarted plans.

The journey back to Chuikuland was solemn. Etana came to her at night and shared her bed, whispering his love for her in her ear. But his passions and companionship helped little. The Priestess's words lingered, keeping her full of worry. No sooner had they arrived home did she prepare for another journey.

Siza paced as Nandi replenished her supplies. Abasi leaned against the wall, his face twisted in disapproval.

"You should not go alone," Siza said. "The Bindamu are most likely hunting you."

"The Priestess summoned me," Nandi said.

"I agree with Siza," Abasi said. "We should be with you."

Nandi stopped packing then gave both of them a hard glance.

"Stay here and rest," she said. "You especially, Siza. I know you've been sick, and I know why."

Siza stood straight, her eyes narrowing. Abasi looked confused.

"You two have much to discuss," Nandi continued. "And you know I won't be alone. Now come kiss me goodbye, both of you."

They both kissed her cheeks then left her room.

"What is she talking about?" Abasi asked Siza.

"I'll tell you, but not now," Siza replied.

Siza hurried away, Abasi chasing her. Nandi grinned then continued to pack.

* * *

Nandi set out at dusk, slipping away during the dinner hour. She was tired of grand sendoffs and the emotions they stirred. She wanted her journey to resemble a simple hunt even though it was far from it. She traveled until darkness forced her to set up camp. Etana appeared and together they started the fire and ate a simple meal. They lay together that night without lovemaking.

"So Siza is pregnant? "Etana asked.

"Yes. She wasn't going to tell Abasi yet but I forced her to. He should know as soon as possible. They have serious decisions to make."

Etana lay on his back, staring into the sky. "What decisions?"

Nandi sat up, pulling her legs to her chest.

"Siza planned to Walk with Abasi before having a child. I believed she wished to do so until her pregnancy was obvious. Now the Mothers won't allow it. They won't risk the life of a child, especially now."

"What about you?" Etana asked.

"I think she should go."

Etana shifted. "No, that's not what I mean. Are you pregnant?"

"No," Nandi answered. "I can't afford that now."

"I see," Etana said.

Nandi heard the disappointment in his voice and chose to ignore it.

"Do not come to me after tonight," she said. "I must be alone when I meet the Priestess."

"Is that the only reason?"

Nandi hesitated before answering. "Yes."

Etana kept his promise and did not return. Nandi was grateful for the solitude. Three days after their encounter she met the Priestess in her cave after the arduous climb up the mountain. Aziza sat before a strange white fire; her eyes locked on the shimmering flames. She spoke to Nandi without breaking her gaze.

"You have come, Sister. I wasn't sure you would."

"We are bound in battle," Nandi said.

Aziza looked at her, her eyes sad.

"Yes, we are. Come sit beside me."

Nandi joined Aziza before the fire. Aziza took her hands.

"Much has happened, and much has yet to be. But you must know the reason so you can prepare your people. Look into the flames."

Nandi turned towards the fire. No sooner had her sight touched the firelight did she find herself soaring over water with no boundaries. Aziza flew with her, their hands still linked. The sea below was replaced by a hard land jammed with roads, cities and people. They veered toward an imposing mountain range then settled into a hidden temple protected by steep peaks. The inside of the temple was warm despite its frigid surroundings, the walls decorated with images which seemed familiar to Nandi. The images transformed into a living scene. Armies marched, divided into units bearing banners emblazoned with . . . tambikos! She recognized them all: Taiku, Temboku; Simbaku . . . all the tambikos of the nKu. One banner flew higher than the others, carried by the spotted warriors: Chuiku.

The scene accelerated. The nKu clans were surrounded by a massive army whose clan banner was unfamiliar to her. Others joined them; Nandi felt anger as she recognized them as the Watoto. Together the unknown clan and the Watoto subdued the nKu clans. The army retreated as the storm children worked their nyama, lifting the remaining nKu into their clouds. Once again Nandi flew over land then sea, following the clouds of entrapped people. The clouds settled over an isolated island, where they rained the captured people across the land. Then the Watoto worked their nyama on the island, calling forth a continuous ring of mountains around the island.

The image disappeared; Nandi once against stared into Aziza's eyes.

"We are prisoners?" she said.

Aziza nodded. "It happened long ago, so long ago that both your people and the Bindamu have forgotten. When the Bindamu first sought you out, they thought your island as some sacred place to claim. They will soon know the truth. When they do, their intentions will change."

"Did the Watoto know?"

"No," Aziza said. "The Bindamu turned on them once they'd sealed the nKu on the island. They've been persecuted since."

"The Bindamu will try to wipe us out," Nandi said.

"Yes."

Nandi stood. "So, the next war we fight will be for our survival."

Aziza stood with her.

"You must fight this battle alone."

Aziza's words hit Nandi hard. She stepped away.

"What do you mean alone? We are bound!"

Aziza tried to smile.

"Yes, we are. But I am tired, Nandi. The Spirits have long offered me a place among them and I am ready to accept it."

Nandi snatched her hands away from Aziza.

"You are deserting me?"

"No, Nandi. I'm not. I am elevating you."

Aziza extended her staff to Nandi.

"You are the nKu priestess now. My staff contains the nKu tambikos and much more. It is yours to wield. You will be stronger than me, for you are a Hunter as well. You have the strength for war. I do not."

Nandi took the staff. It was warm and familiar. She looked at her sister, her emotions swirling like a storm.

"Aziza, I don't . . ."

"You can and you will," Aziza said.

She touched Nandi's chest with her hands then kissed her.

"Goodbye sister."

Aziza disrobed then stepped into the white flames. Nandi stared in wonder as Aziza's form faded, the staff glowing as she transcended. Then she was gone and the flames subsided.

Nandi stared at the dying fire a moment longer before gathering her possessions. She secured the staff across her back then ambled to the cave entrance. When she looked back again the flames had decreased to embers. She looked away to the land before her, the land she was now charged to protect.

"I hope I'm strong enough," she whispered. "I hope I'm brave enough."

She took a deep breath, and then began the descent.

PART FOUR:

THE FULL CIRCLE

TWENTY-NINE

A full moon shone in the cloud dusted sky over Asis, capital city of the Menu-Kash Empire. The pinnacle lamps of the pyramids and obelisks overwhelmed the starry illumination above, just as the alchemists built them to do. For the Menu-Kash, power did not exist in the hands of invisible gods or man-made idols; it manifested in the city controlled by the family which ruled the vast empire for 500 years. So it was no surprise that Siris XXIII shook in his throne as his djeli read the report of the uprising in Awere. The Pharsa shifted his bulk on his cushions, growing angrier with each word uttered from the djeli's mouth.

"Enough!"

He turned to Olagun Basha, the commander of the army of the Eastern Realm. The commander met Siris's gaze, but the sweat running from his forehead betrayed his fear.

"You told me . . . no, you promised me the Rain Prayers were no more," Siris said.

"There were only three," Basha said. "Finding three in the vastness of their land . . ."

"My land," Siris said.

"My pardon, Pharsa. Finding them in the vastness of Menu-Kash would be nearly impossible."

Siris sat back in his throne then pulled at his voluminous beard.

"So, you believe these were the last three?" he asked.

Basha swallowed hard. "Yes, Pharsa."

Siris's eyes shifted toward the djeli.

"Mawdou, I believe I heard you say that one of the Rain Prayers was a woman."

Mawdou nodded his turban covered head. "Yes, great Pharsa. I did."

"Basha, did it occur to you that this woman may have had children? Did it occur to you that there may be other women and men? Did it occur to you that it may be possible that there are more than three Rain Prayers still alive soiling my realm with their trickery?"

Basha stepped away. "My Pharsa . . ."

Siris's was quick. He raised his metal gloved hand then fired a bolt into Basha's chest. The light enveloped the olagun's body then incinerated him, leaving a pile of smoldering ashes. He cut his eyes at the shivering servant standing to his left.

"Clean up that mess," Siris ordered. "Mawdou, summon Olagun Akinbola."

The djeli glided from the royal chamber then quickly returned, followed by Olagun Akinbola. Siris smiled at the sight of his greatest and most loyal Olagun. Akinbola was pure Menu-Kash, seven reeds tall and 300 stones of hardened muscle. His dusky skin revealed his northern roots and his short-cropped hair gave away his Great Grasses origin. Siris couldn't think of a better man to lead his elite Skadr, which Akinbola had done with distinction for over 30 winds.

Akinbola glanced at the servants sweeping up the ashes that once were Basha.

"I see Basha failed my Pharsa," he said.

"You warned me long ago," Siris said.

"It was only a matter of time," Akinbola replied.

"I need you to take the Skadr east. It seems the Rain Prayers still exist. Do not return until Rains sing no more."

"As you wish," Akinbola said.

"When you are done, return to me. I have another task for you."

Akinbola's eyebrows raised and Siris grinned.

"We've dallied with the nKu long enough. It's time to bring that island into the Empire."

"And what of the nKu?" Akinbola asked.

"What of them?" Siris said. "They will join the Rain Prayers."

Akinbola fell to his knees then touched his forehead to the marble floor.

"It shall be done," Akinbola said.

He marched from the room. Siris's smile faded as Akinbola took his leave. He knew more of the nKu than he revealed, knowledge that if shared would shake the foundations of the empire. The nKu had to be annihilated at all cost.

THIRTY

Nandi cradled Goma in her arms, her heart filled with unspeakable joy. She looked at Siza and her best friend smiled back. Abasi stood beside Siza, a proud grin on his face.

"She's beautiful, just like her mother," Nandi said.

"And her father," Abasi said.

They shared a laugh together and it felt good. There had been so little to laugh about lately and Goma's birth was a much-needed respite. So many died fighting the Taiku and the Watoto that any birth was a precious event.

"Give her back now," Siza said.

Nandi frowned in mock anger. "You're so selfish!"

She gave Goma back to her mother. Siza held her daughter tight and hummed to her.

"I must go," Nandi said.

"So soon?" Abasi asked.

"Yes. The elders and the Hunters are waiting for me. We have much to discuss."

Siza's expression turned serious. "I will be ready when you call."

"You won't be called," Nandi said. "You are a Mother now."

"Yes, you are," Abasi said.

Siza glared at Abasi. "This is women's business. What do you know of it?"

"I know that you hold our child in your arms. That is enough," he said. "I will fight beside Nandi in your stead."

Siza laughed. "You can't shoot a bow."

"You'll teach me," Abasi said.

Nandi rolled her eyes. "I'll leave you two to your discussion."

"You'll come back soon, won't you?" Siza asked.

"I don't know," Nandi replied.

She hurried from the house before Siza could ask another question. Her time was no longer her own. She wore three taji now: Chuiku Hunter, nKu First Hunter and priestess. Her responsibilities rode her from sunup till sun down. There was little time to rest, let alone visit. As she arrived at the council house the expressions of those waiting reflected their impatience.

"Welcome, First Hunter," Zalika said. "It is good our time waiting for you was not in vain. How is your niece?"

Zalika's words dripped with sarcasm. She was the new Hunter of the Temboku, chosen more for her skill than for her diplomacy. Just looking at her made Nandi miss Winda.

"She is strong," Nandi said. "And more patient than you."

Zalika's eyes narrowed. The woman would challenge Nandi if given the opportunity and she would fail. She was nowhere near Winda's skill. The fact that she was chosen First Hunter revealed how dire the Temboku situation was.

"We are not here to trade insults," Nandi said. "We are here to prepare. It has been a year

since we fought the Taiku. The Bindamu have regained their courage and are venturing outside
Awere. Soon they will cross the river. We must not
let that happen."

"We will be ready when they do," Zalika said.

"It's not about them crossing the river,"
Nandi said. "It's about their very presence. It's time
we put an end to this."

"What are you proposing?" her mother said.

"We must attack Awere and drive the
Bindamu out. Once they are gone, we will burn the
city then seal the tunnel."

"I believe we can take the city," Orma of the
Nyatiku said. "But we cannot close the tunnel. We
have nothing that powerful."

"We have this." Nandi raised the staff bestowed to her by Aziza. It glowed brightly as if sensing her words.

"How can you be sure it will work?" Zalika
said. "You are not the Priestess."

Nandi ignored her words. "I'm setting out for
the river tonight. Our men patrol the shores and
will update me on the situation. When I return, we
will plan our attack."

Nandi had turned to walk away when Zalika
spoke.

"Is it information you seek, or a night with
Etana?"

Nandi stopped as the others fell silent. She
was a priestess and should be beyond such insults,
but the Hunter in her told her different. She took off
her weapons then placed them at her feet.

"Mama?" she said.

Her mother came to her. Nandi handed her
the staff.

"Daughter, this is not necessary."

"Yes, it is," Nandi said.

She strode toward Zalika.

"Come sister," she said. "Express yourself."

Zalika jumped to her feet then ran at Nandi. She was faster than Nandi anticipated; she barely avoided Zalika's first ax swing. The Temboku hunter attempted to backswing but Nandi struck her elbow, sending searing pain up Zalika's arm. She dropped the ax as Nandi kicked her in the stomach, doubling her over into Nandi's rising knee. Nandi punched her twice in the face before she fell onto her back; she kicked the woman onto her stomach then sat on her back as she wrapped her into a strangle hold.

"You are not worthy of taking Winda's place," Nandi whispered. "She was a proud and kind woman, and a much better fighter. Challenge me again and I'll kill you."

Nandi shoved Zalika's face into the dirt. She sauntered back to her possessions then took the staff from her smiling mother. She turned to the others, acknowledging their nods.

"I'll return in one week," she said.

She ran through the cheering Hunters then disappeared into the forest.

THIRTY-ONE

Dhoruba Mlima towered over the verdant valley, its snow kissed peak shadowed by black storm clouds. Olagun Akinbola looked upon the summit as his warriors took position. He knew his pursuit would eventually end here; their pursuit had been a mere formality. He expected the Watoto to flee to their traditional homeland when pressured. His initial plan was to station a division of his men to meet them as they returned but he determined such a move would only capture a few. He wanted them all. So, he placed his men throughout the east, rooting out the conjurers by spreading rumors of a Kashite attack. They were all here now. He was sure of it.

"Your helmet, bwa." His servant handed the strange headpiece to him and he placed it over his head. He connected the dangling metal straps to his breastplate as his servant secured the breastplate straps to his hip armor and his metal boots. The armor was cumbersome but necessary. Facing the Watoto in anything less was suicide, which made him wonder how the nKu were able to defeat the conjurers among them, even if there were only three. He cleared his mind of the distracting thoughts. Time to concentrate on the battle before him.

He emerged from his tent. The others waited, five hundred of his best warriors in similar armor. He wished he could take more but there was
little of the armor in good condition. This was not
the first time Menu-Kash fought the Watoto; many
lives had been lost before they developed the means
to defeat them.

"Each warrior inspect your companion," he
shouted. "Make sure your straps are secure!"

He walked among the warriors as they examined one another. Nzali, his artillery officer, approached him as he completed the inspection.

"Olagun, the catapults are in position," she
said. "We have secured enough explosives to sustain
a two-hour bombardment."

"Good." he said. "How about mobility?"

"We've mounted each catapult on wheels and
harnessed them to the local oxen."

"Well done, Nzali. Wait until we are halfway
up the mountain before commencing."

Nzali hesitated. "Bwa, are you sure?"

"Yes," Akinbola replied.

Nzali nodded. "As you command."

The artillery commander returned to her
post. Akinbola watched her give the command to
her signalers, who immediately drummed a rapid
cadence. The clouds responded with a deep rumble.

Akinbola raised his hand and his warriors
gathered about him. He looked at each one of them
in the eyes. They were veterans and needed no encouragement.

"You know what to do," he said.

The warriors parted ways to let him through.
Once clear his eyes met Nzali and he nodded. Nzali
spoke to the signalers and the drum cadence
changed to a slow steady rhythm.

"Light fuses!" she shouted.

The catapult crews went into motion, lighting the fuses on the powder bombs then loading them into the catapults. Nzali watched the fuses burn down, waiting to make sure they would explode close to their target.

"Release!"

The catapults fired in sequence, the bombs arching across the grey sky then exploding on the distant peak. Moments later tendrils of electricity ran across the clouds, forming bolts that flashed to the ground. The first catapult crew was too slow; the catapult shattered into wood and rope as the lightning struck it. Akinbola and his warriors raced up the mountains as the battle between the catapults and the clouds raged. They had to reach the summit before all the catapults were destroyed and the fury of the storm turned on them. They were almost to their objective when Akinbola noticed movement before them. A herd of mountain deer bounded toward them. At first Akinbola suspected they were hapless animals trapped between warring men until he saw their fur clad riders. He crouched behind the nearest boulder, turning his up his left palm then tapping his wrist. Tiny bolts flashed from his fingertips, forming a blue ball of light over his palm. A familiar face appeared within the luminescence.

"Kalat! I'll need you sooner than I thought," Akinbola said. "It seems the Watoto have hired mercenaries."

"I see them," Kalat said. "We're on our way."

Akinbola closed his hand just as a faint shadow blanketed him. A deer rider's spear tip sparked against his helmet, the force of the blow knocking him onto his back. He batted the second thrust aside with this right arm then jumped, wrapping his arms around the deer's neck then pulling animal and rider down. He twisted hard, snapping the beast's neck and throwing the rider free. The deer was dead before it struck the ground, the rider stunned. Akinbola finished the rider with a quick stab to the throat.

Another deer rider appeared on the boulder then just as suddenly was swept away by huge claws. Take looked up then smiled as the kipanga and its handler flew by then dropped its catch onto the rocks below. Apparently Kalat was on his way long before Akinbola's call, anticipating a quick victory. With the deer riders involved that victory would not be as quick as he anticipated. The deer riders dispersed, driven away by the swarming kipanga. Akinbola was about to continue his climb when the first lightning bolt hit him. The armor performed its function, channeling the electricity though him then into the ground. The second bolt sent him to his knees, his body tingling. The third bolt knocked him flat. He lay still for a moment, the numbness dissipating with the heat. When he regained his feet, he looked about. The other warriors had endured the onslaught as well. Not all of them survived.

Akinbola grimaced as he sprinted up the mountain. By the time he reached the rim the others had gathered around him in attack formation. The deer riders had dismounted, forming a ring around the Watoto. Akinbola drew his sword and ax then charged forward. Skadr met deer riders and the slaughter began. The riders were no match for the heavily armored and highly skilled warriors, although they fought valiantly. Akinbola was the first to break their line; he immediately set upon the

Watoto. The storm sorcerers did not move nor did they try to defend themselves. They stood still; their arms lifted to the clouds. Akinbola noticed a flash of light with each Watoto he killed, the clouds growing less dense with each death. As the last Watoto died, the clouds dispersed.

Akinbola scanned the scene, his mood heavy. This was not a warrior's work, but it was what his Pharsa demanded of him. As he turned to walk away a large kipanga landed before him, its handler jumping from its back. The handler unraveled the fabric protecting his face, revealing a man who looked like a younger version of the Skadr commander.

"Grim work, brother," he said.

"Grim work indeed, Tunde."

"At least mine is done," Tunde said. "Rumor is that you will travel to nKuland."

"Not rumor, truth," Akinbola said. "Now that is a campaign I look forward to. I hear they are formidable warriors."

Tunde nodded. "It will be a good victory or a good death."

Akinbola looked at his brother then patted his shoulder.

"If the gods bless me, it will be both."

THIRTY-TWO

Nandi stared down into the gorge from atop her farasi, the perspective making her dizzy. Etana and the others surrounded her, amused by her uneasiness. It had taken her a few weeks to get used to the beasts, a gift from the recently allied Farasiku. She preferred nyati, but the farasi were much more agile and fit for patrolling the river. The Farasiku gifts were not entirely innocent; they'd lost many clan members to the invaders, especially men. The Chuiku had an abundance of marons, so the recent peace was an opportunity for the Farasiku. The farasi Etana rode was a particularly handsome beast, given to him personally by Keteke, Mai of the Farasiku. The animal came with a marriage proposal Etana politely refused. Still, it bothered Nandi that he kept the beast. She would have to discuss that with him later.

They came upon a narrow section of the river blocked by rushing rapids. Etana signaled for everyone to stop by raising his hand. Nandi rode up to him.

"Why are we stopping here?" she asked Etana. "This section of the river needs no defense. It is an obstacle in itself."

"We can't be sure," he said. "There are rumors the Bindamu have the ability to make paths anywhere they desire."

"Those are rumors," Nandi said.

"After our encounter with the Watoto we have to take every claim seriously until we know otherwise."

Nandi nodded in agreement.

"There's something else," Etana said.

"What is it?"

"Another army is coming," he said. "The Awere commander has received word that their ruler is sending his elite warriors to deal with us. It seems we have captured his attention."

Etana's humor was lost on Nandi. She was responsible for this.

"We must attack as soon as possible," she said. "Once we capture Awere and seal the tunnel we'll be done with the Bindamu."

They rode back to their camp in the lowlands, reaching the valley by nightfall. Nandi and Etana settled a distance away, reacquainting themselves with each other's bodies. So much had changed between them. Before, she kept Etana at bay; now she craved him. She thought her status as priestess would drive them apart but instead it had brought them closer. He'd become her confidante, a role formerly held by Siza. Siza didn't seem to mind, especially with the baby to tend to.

"How are things in the city?" Etana asked.

The question was meant to distract her and it did.

"Siza and Abasi are parents now," she said.

"I'm happy for them. Abasi will be less reckless now."

Nandi laughed. "I doubt it. He's already insisting that Siza teach him the bow."

"No one is safe," Etana said.

"Would you be less reckless if we had a child?" Nandi asked.

Etana sat up. "Are you . . ."

"No," Nandi said. "But if I was, would you be?"

"Of course, but that is something that will not happen."

Nandi didn't reply. It wouldn't happen until the Bindamu were gone.

"I need more information," she said.

"About children?"

"No, about this new army. Where can we obtain it?"

"We'll need to find someone close to the commander," Etana said. "The only way we can do that is to go into Awere."

"Then I will go," Nandi said.

"We're not ready," Etana said.

"No, I said I will go. With this."

She touched her staff.

"I don't think that's a good idea," Etana said.

"Aziza gave me this staff to help our people. It's time I learned what it is capable of."

"Take me with you," Etana said.

"No. I'll go alone. Do not follow me."

Etana laughed. "You know I will."

Nandi rolled onto him.

"Wait two days then before you come. For now, be quiet. You have work to do."

THIRTY-THREE

Thutmos felt contact in his temples, forcing him to rise from the filthy cot which had been his bed for three years. Ever since Commander Adan threw him in the city prison for his contact with the Rain Prayers he'd waited for this day. Menu-Kash was reaching out to him, forcing contact through the thick walls the commander was sure would keep him isolated. Whatever the reason for the extra effort, it was hope. They could not deny him now.

He struggled to his feet. Oh, how his knees ached! Once he was free, he would make sure his captors suffered the same fate. Thutmos picked up his battered l drinking cup then pounded it against the metal barred door window.

"Guard! Guard!

The guard took his time. He looked through bars then snarled.

"What in the Seven Moons do you want now?"

"I want to see the commander," Thutmos said. "I have a message for him from the Pharsa!"

The guard laughed. "You've finally gone mad. Good. It will make your time here shorter."

"I see you need convincing," Thutmos said. He stepped away from the bars then spread his arms. He then opened his hands turning the palms toward each other. Purple bolts flashed down his arms to his hands. They flashed between his palms, coalescing into the puzzled countenance of the Pharsa.

"Thutmos," the Pharsa said. "Where are you?"

The guard's faced disappeared, replaced by the sound of running feet. Moments later Thutmos smiled as he heard rattling keys. The door squealed open on its rusty hinges. Thutmos strode by the man as if he's only spent a moment confined, his pompous attitude returning with a vengeance. The guard followed him in a half bow.

"Forgive me," he said. "I didn't know!"

"Shut up, fool!" Thutmos said. "Walk ahead of me and announce my arrival. I may spare your life."

"Thank you! Thank you!"

The man shuffled ahead, making sure every door was open before Thutmose reached them. Commander Adan was seated when Thutmos entered his office. He jumped to his feet; his anger obvious.

"What are you doing here?" he said.

Thutmos answered by opening his hands. The current appeared again and the Pharsa's face appeared. Adan eyes went wide and fell to his knees immediately.

"My Pharsa!" he said.

"Who is this man, Thutmos?" the Pharsa asked.

"He is Commander Sisook Adan, a worthless piece of trash."

"Rise, commander," the Pharsa commanded.

Adan stood, his eyes averted.

"What is the situation in Awere?"

"We are in dire need," Adan said. "The Bindamu have united under an nKu known as the Chui. They are led by a priestess. Her name is Nandi."

"It seems our timing is perfect," the Pharsa said. "How many warriors are we dealing with?"

"I'm not sure, my Pharsa. At least five thousand, no more than ten."

"Olagun Akinbola and my Skadr are on the way," the Pharsa said. The mention of the elite troops caused both Adan and Thutmos to flinch.

"You will send out patrols to assess the situation," the Pharsa said. "From this day until Olagun Akinbola arrives you will answer to Thutmos. Do you understand, Adan?"

"Yes, Pharsa. I do."

"Good. Now break this communication before you kill yourself, cousin. I will reach out to you when needed."

Thutmos closed his eyes and the bolts subsided.

"Get out of my office," Thutmos said.

Adan looked puzzled. "Your office?"

Thutmos leered. "Yes, my office. I'm in command now. And send your servants to prepare a bath. I stink."

"Yes," Adan said. "Of course." He exited the office, cutting his eyes at Thutmos.

Thutmos didn't care. His fortunes had taken a sudden turn. He'd lose his status once Akinbola and his killers arrived, but for now he was in command. He intended to take full advantage of it.

THIRTY-FOUR

Zalika gazed into the dancing fire, still seething from her defeat at the hands of Nandi. The other Temboku warriors milled about, distracting themselves with other duties. No one would approach her, for her temper was bad enough when she was in a good mood.

Zalika stood."Everyone to me," she shouted.

The warriors gathered around her.

"When Nandi returns, I will challenge her for leadership of the nKu," she said.

The warriors looked away, all except one. Dinka, fearless Dinka, stared back at her as she shook her braids.

"You are a fool, Zalika," she said

Zalika rushed over to Dinka then pulled her to her feet. Zalika towered over the woman.

"You dare to say such words to me? You forget yourself!"

"And what will you do, Zalika? Beat me? There is no honor in defeating one who is weaker than you. There is also no purpose in challenging someone who has already proven her superiority over you."

Zalika let Dinka go.

"Nandi didn't defeat me. It's that damned staff. Take it from her hands and she is no better that a worm."

"Now is not the time to feed your vanity," Dinka said. "Nandi did not possess the staff when she bested you. We have a war ahead of us and everyone trusts Nandi, not you."

"They would trust me if I possessed the staff," Zalika said.

"Then wait until we have defeated the Bindamu before challenging her," Dinka advised. "I'm sure Nandi would have no problem defeating you again."

Zalika spit at Dinka. "I won't kiss at the feet of the Chui like you and I will not wait."

She strode back to the fire. "Gather around and I will tell you how we will take the staff from Nandi. The nKu will follow the Temboku to war, not the Chuiku."

The warriors gathered about, all except Dinka.

"You will have us all die to serve your pride," she said. "Our elders did not pledge us to this war to betray our allies."

"If you die then you were not worthy to follow me," Zalika said. "As for the elders, they are fools."

Dinka gathered her things.

"Where are you going?" Zalika asked. "Are you running to warn your Chuiku masters?"

"I will not betray my fellow warriors; not even you," Dinka said. "But I will not take part in foolishness. I advise you to let your anger cool. Do not do this."

"My mind is clear," Zalika said. "It will be done."

"Then I hope you all die a good death," Dinka said. She walked away, fading into the woods.

Zalika hissed in her direction.

"The rest of you pay close attention," she said. "This is how we will regain the honor of the Temboku."

* * *

Etana dragged the Bindamu warrior to Nandi as she sat by the river's edge. The man was battered and bruised but still conscious. The beating was unnecessary but she knew how Chuiku marons could be. She hoped the man could talk.

"What is your name?" she asked.

The man tried to speak then spit up blood. Nandi glared at Etana.

"He resisted," Etana said.

Nandi stood then ambled to the man. She knelt before him then lifted his head.

"What is your name?" she asked again.

The man managed to smile. "You're a pretty little savage."

He spit blood into her face. The Chuiku marons raged then pulled their blades.

"No!" Nandi said. She wiped her face with her sleeve.

"We will do this a different way," she said.

She touched the man's forehead with the tip of her staff. He howled, his body flopping like a fish dragged from its watery lair. Then he stiffened, his eyes locked on Nandi's.

"What is your name?"

"Akello," the man said.

"What preparations does the city make for war?" she asked.

"Thutmos rules the city now. The Pharsa has given him command until the Skadr arrive."

Nandi scowled at the mention of Thutmos's name. It was his trespass that sparked the first war against the Bindamu.

"Who are the Skadr?"

The man lost his timid gaze, his smile confident. "They will be the death of the nKu and you!"

Nandi pulled her staff away too late. Paralyzing pain flooded her mind as the image of a face she did not recognize formed before her.

"So, you are the priestess," the man said. "Weak as I suspected. I will crush you first; the others I'll leave for my . . ."

The foul countenance shimmered.

"What is this? Who...Ahhh!!!!"

The face vanished, replaced by the worried appearance of Aziza.

"Sister, wake up! You are safe now. Wake up!"

Nandi opened her eyes. The Chuiku marons surrounded her, their faces grave. Etana held her hand with tears in his eyes.

"Nandi," he said.

Nandi struggle to sit up then stand. Etana reached out to her but she waved him away. There was another sight before her, the body of the soldier hacked to pieces.

"What happened?" Etana asked.

"Their . . . Pharsa attacked me through the warrior," she said. "He meant to kill me, but Aziza saved me."

The marons nodded.

"He revealed his plan thinking I wouldn't live to share it," Nandi said. "You were right. More warriors are coming, warriors more formidable than those we fought before."

"We must return to the city and prepare," Etana said.

"Yes. Take the marons, Etana. Gather the others along the way."

"You aren't going with us," Etana asked.

"No," Nandi replied. "I must see what we're up against."

She raised her staff to the sky.

"Aziza, guide me," she said.

She felt Aziza's embrace as she lifted from the ground into the night sky.

"Where to you wish to go, sister," Aziza said.

"To Awere," Nandi replied.

THIRTY-FIVE

The Pharsa tumbled from his throne before his servants could catch him. He struck his head hard on the stone floor, almost blacking out. As his servants reached for his arms, he swatted them away.

"Leave me!" he shouted.

The servants fled for their lives. The Pharsa rolled onto his back, shaking his head in a physical attempt to clear the darkness. After a brief panic he fell back on his training. He concentrated on his safe symbol, a bright pulsating light. The darkness dissipated, his breathing calm and rhythmic. His mind finally cleared and he opened his eyes then sat up. He immediately wished he hadn't sent his servants away. The Pharsa struggled to regain his feet then staggered to his throne.

He raised his arm the touched his wristband. The image of Supreme Alchemist Raman Rai appeared. The man looked more warrior than scientist, his muscled neck bordered by broad shoulders. His thick upper body tapered down to his narrow waist; he stood on legs that rippled under his tunic. The alchemist was preoccupied with a reddish concoction on his table, stirring it with a glass rod.

"Yes, my Pharsa?" he said without looking up.

"You must come," the Pharsa said. "She is stronger than we thought. I've been attacked."

Raman looked up, peering over the top of his square spectacles.

"Attacked you say? How? Have they managed to cross the Breach?"

"No," the Pharsa said. "They attacked me here."

The Pharsa pointed at his head.

Raman straightened.

"I'll be there right away."

Twenty minutes later the palace vibrated as Raman's scarab landed on the nearby platform. The palace guards had been informed of his arrival and quickly escorted him to the Pharsa. The servants returned, their movements displaying their fear. They were in the presence of the two most powerful men in all of Menu-Kash. Raman hurried to the Pharsa, extracting a thin metal object from his top pocket.

"Raman, I think . . ."

Raman waved him silent. "Your eyes. I must examine them."

The Pharsa leaned back into his throne, raising his chin. Raman twisted the metal tube and a beam of light emerged. He used the light to examine the Pharsa's eyes. After a moment he nodded as he shut off the light.

"There was no damage," he said. "You are lucky."

"I'm angry," the Pharsa said. "How could she do such a thing? She is only a warrior."

"Apparently she's much more than that," Raman said. "Are you sure it was only her?"

"She was the only person torturing our mark," the Pharsa said.

"Then she is no warrior," Raman said. "This is the same woman who defeated the rain folk, is it not?"

The Pharsa nodded.

"She must be killed immediately," Raman said.

"I have sent Akinbola."

Raman frowned. "He may not be enough. We will send our troops as well."

The Pharsa's eyes widened. "Is that wise? The city will be undefended."

"If we do not stop this woman now, nothing we possess will stop her. Remember your history, Pharsa.

The Pharsa shivered. "Yes, you are right. Send your troops. I'll inform Akinbola that they are on their way."

"He won't be happy," Raman said. "Olagun Akinbola is selfish with his glory."

"This is not about his glory," the Pharsa said. "It's about the survival of Menu-Kash. The nKu almost destroyed us once. They will not get a second chance."

Raman nodded in agreement.

"I will leave you, then. Our troops will be ready in a fortnight."

"Thank you, Raman," the Pharsa said. "I know you could have refused."

"We have our differences Raman but as long as we hold Menu-Kash high we will always remain allies if not friends. You can rest assured that the Alchemists will do everything in our power to defeat the nKu. Or should I say the NKulu."

Hearing their true names said caused Raman to shiver.

"We will never return to those days," he said. "Never."

* * *

Nandi would never get used to flying. Of this she was sure. She fought the queasiness in her stomach as she soared over the forest then crossed the empty expanse between the trees and Awere. She bypassed her destination, crossing into the mountains. She felt Aziza's embrace and was comforted. Although the priestess no longer existed physically, she had not abandoned her. She continued to guide her, but for how much longer Nandi had no idea.

The sprawling city was replaced by gray mountains. Nandi searched for signs of life among the bleak valleys, occasionally spotting a mountain sheep or goat herd. Rarer still were small villages tucked into the thin crevasses, groups of hardy people who had somehow managed to survive in the harsh peaks. These people were oblivious to what happened beyond their cold world; barely existing off the local fauna and edible lichen which thrived on the damp stone. Empires could rise and fall and they would not notice for their homeland did not appeal to anyone with powerful ambitions. She wished it was the same so for her people.

Nandi broke off her delay then flew to Awere. She chose a quiet district to descend, one where she would less likely be noticed. As soon as her feet touched ground, she covered herself with the cloak she brought with her, hiding her features under her hood. Nandi walked the near empty streets, her staff clicking against the stone streets. She let her senses drift; infiltrating the shops and homes she

passed, brushing the minds of the people seques-
tered within. The anxiousness that filled the minds
of her people was not present here, at least in this
district. She worked her way from the market district to the Taiku district. A different sensation prevailed; a melancholy weight that brought sadness to
her as well. Though they were of different tambikos
they were nKu, bound by land and tradition. Their
feelings were closer to her than the Bindamu. She
almost felt sorry for them, but her Chuiku pride
wouldn't allow it. She knew her people well. They
would fight to the death before allowing anyone to
rule them.

She ended her journey in the Awere's central
district, the Bindamu district. Confidence pervaded
her mind. These people were sure of their rule and
seemed totally unaware of the war about to befall
them. Still, there was nothing that indicated a
threat. The Bindamu of Awere were complacent.
They were not preparing for war.

Nandi was not satisfied with her reconnais-
sance. She found an empty alley then soared again.
This time she flew across the wide mountain range
separating nKuland from the coastal region, her
destination Kilindi. The coastal town served as the
landing for the Bindamu; the tunnel leading to
Awere originated there as well. The mountains ended abruptly and the black sands leading to the sea
took precedence. Nandi reached out and felt the focus of those below. As she swept her senses across
the land a sudden burst of malevolence gripped her
mind then dragged her attention beyond the horizon. She followed the emotions out into the sea, lo-
cating its source. A fleet sailed toward the harbor,
ships filled with men and beasts whose thoughts
were clear.

"There you are," a voice said.

Nandi jerked then fell for a moment. She regained her composure before the voice spoke again.

"You are not afraid," it said. "That is good. You will be a worthy adversary."

"Who are you?" Nandi said silently.

"You will find out soon enough, First Hunter. I suggest you return to your people and prepare. I wish this to be a glorious battle."

"We will bury you," Nandi said.

"We shall see," the voice replied.

Nandi turned about, flying for the mountains. Once again, she would face a powerful foe from the Bindamu. She hoped the priestess would be by her side.

Nandi flew throughout the night, landing a few yards away from Jikubwa. She was careful not to let anyone see her fly. It was a skill best kept to just a few, a talent that could have strategic advantages not only against the Bindamu but other nKu as well. As much as she would like to think the old feuds had died, she knew that was not the case. For now, a common enemy brought them together. Once that enemy was defeated the old ways would reassert themselves if allowed.

"You possess all the tambikos," Aziza said in her head. "They will do as you ask."

"Will they?" Nandi shrugged. "You seemed to have forgotten Zalika."

"The Temboku knows her place now," Aziza said. "You will see."

Aziza's words were prophetic. As she entered Jikubwa she saw Zalika and two Temboku sitting under the meeting tree with her mother and the elders. They all looked in her direction as she approached.

"Your timing is fortuitous," her mother said. "Zalika has journeyed far to speak with you."

Nandi planted her staff in the dirt then leaned against it, suspicion bitter in her mouth.

"Is that the reason you have come, Zalika?"

The Temboku first hunter stood then prostrated before Nandi, touching her forehead to the ground then sprinkling dust onto her head. It was a gesture of total submission, one that the other nKu had yet to make despite their defeat.

"I come asking your forgiveness," Zalika said. "I have disgraced my nKu and Winda's memory."

Nandi glared at Zalika for moment then calmed herself. She was priestess now and could not let her emotions rule her decisions. The Temboku were needed for the coming war, even Zalika.

"You are forgiven," she said.

Zalika raised her head, looking into Nandi's eyes.

"Thank you, priestess," she said. "I would like to ask another favor. Our elders wish for you to accompany us to Tembokuland for a celebration to confirm our commitment to the alliance."

"We have no time for celebrations," Nandi said sternly. "Our enemy's forces have landed at Kilindi."

A nervous murmur rose from the elders.

"Then let us be your escort," Zalika asked.

Nandi hesitated. She looked to her mother who nodded in agreement with Zalika.

"It would be a proper gesture," Aziza said.

Nandi finally nodded.

"You can accompany me. Furaha and Tumaini will come as well."

"I will send for them," her mother said.

"We will leave in the morning. I must rest."

The elders dispersed. The Temboku were taken to the visitors' lodge; Nandi followed her mother to the family compound.

"It is a generous thing you do," Mama said. "You are proving to be a good leader."

"I don't trust them," Nandi said. "I agreed only on your word and that of Aziza."

"The priestess is still with you?"

"Yes, but I don't know for how long."

"If she urged forgiveness then it was the correct decision."

"Aziza was our priestess," Nandi said. "She was wise, but she was not perfect."

Her mama shook her head. "My Nandi. Always the suspicious one."

"It has served me well," Nandi said.

"So, you say," her mother replied. They shared a smile only a mother and daughter could, a smile filled with past memories and secrets.

Nandi followed Mama into the home. It had been months since she slept under the familiar thatch roof. The smell was still the same; her mother loved lavender and cinnamon. A small pot of kelek stew simmered over the modest fire in the stone fireplace, its subtle aroma complementing the other scents. Nandi was glad she had come home. She felt more relaxed than she had in months. Mama scooped the savory stew into a bowl then sat it on Nandi's mat covered lap. She brought Nandi a drinking gourd of mango juice then they sat together and ate.

"Have you seen Etana?" her mother asked.

Nandi nodded; her mouth full. She carefully swallowed the hot stew before answering.

"He patrols the river with the other marons. They have chosen him as their leader."

"Maybe because he is your pair," Mama said.

"Etana is a good choice," Nandi said. "He is a good hunter."

Mama scooped stew into her spoon then blew on it.

"Did you see your baba?" she asked.

"Of course, I did," Nandi replied.

"Is he well?" Mama asked.

"You should send for him and ask him yourself."

Mama sucked her teeth. "Old women don't send for old men."

"I think he would be happy to see you," Nandi said.

"Would he?" Mama's face brightened.

"He would," Nandi said. "He misses you. He misses us."

Mama's face went cold. She knew where this conversation was heading.

"Always the bee stirrer," she said.

"I think Siza is going to leave with Abasi," Nandi said.

Mama's eyes went wide.

"She can't! It's forbidden!"

"She wouldn't be the first," Nandi said.

"The Chuiku would disown them both."

Nandi continued to eat her stew.

"I hope you're not planning on doing such a thing with Etana."

Nandi shook her head. "I can't. I'm the priestess of nKu. There is no future for us."

Mama touched her shoulder. "Maybe when this is all over . . ."

"It may never be over," Nandi said. "And even so I will still be priestess. The nKu are my children now."

There was firmness in Nandi's voice that she did not feel in her heart. They finished the meal in silence. Nandi helped mama clean the room then retired to her room. She discarded her weapons then leaned her staff beside the bed. She slept before head touched the headrest, falling into a dreamless sleep.

THIRTY-SIX

Olagun Akinbola waded ashore flanked by his officers. The transport ships had yet to disgorge his warriors, the huge vessels bobbing out in the harbor. The ships were too large to dock, requiring the warriors to be ferried to shore. Akinbola took the first ferry with his officers, eager to set foot on this historic land. He grinned as the black sands crunched under his boots. A delegation of rough looking men approached, prostrating before him before speaking.

"Welcome, Olagun Akinbola," the lead man said. He was bald with a voluminous beard covering the bottom half of his face. His perfunctory smile was barely visible. A thin gold band circled his head, designating him as *mtemi* of Kilindi.

"What is your name?" Akinbola asked.

"Dandu. We have prepared lodging for you and your army."

"That was not necessary," Akinbola replied. "What we need is transport. We intend to set out for Awere immediately."

Dandu and the others looked at each other in confusion.

"Olagun, it has been a long journey for you and travel through the tunnel is arduous. Surely you wish to . . ."

"Don't second guess me, Dandu." Akinbola glared at the mtemi. "Do you have sufficient transportation for my warriors?"

Dandu looked over Akinbola's shoulder. "I don't think so. We could take them in shifts, but that would take weeks."

"We don't have weeks." Akinbola scanned the city and its surroundings. The buildings were sturdy yet small and whatever trees growing at the rim of the mountains were few and weak. He then looked to the transports.

"Nzali!"

The engineer stepped forward.

"Yes, bwa?"

"Once the warriors are ashore bring the transports in and run them around. We will harvest them for building transports to Awere."

Nzali bowed then trotted off to the docks. Akinbola looked into Dandu's stunned face.

"Dandu, I will need all the workers you can spare. I want these transports ready by week's end."

"Olagun, you will destroy your ships? How will you return to Menu-Kash?"

Akinbola grinned. "I have no intentions of returning to Menu-Kash," he said. "There is much to be done to restore NKumala to its former self. Besides, there is plenty wood beyond Awere. Once the nKu are subdued we will have all we need."

Dandu and the others stared at Akinbola.

"You have your orders, Dandu."

"Yes . . . yes Olagun!"

It was near nightfall before the ships were emptied of men and supplies. The Skadr set up camp outside Kilindi, the tent city rivaling the nearby settlement in size, the fires resembling earthbound stars in the moonless night. Akinbola strolled through the encampment, oblivious to his chattering entourage. He was still savoring his encounter with the nKu priestess. He could have pulled her from the sky and confronted her; but she was a true warrior and deserved an honorable death. It had been too long ago since he'd met an adversary with such power.

"Bwa, did you hear me?"

Akinbola broke his musing to take Nzali's report.

"What is it?" he asked.

"The lumber from the ships with give us sufficient wood to build enough transports to take us through the tunnel to Awere."

"Excellent," he said.

"There still remains one serious obstacle."

"And that is?"

"There are not enough beasts to pull the wagons."

"We need engines," Akinbola said.

"We don't have enough materials for engines . . . but we can build one engine!"

Akinbola had no idea what Nzali had planned but he knew it would be sufficient. The engineer hurried away, yelling orders to her assistants.

It was late into the night before the encampment slept. Akinbola lay in his massive tent, too excited to sleep. Once he was sure no one was awake he dressed then exited the tent, ambling alone through the camp then skirting the borders of Kilindi. Moments later he stood before the tunnel entrance peering into the darkness. The moment the island was discovered he knew. The legend of its existence had been passed down through his family for generations. It was a story that made him proud as well as ashamed, but he could not change the past. His ancestors had done what was required to survive. Ever since that fateful time they'd work to redeem themselves, and now that redemption rested in his skilled hands. He was the culmination of their efforts. Akinbola gazed into the darkness a moment longer before returning to camp.

The next morning the camp hummed with activity. Those who were not involved in building wagons labored on Nzali's new project. It was a massive engine, a contraption that would not only pull the wagons through the tunnel but also generate sufficient light to illuminate the pathway. Akinbola spent the day in his tent surrounded by his subordinates, pouring over battle plans. He was in deep discussion when a young officer burst into the tent.

"Olagun! I apologize for the interruption, but Nzali said you must come immediately!"

Akinbola followed the officer out of the tent to the construction site. Nzali's face was grim.

"What is it?" Akinbola asked.

Nzali gestured to the sky. Akinbola looked and his expression became just as dark.

"Alchemists."

Four oblong objects cruised toward them from over the sea. As they neared their details became clear; large black dirigibles decorated with royal glyphs filled with lighter than air gas produced in the Alchemists' secret cities. Large fuselages hung under the dirigibles connected by thick metal cables. A pair of large propellers extended from either side of the fuselages to the rear, their spinning providing propulsion for the airborne juggernauts. The aircrafts drifted over the camp to a clearing then descended to a few hundred feet.

Thick supports extended from the base of the ships; the propellers shut down then folded into the fuselage as the craft neared the ground. Despite their size the ships touched down with barely a sound. Ramps emerged from the fuselages and Alchemist's slave-warriors, *mulaks,* streamed out, followed by their masters. The warriors formed ranks, surrounding the flying crafts as the Alchemists ambled to the Skadr camp, draped in their colorful robes and gaudy headwear. Raman led them, his golden jackal helmet signifying his rank.

Akinbola's officers formed around him and they strode toward the Alchemists. The met halfway between the armies.

"Raman," Akinbola said.

"Akinbola," Raman replied.

The Supreme Alchemist stood a head taller than Akinbola, but there was no doubt both men were equals in the Pharsa's eyes.

"Why are you here?" Akinbola asked.

"The Pharsa had an 'incident' with the nKu woman," Raman said. "He felt that this was a situation which required a serious response."

"Which is why I am here," Akinbola said.

"Do not take this as the Pharsa's concern about your success," Raman said. "Consider our presence as a guarantee."

"You misunderstood my question," Akinbola replied. "Why are YOU here?"

"I felt this was a situation that required my supervision," Raman answered. "Again, don't feel threatened, Akinbola. I am here only for support."

Raman's attention drifted toward Nzali's project.

"I see your engineer has been busy," he said.

"Yes. We are constructing an engine to take our transports through the tunnel to Awere."

Raman's eyes brightened. "Ah, a locomotive! Very ingenious of her. We constructed such a vehicle decades ago. Maybe our technicians could share their expertise with her team."

"We would be grateful," Akinbola answered.

Nzali stepped forward then bowed to Raman. "I would be happy to take them," she said.

"Ram! Iset! Go with Nzali."

A man and woman stepped forward. They bowed to Nzali then followed her to the work area.

"If you'll excuse me, I have battle plans to complete," Akinbola said.

"I will accompany you," Raman said.

Akinbola frowned. The last thing he needed was Raman's interference but he could not refuse him.

"So be it," he finally said. "Follow me."

Raman followed Akinbola to the command tent. The officers surrounded the table awaited Akinbola to reinitiate the discussion.

"We do not want this to become a forest war," he said. "The nKu know the woods and terrain. Although I'm confident we will eventually defeat them, the cost would be high."

"We must find a way to draw them into the open," Daraja said. "We could end the war with one decisive battle."

"Might I suggest something?" Raman asked.

Akinbola closed his eyes in annoyance. "Of course."

"If the forest is an obstacle, we should remove it," he said.

"So, your suggestion is that we uproot every tree?" Daraja asked.

"Of course not," Raman replied. "Don't be foolish."

Daraja stiffened at Raman's insult. Raman continued, oblivious to Daraja's mood.

"There are certain substances that when properly applied can defoliate the forest, giving us excellent visibility of our enemy."

"We did not come here to destroy the island," Akinbola said. "We came to defeat the nKu."

"What is the difference?" Raman replied. "The Pharsa has no use for this island. His desire is to see the nKu defeated anyway necessary. Destroying the foliage also eliminates the nKu food source."

Akinbola stared at Raman until the alchemist began to shift nervously.

"It is only a suggestion, nothing more," he finally said. "You are the commander. I am only a servant of the Pharsa here to assist."

Akinbola turned back to his commanders. "We will assess the situation when we arrive in Awere. In the meantime, have your warriors assist Nzali and the engineers in any way possible. I wish to be on our way within the week."

Akinbola nodded, dismissing the commanders. Raman spoke as soon as the tent was empty.

"I apologize for the intrusion," he said. "I forgot how determined warriors are to spill blood, even when it's not necessary."

"This island is a valuable resource," Akinbola said.

"You've seemed to have forgotten what this island once was," Raman replied. "Are you sure you have the Pharsa's best interest in mind, my brother?"

"I will handle this situation the best way I see fit, as I always have, my brother," Akinbola said.

"And I will remind you of your promise not to inter-fere."

Raman raised his hands in surrender. "And I keep that promise. That doesn't stop me from expressing an opinion, does it?"

"No," Akinbola said. "But if you wish to offer any suggestion that directly conflicts with my orders make sure you do so in private. The warriors don't need to see disagreements among leaders."

"Agree. I do however have a suggestion you might find advantageous."

Akinbola's eyes narrowed. "Yes?"

"We can take small force over the Wall to Awere in the scarabs," he said. They can study the situation before the bulk of your army arrives and have coherent plans in place."

Akinbola smiled. "That's an excellent idea. I'll select a team to accompany you and the others."

"You're not going?" Raman asked.

"I travel with my warriors. It's tradition."

"As you wish. We will leave in the morning. Make sure your warriors are ready."

"I will," Akinbola said.

Akinbola waited until Raman was gone before summoning a servant.

"Bring Bala to me," he said.

Akinbola occupied himself with a gourd of warm wine and cama bread as he waited. Bala, commander of Akinbola's elite Shadow Blades, entered as he was finishing his wine. He was almost as tall as an Alchemist soldier, twice as broad with a head crowned with braids which fell over his shoulders to his thick biceps and the middle of his back.

"Bwa," he said with a rumbling voice. "You summoned me?"

"Sit," Akinbola ordered. Bala sat cross-legged on the ground before Akinbola. Akinbola sat down his gourd then leaned toward Bala.

"Tomorrow you will go with Raman to Awere. You will ride the scarabs."

Bala nodded. "What are your orders?"

"You are to secure the city and prepare it for our arrival," Akinbola said. "All resistance within the city must be eliminated. You understand?"

Bala nodded. "Yes, bwa. We will prepare to leave immediately."

Bala stood, bowed, and then exited the tent. Akinbola sat erect on his stool.

"More wine!" he called out.

A servant appeared with a new. Akinbola sipped as he mused. This campaign was getting more interesting by the moment. He realized was now fighting two wars. He was determined to win them both.

THIRTY-SEVEN

The Chuiku/Temboku war party worked their way through the forest, slowed by frequent rains. They abandoned the narrow path which had become a river of water and mud due to the almost constant downpour. Rainy season was traditionally not a time of war. It was a time of planting, a time which occupied everyone even the marons. But the Bindamu did not care for seasons; they were a people who waged war continuously, so the nKu adapted.

The party set up camp on high ground then set about building a temporary lodge. The Temboku packed the large waterproof leaves native to their land which were used for the roofing. Branches and saplings were cut then tied together to make the walls. Nandi and the other Chuiku were assembling their pots for the evening meal when Zalika approached.

"Please Nandi, allow us to prepare the meal," she said.

"We can cook on our own," Nandi replied.

"Please," Zalika insisted. "It will honor us."

Nandi looked at the others and they nodded their approval.

"So be it," she said.

Zalika hurried off, shouting orders to her sisters. Nandi sat to rest. Furaha and Tumaini joined her, setting down their loads and stretching out on the damp ground. If the journey to the river was to be a healing salve it had failed. The Chuiku trio kept close to each other, barely speaking to their Temboku compatriots. It was Nandi's fault, she realized. She still held a grudge against Zalika for challenging her authority. It was not the way for a priestess to react, or at least she assumed as much. A priestess must be impartial and fair to all she serves. But how many priestesses had been nKu before? The songs said that priestesses were their own separate kind, raised as children to one day serve all. They did not have children; each nKu gave girls to them to be trained up and taught the mysteries of their kind. The children given were usually orphans, those who mothers had perished during childbirth and no others would claim them. But Nandi was a woman of family, position and a First Hunter. It would be hard for her to shed old ways.

Her musing was interrupted by Zalika and the other Temboku. The wood was too damp to start a fire so they brought bowls of edible leaves, fruits and nuts with them. Together they ate, the meal mundane yet satisfying. The Temboku did not speak. While the others looked into their bowls, Zalika stared at Nandi as she chewed her food.

"How is it?" Zalika asked.

Nandi's throat tightened and she coughed in response. Moments later Furaha and Tumaini coughed as well. The coughing became uncontrollable; she looked at Zalika and the woman smiled. The other Temboku were staring at them now, their expressions ranging from curiosity to fear. Nandi attempted to stand but vertigo sent her reeling to the ground. She looked to her side and saw her Chuiku companions writhing on the ground, foam leaking from their convulsing mouths. She jerked her head away as her body began to spasm then stared into Zalika's grinning visage.

"Die, Chuiku," she said.

Nandi tried to curse but her throat was swollen shut. Her body shook as her vision failed and she fell into painful darkness.

*　*　*

Thutmos was bored. He lounged on his chaise, rolling a grape between his fingers as he watched the dancers cavort before him for the one hundredth time. All his life he strived for a life of luxury, a life without want or need and now he had it and it was the antithesis of everything he thought it would be. He dropped the grape back into the golden bowl then sipped his wine as a dancer gyrated her way toward him. He frowned then waved her away.

"Get out, all of you," he said. "Get out!"

The musicians stopped playing. Thutmos threw a handful of coins at them which they gathered from the carpeted floor. One of the dancers strode to him, a scowl marring her otherwise lovely face.

"We are not *faa*, Bindamu!" she said. She said the word Bindamu like a curse.

Thutmos smiled.

"Finally, some spirit!" he exclaimed. "You can stay."

"I'd rather jump into a fire," she replied.

She stomped out the room as the others continued to pick up coins.

"Drummer, come here," Thutmos called out.

The drummer approached Thutmos, fear clear on his face.

"Yes, bwa?" he asked.

"Who was that woman?"

The man frowned. "Dala. She's Taiku. I don't see why they're allowed to remain in Awere. We should drive them into the woods with the others!"

"And yet you hired her," Thutmos said.

The man shrugged. "She's beautiful and she's a good dancer."

Thutmos reached into his pouch then took out a golden eagle.

"Give this to her," he said. "Tell her if she changes her mind to show it to my guards."

The man's eyes went wide. "Thank you bwa! I will!"

The man hurried the others from the room. Thutmos knew there was a slim chance the Taiku woman would see that coin, but it was the thought that counted. He took a long drink of wine then nestled his head against his headrest. Sleep was about to take him when his servant burst into the room.

"Bwa! Bwa! They are here!"

Thutmos almost tumbled from the chaise.

"Who's here?" he said.

"The warriors from Menu-Kash!"

Thutmos sprang to his feet.

"So soon?"

Yes, bwa!" the servant said. "They came from the sky!"

Thutmos was dumbfounded. Akinbola's forces had no flying craft. For them to arrive such a way was impossible . . . unless it was not Akinbola!

"My clothes," Thutmos commanded.

The servant dressed him in his finest garments then the two of them rushed to the city ramparts. Thutmos grinned when he looked out into the plains separating Awere from the river and the nKu forests. Three Alchemist scarabs rested in the field, their ramps lowering into the short grass. Ranks of mulaks marched out of the craft, towering men covered in golden armor. Thutmos's joy was muted by another sight. As the last of the Alchemist warriors emptied from the scarabs, they were followed by other warriors covered in white cloth, their faces and heads hidden by loose turbans.

"Shadow Blades," he whispered. "So Akinbola, you did come."

The Shadow Blades spread out, forming a semi-circle perimeter around the Alchemist soldiers. Their leader, the warrior with a golden broach in the center of his turban, drew his sword. The other Bladesmen did the same. He faced his men then pointed his sword at the soldiers. When he dropped his sword, The Shadow Blades fell upon the mulaks, killing them with ruthless efficiency. Half of the soldiers were dead or dying by the time they overcame their shock and began to fight back. The soldiers' armor aided them, but they were no match for the Shadow Blades' skill and experience.

"Bwa, what is happening?" Thutmos's servant asked.

"The Pharsa has been betrayed!" Thutmos said.

He ran from the ramparts, his servant following.

"Close the gates!" Thutmos shouted. "Summon the city guard! Do not let those traitors inside the city!"

Thutmos did not stop running until he reached his palace, which required uncommon stamina. He burst into his room then collapsed onto his bed, gasping with fatigue and terror. He had to let the Pharsa know what was happening. He forced himself from the bed then stumbled to his dresser, shuffling through his trinkets until he found his communication bracelet. He slid the bracelet over his chubby hand then attempted to calm down as he reached out to his cousin. He anxiousness eased as an image formed his mind. His hope fled when that image coalesced into the face of Olagun Akinbola.

"I see you witnessed my surprise," he said.

"The Pharsa will see you tortured for this!" Thutmos said.

"The Pharsa will know what he needs to know when the time comes," Akinbola said. "In the meantime, I suggest that you order your militia to stand down and open the gates. I will arrive in a week's time. If my men are still outside the gates, I assure you that once we breach the gates it will be you who will be tortured."

"How do I know you'll keep your word?" Thutmos asked.

"You don't," Akinbola replied.

Thutmos broke the link. He yanked the bracelet from his wrist then threw it across the room. His servant approached him warily.

"Bwa? Are you well?"

Thutmos's shoulders slumped. He was a rat trapped in a cage. He went to his dresser again then found his seal then handed it to his servant.

"Show this to the militia captain. Tell him to open the gate and allow the Shadow Blades inside."

"Yes, bwa!"

The servant took the seal then hurried off. Thutmos waited until the servant was well on his way before scurrying around the room, collecting his essential items. He would not wait for his death like a beast for slaughter. He would hide in the merchant district until the incident was over. Once Akinbola's forces subdued the nKu he would flee for the forests and lose himself among the defeated until he felt the time was right to escape to Menu-Kash. His life of luxury was at an end. It was time to run.

THIRTY-EIGHT

Etana and the Chuiku marons watched the Bindamu forces fight each other from wooded ridge before the river. The other marons laughed and yelled insults at their enemies, but Etana observed the forces carefully.

"They fight like children," Taabu said. "I'll take them on with my food knife."

The others laughed as they whistled.

"They're not worth the edge of my porridge spoon," Waiyaki said. "I'll fight them with stones."

More laughter and more whistles. Etana was not fooled by his brothers' bravado. He'd been among them long enough to know that the more the boasting, the more unsure the nKu. These white-robed warriors would make a daunting enemy. If the others were as skilled, they would need all of Nandi's talent to defeat them.

Etana set off for the rendezvous point in silence. The others followed instinctively, falling into a warrior's pace. They ran the remainder of the day, stopping only for a brief respite. It was dusk when they arrived at the gathering point, a wide grassland surrounded by the dense forest. The other warriors turned as they entered the clearing; Etana knew as soon as he saw their faces something was amiss. These were Temboku, not Chuiku. Where was Nandi?

The warriors parted and the Temboku strode toward them. Zalika led the procession, a smug smile on her face. Etana's eyes focused on what she held in her hand; the priestess staff. His hand went to his hilt; the other Chuiku marons did the same.

Zalika and the other Temboku continued to advance. She faced Etana with a frown.

"Is this how you greet the First Hunter?" she said.

"How did you get that?" he said, his eyes cutting to the staff.

"How else would I get it? I defeated Nandi."

"That's impossible," Etana said. "She beat you easily."

"Then how do you explain this?" Zalika waved the staff.

"Where is she?" Etana asked.

Zalika smiled. "Dead."

Etana yanked his sword free and the Chuiku marons did the same. The Temboku warriors surged forward, as did the others. The Chuiku were not well-liked among the other nKu, and many of them would love to have Etana's head as a trophy. As much as he wanted to slit Zalika's throat, something told him that this was not the path to take.

"I hold the priestess staff," Zalika said. "I earned it by right of battle. Those who followed Nandi are now obligated to follow me!"

The warriors prostrated before Zalika. The Chuiku marons did not. Instead they left the field as the others paid homage, following Etana. No matter what Zalika said, Etana knew Nandi was not dead. He would find her and discover what happened.

* * *

Nandi opened her eyes. Rain splattered her face, yet she could not lift her hands to wipe away the water. Breathing pained her chest, each breath like being stabbed. She was not dead, yet she was barely alive. She did not know how much time passed before she could move her head, turning it to the right to avoid the drizzle. What she saw sent her into despair. Furaha and Tumaini lay side by side, their bodies twisted in odd positions. They were dead; killed by the poison that almost killed her. As darkness approached her breathing became easier; sometime during the night she was able to sit up then crawl to a large tree with a dense canopy which protected her from the rain. A wave of nausea swept through her and she retched. The effort drained her; she closed her eyes then passed out.

Something warm touched her cheek and she opened her eyes. It was a hand, one rough and familiar.

"Etana?"

Strong arms cradled her then lifted her from the ground. She was moving, slowly at first, then at a running pace once her carrier reached smoother ground. Nandi kept her eyes closed. She was afraid to open them; afraid he might see a Temboku carrying her to her death. She searched for Aziza but could not find her.

Familiar sounds and smells filled her senses and she dared to open her eyes. She was home. The runner stopped; his breathing heavy. The next voice Nandi heard filled her with hope.

"Etana!" Mama exclaimed. "What happened?"

"We found her like this," Etana replied. "Furaha and Tumaini are dead."

A piercing series of wails filled her ears. She felt herself being passed into another's arms.

"Abasi, follow me," Mama said. "Siza, fetch the healer."

"I must go stop Zalika," Etana said.

"She did this?"

"Yes. She plans to lead the nKu against the Bindamu. It is not her place."

"No, stay with us," mama said. "She will need your strength."

"It is not permitted," Etana said.

"It is today," mama replied.

As Abasi carried her to the house Nandi managed to open her eyes. Siza looked back at her, a cautious smile on her face.

"You will be fine, sister," she said. "We have you now."

Nandi wasn't as confident. She'd never felt weaker in her life. She wanted to believe she would survive, but she couldn't understand how Aziza permitted Zalika to poison her.

"I could not prevent this," Aziza said. "You went against your instincts. This is why you are here and your friends are dead. Some lessons cannot be taught."

Nandi closed her eyes to stop the tears from flowing.

"Nandi," Mama whispered. "Can you hear me?"

Nandi nodded.

"The medicine priest will be here soon," Mama said. "Stay with us."

Nandi drifted in and out of consciousness. She felt a thin tube pushed into her mouth then a warm trickle of liquid flow down her throat. The elixir calmed her and made her sleepy. She drowsed, her rest interrupted by the images of Furaha and Tumaini twisting in agony as the poison claimed them. In the background Aziza's words echoed.

There came a time when she was strong enough to sit up. Her head spun and she grasped it with both hands hoping to steady it. After a moment she opened her eyes. Siza slumped in a chair beside the bed, cradling little Goma in her arms. Both she and the baby slept.

"Siza," Nandi said.

Siza jumped. She opened her eyes and a wide smile creased her face.

"Nandi!"

Her shout woke Goma. The little girl cried as she grasped at Siza's breasts. Siza nursed her and Goma fell silent.

"I must go tell your mother!" Siza said.

Nandi shook her head.

"Mama!" she shouted. "Mama!"

It was good to hear her own voice so strong and sure even though her body was still weak. Mama ran into the room followed by Etana. Mama wrapped her into a tight hug; Etana kept his distance although his face expressed his joy. His presence took her mind to more serious matters.

"What is the situation at the river?" she asked him.

Etana's smile faded.

"I don't think this is the time to discuss such things," he said.

"Tell me," Nandi said. "Now."

Etana straightened. "Zalika leads the nKu now. They are preparing to attack Awere."

Nandi swung her legs over the edge of the bed.

"They will fail," she said.

"How?" Etana asked. "She has the Priestess staff."

Nandi dropped her head.

"I know. I take the blame for losing it. I also take the blame for Furaha and Tumaini. But Zalika cannot defeat the Bindamu. She doesn't possess the tambikos. Without them she will not be strong enough."

"This is no longer our fight," Mama said. "The nKu have chosen to follow Zalika despite her treachery. If they die, so be it."

"If they die, we die too," Nandi said. "The Bindamu will not stop until all of us are defeated."

"We stopped them at the river before," Etana said. "We will stop them again."

"You don't understand, Etana," she said. "The Bindamu are a vast people. They will keep coming until they have overwhelmed us. The only chance we have is to defeat them in such a way that they will fear us too much to continue to fight us. I was given this task and I will see it through."

Nandi stood. She swayed and everyone lurched toward her. She waved them away then steadied.

"Bring me my armor and my weapons," she said. "We leave for the Hagosa today."

"Nandi, you're not well enough!" Mama said.

Nandi closed her eyes then took a deep breath. Aziza urged her to trust her instincts and her instincts told her that now was the time to leave.

"It's time," she said. She turned to Etana.

"Gather the warriors."

Etana left immediately.

"Mama, I need the hunters as well."

Mama's eyes went wide.

"Hunters and marons can't march together! It's forbidden!"

"Summon the hunters, Mama," Nandi said. "Now."

Nandi bent to pick up her armor then felt woozy. She sat hard on her bed.

"I will help you."

She looked up into Siza's face. Nandi smiled at her best friend then nodded.

Siza knelt before her then strapped on her shin guards.

"Where's Goma?" Nandi asked.

"With Abasi."

Nandi grinned. "Are you sure that's wise?"

Siza laughed. "He's very good with her. If he had breasts, he would steal her away from me."

They laughed as Siza secured her leather skirt.

"You are leaving too soon," Siza said.

"Don't Siza," Nandi warned.

"I'm not trying to stop you," Siza said. "I know you're doing what you feel you have to do. But the Chuiku have survived without the others. We can do so again. We are the ones who held the border at the river."

"We need every warrior to stand against the army that is coming," Nandi said. "This is a battle we cannot win alone."

Siza held Nandi's breastplate in her hands.

"How bad will it be?"

Nandi's face became solemn. "Very bad. Many will not survive. The mourning fires will burn for a long time. I don't do this for us. I do this for Goma."

Siza strapped Nandi's breastplate into place. "Will you return?"

Nandi lowered her head. "I don't know."

Siza kissed Nandi's cheek and they hugged.

"You will come back," she whispered. "Goma needs her auntie."

Nandi closed her eyes then squeezed Siza tight.

"I will try."

Siza help Nandi to her feet. Nandi's serious face returned.

"Promise me that you and Abasi will not separate."

Siza's eyes widened. "Why are you saying this?"

"Just promise me. The old ways make no sense. This war will change us, Siza. In order to win marons and hunters will fight together. We should stay together afterwards. You and Abasi will be the example for others."

Siza gripped Nandi's hand. "We will."

Nandi smiled. Her legs were steadier than before; as she took a step, she felt her strength building.

"I must go now," she said. "The war waits."

She strode from the house and into the courtyard to the waiting warriors.

THIRTY-NINE

Akinbola shielded his eyes from the sunlight he had not seen for seven days. Nzali and the others in the cabin of the steam engine did the same. As his eyes adjusted to the intense light the city of Awere came into focus, its spires rising over the white-washed walls. Despite its swiftness the journey through the tunnel had been unpleasant. The lights helped, but the perpetual darkness had a despondent effect on the warriors. Emerging into the world again would surely be an uplifting experience for them all.

Raman sat on a stool at the rear of the cabin, his legs, arms and mouth bound. The Alchemist leader learned of the massacre of his men as they traveled through the tunnel. His reaction had been surprisingly muted; the man collapsed before Akinbola and his men quickly surrendered. Akinbola was relieved; his warriors would have found it difficult to kill their own, unlike the Shadow Blades. They were assassins who know no loyalty except to their own and Akinbola, which is why they were so valuable. The Blades were the ultimate enforcement, and if things went awry, the ultimate protection.

They followed a road which snaked through a narrow valley. The steep rocky slopes hemming them in were sparsely forested with narrow evergreen trees and squat shrubs peppered with small red berries. The hint of nature helped brighten the mood as they left the gloom of the tunnel behind. Horns blared from the distance as the rear gates swung open. Akinbola raised his eyeglass then smiled. The ramparts were manned by Shadow Blades.

They were a hundred spans from the city when Akinbola touched Nzali's shoulder.

"Stop the train," he said. "I think we need to stretch our legs. We'll march from here."

"As you wish, bwa," Nzali replied. She shuffled to the control panel then grasped the acceleration lever with both hands. She eased the lever down while pushing the brake down with her right foot. The engine slowed then stopped.

Akinbola grasped the megaphone hanging from a brass hook near the control panel. He waited as the door opened and the ladder lowered to the ground. Two of his men climbed down first then stood guard by the ladder; Akinbola climbed down then stepped away from the train.

"My warriors! Today is a beautiful day for a walk. Join me!"

The transport doors opened and the Menu-Kash warriors spilled onto the field. They fell into formation behind their commanders as the cadence drummers and standard bearers made their way to Akinbola.

"Give us a brisk rhythm to stretch our legs," Akinbola commanded.

The drummers played and the army glided across the field to the city. They shifted to single file to accommodate Awere's narrow gate. Bala met Akinbola as he entered, walking stride for stride.

"Welcome, bwa," he said.

"Thank you," Akinbola replied. "I see you have fulfilled your duties. Were the Alchemists a problem?"

"No, bwa."

"Where is Thutmos?"

"He is being held in the dungeons, bwa."

Akinbola laughed. "He's very familiar with them. Have the Nkulu shown themselves?"

"No bwa, but they are massing. We have seen so from the scarabs. I'm sure they will attack soon. Your arrival is timely."

"Good. The sooner we defeat them the better."

"We have prepared barracks for our warriors in the merchant district and the city center. Thutmos's palace has been selected as our headquarters," Bala said.

"You've been very busy," Akinbola replied.

"Yes, bwa."

"Send scouts across the river," Akinbola said. "I need an assessment."

Bala did not reply, which caught Akinbola's attention.

"What is it?"

"Bwa, we have sent scouts. None have returned."

Akinbola stopped walking. "None of them?"

"No," Bala said.

"That's interesting," Akinbola said. His response was an understatement. Never before had a Shadow Blade not return from a scouting mission.

"How many scouts were sent?" Akinbola asked.

"Three, bwa," Bala replied.

"Take me to Thutmos."

As the warriors marched to their new barracks, Bala and Akinbola strode to Awere's stockade. They found Thutmos at the bottom level in his familiar cell. His expression was not pleasant.

"Traitor," he said to Akinbola.

Akinbola smiled. "You should watch what you say to the future Pharsa."

"You assume too much," Thutmos shot back. "You have yet to defeat the nKu, let alone Menu-Kash."

Akinbola leaned against the damp wall then folded his arms across his chest.

"Menu-Kash will be easy. It's like an old person waiting for its final breath. The Pharsa and those like you depend on the complacence of your subjects enforced by their fear of the Alchemists. Now that they are no more no one stands between me and the Stool.

"Your bloodline should have been imprisoned with the others!"

"My bloodline created this empire!" Akinbola shouted back. He closed his eyes, admonishing himself for losing his temper, especially before someone as useless as Thutmos. He was tired; he would rest before planning the defeat of the nKu.

"When I am ready you will join us. I'm sure there are details you know about the nKu that will be useful."

"I'll tell you nothing!" Thutmos replied.

Akinbola laughed. "You are not a brave man, Thutmos. You've never been. You'll tell us what we need to know because you know what will happen if you don't."

"I'm probably going to die either way," Thutmos said, resignation heavy in his voice.

"True," Akinbola said. "That death can be either quick and peaceful or long and painful. I'm a reasonable man."

"There is nothing to tell," Thutmos said. "You are here now. All the answers you seek wait for you on the battlefield."

"And you will be there to advise me."

Thutmos drew away from Akinbola.

"Me? Didn't you hear me? I can't help you!"

"We will see when the time comes, won't we?" Akinbola replied. He looked to Bala.

"Find him some suitable armor. The Pharsa's cousin should take part in our victory."

* * *

Zalika strode to the river's edge, the priestess staff gripped in her right hand. Its power pulsed against her palm, the warmth sending waves of energy throughout her thick muscled body. This was true strength; this was ultimate power. She realized she could never have defeated Nandi as long as she had such a powerful talisman in her possession. True, she did not possess the tambikos but she would not need them. They were fighting Bindamu; their victory was a mere formality.

She waded into the cool river waters surrounded by her sisters. The other nKu followed, ready to end the dominance of the invaders once and for all. The Simbaku were the first to begin singing as was their way. Soon the others joined in, their voices filling the open grassland. Zalika jabbed the staff over her head in rhythm with the singers, their song a chant and a challenge.

The gates of Awere swung open. An army emerged, one that did not resemble the army the nKu had skirmished with for so many seasons. This was not a half-disciplined group of conscripts bolstered by a handful of warriors and nKu traitors. This was a professional force that advanced toward the nKu horde with disciplined precision. Zalika wasn't the only one to notice; the First Hunters of the other nKus quickly gathered around her, anxious for her strategy.

"The Temboku will hold the center," Zalika said. "The Vifaruku and Nyatiku will stand with us. The Pundaku and Paaku will take the flanks. The Simbaku and Mambaku will stand in reserve."

"No," Niko said. "The Simbaku follow no one into battle. We either lead or we do not fight."

"You would have followed Nandi," Zalika said.

"You are not Nandi," Niko replied.

It was a clear challenge, ill-timed and unnecessary. Zalika's first instinct was to smash him with the staff but she glanced at the Bindamu army gathering before the wall, an army much larger than she anticipated.

"So be it," she said.

Dijito of the Mambaku stepped forward, covered in her serpentine armor.

"I will not follow a Simbaku!" she shouted.

"Nor will I!" Awacho of the Fisiku yelled.

Zalika raised the staff. The talisman emitted a blinding light that forced the others to turn away.

"You will do as I say!"

The brilliance dissipated as she lowered the staff. The Simbaku took their place before the army. Badatisha, her second, whispered in her ear.

"Why are you doing this?"

"Let the Simbaku have their pride," Zalika said. "They will rush ahead, hoping to grab the glory first. Then we will see how these Bindamu fight. Their sacrifice will be our gain."

Badatisha grinned. "You are a formidable Hunter."

Zalika grinned back. "Yes I am."

* * *

Akinbola and the others on the ramparts covered their eyes from the blinding flash among the NKulu. He raised his spyglass after it subsided, looking toward its source. The woman holding the staff seemed to be a powerful warrior, but she was not the woman he'd confronted weeks ago. He was disappointed.

"Nzali!" he shouted.

The engineer came to his side.

"Are the slings in place?"

"Yes," she replied.

"Wait for my signal," he said.

Nzali nodded then stepped away.

Bala came to Akinbola's side.

"They are not as stupid as they seem," he said. "They are taking formation."

"Yes," Akinbola said. "Somewhat surprising, but it doesn't change the outcome."

"Will we use the scarabs?" Bala asked.

"I don't think we'll need them. The slings will do the most damage."

"The Chuiku are not with them. She is not with them," an irritated voice spoke.

Akinbola and Bala turned their attention to Thutmos. The man's hands were still bound and his ankles shackled, but he was allowed to wear his best clothing. His servant stood by his side.

"The Chuiku?" Akinbola asked.

"They have clans," Thutmos said. "Each clan has a tambiko spirit. The Chuiku are the most powerful clan. Their First Hunter, Nandi, is the one who has vexed us for so long. She and her clan are not present. If we defeat this rabble our troubles are far from over."

"We will deal with that later," Akinbola said. "Send the skirmishers."

Bala raised a green flag. Lightly armored men with throwing spears sprinted forward, followed by ranks of similarly garbed men on horseback. The dust they churned in their charge obscured the movements of the remaining army. The NKulu seemed to be holding back as well. A portion of their army surged forward, warriors wearing circular crowns of woven grass that haloed over their heads. They shook their spears and swords, chanting as they advanced toward the skirmishers. The Kashites threw their spears which the nKu warriors easily evaded; the nKu threw their spears and dozens of Kashite skirmishers fell. The forces crashed together, a roar rising from them like an angry beast. The skirmishers held their own for a moment then collapsed. They sprinted away as quickly as they attacked, their retreat covered by the cavalry. The other nKu warriors could not hold themselves back. Akinbola watched as the horde charged into range.

"They are in range," Nzali said.

"Fire the slings," Akinbola ordered.

Nzali looked into the city then raised a black flag. Bare-chested men turned huge cranks, compressing the springs which served as propulsion for the formidable launchers. Once the springs reached the appropriate tension a large container of explosive power was gently place into the wide cushion

cradle. The sling master stood on the wall beside
Nzali, adjusting her target gauge as she scanned the
battlefield. She shouted commands to the slingers
and they positioned the slings according to the co-
ordinates. Satisfied, the sling master nodded to
Nzali, who then nodded to Akinbola.

"Bring the storm," Akinbola said.

* * *

The Simbaku clashed with the Bindamu
skirmishers, their terrifying roars rising over the
battle din. Zalika held the others back, her arms
spread wide as the arrogant nKu took the brunt of
the attack. She was waiting until most of the
Simbaku were slain before committing her full forces. With their warriors depleted the Simbaku would
be one less challenge to confront once the Bindamu
were dealt with. She would need all her energy for
the Chuiku. They would certainly seek revenge for
Nandi's death, and with the staff she would be more
than ready.

A cheer rose among the Simbaku. The
Bindamu attack faltered, the skirmishers turning
and fleeing for the safety of the city. The others
crept beyond her invisible line, eager to taste victory. She raised her arms then pointed forward; the
nKu army surged after the Bindamu. The Temboku
remained, looking at her with anxious eyes.

"Go!" she said.

They blew their trumpets then joined the
pursuit.

Zalika and her personal guard trotted forward. This had been much easier than she'd anticipated. There was still a city to claim, but these
Bindamu were a disappointing lot. The Chuiku

could have defeated them on their own, which confirmed her suspicions. Nandi had used the so-called Bindamu threat to bring the nKu under Chuiku control. It was a shrewd plan that worked now in the Temboku favor.

A sound like thunder swallowed all others, the ground jolted beneath her feet. A few strides before her bodies sailed through the air. The sound repeated to her right, followed by a ball of smoke and fire. More bodies flew, this time accompanied by cries of pain and terror. The grassland erupted around them as Zalika searched for the source of such vile destruction. Then she saw it, a large barrel-like object falling from the sky directly toward her.

"Run!" she shouted.

But Zalika did not move. She closed her eyes then concentrated on the staff. The object glowed in her hands; once she determined it was enough, she locked her eyes on the falling object then swung the staff. The barrel jerked then flew in the other direction toward the city. It exploded over the Bindamu ranks. With a grim smile she raced across the grasses, repeating the gesture. Some of the barrels exploded in the air, others in the Bindamu ranks, a few in the city. She had turned the Bindamu's weapon against them.

* * *

"Cease fire!" Akinbola shouted.

Below him his army struggled to reform the ranks after the unexpected barrage. Behind him the city burned from the barrel that crashed within the walls. He was angry yet impressed; the NKulu was aware of her powers with the talisman. Still, he sensed she was not worth his efforts.

"Bala, the Shadow Blades will form our vanguard. Bring me that staff."

Bala smiled. "Yes, bwa."

Akinbola grabbed Thutmos's arm.

"It's time you served you cousin honorably."

"No! No!"

Thutmos broke free and ran. Akinbola eyes met Bala's and he nodded his head. Bala snatched a spear from one of his warriors then threw it. The spear struck Thutmos in his back then burst from his chest. The man was dead before he hit the stone.

"So much for the honor of the Pharsa," Akinbola commented. "Bala, the army is yours to command."

Bala smiled. "Thank you, Olagun!"

He hurried from the ramparts, his brethren following. Moments later they appeared before the army in classic V formation. Bala looked up to Akinbola; Akinbola nodded his head. The Shadow Blades ran forward, the army marching close behind.

* * *

Zalika circled the staff over her head to draw the fleeing nKu attention.

"To me!" she shouted. "To me!"

Some of the warriors responded; others continued to run. As they arrived her commanders did their best to form them into ranks.

"Zalika!" Badatisha shouted. "Look!"

The Bindamu were advancing, led by the warriors in the white cloaks and turbans. Zalika ran toward them, axe in one hand, the staff in the other.

The Temboku formed around her, the other nKu warriors following. As they neared the Temboku blew their trumpets then threw them to the ground. They smashed into the cloaked ones, their fury and momentum temporarily pushing the Bindamu back. Zalika chopped a man's head from his neck as she crushed another's skull with the staff. She sidestepped a sword thrust to her gut, punched the axe head into her attacker's face then kicked him away. Another cloaked warrior jumped before her, a thin gold band surrounding his turban. This man was skilled. He parried the axe and staff while delivering quick slashes and stabs with his sword and knife which she barely avoided. Their fight took her full focus. She managed to bring down the staff on his left shoulder; he dropped the knife as he grunted. She paid for her brief victory with a slash across her abdomen that drew blood but did not disembowel her. Soon after she felt weak; the blade had been poisoned. Zalika fought as best she could, but the cloaked one's sword continued to cut. A grim smile came to her face. She would be undone the same way she'd killed Nandi. She felt the cloaked man's sword plunge into her stomach but she did not cry out. Instead she pulled the man close.

"You may defeat us, Bindamu," he said. "But you will not live to see it!"

She bit down on the man's neck then ripped his flesh away. He pushed away from her weakening arms then grabbed the wound, blood pouring through his fingers. Zalika fell to her knees. The battle around her faded with her vision. As she died, the staff shimmered then exploded in a flash of light.

FORTY

Nandi's strength increased the closer they came to the Hagosa. The Chuiku moved as fast as she allowed, so their pace quickened with each day. Soon they were only a half a day from the river. It was then that they came across the first straggler. Etana brought the warrior to her, a young Mambaku with a wicked wound across his cheek.

"What happened?" Nandi asked.

"Zalika led us against the Bindamu," he said wincing with each word. "We were winning until the ground began to erupt. That's when I ran. I've been running since."

"Where is Zalika now?"

The man shook his head. "I don't know and I don't care. The Bindamu cannot be defeated! We should hide in our forests and let them have what they claimed."

"Cover his wound," Nandi said. "He marches with us. Any straggler will do the same. Make sure . . ."

It began as a tingling in her fingers then became a coursing flow of energy. Nandi stretched her hands out and light particles appeared over her palms. The particles coalesced then extended as they took solid form. Nandi smiled; Aziza's staff had returned to her. No sooner did the carved wood touch her hand was she swallowed in the images of

Zalika's last moments as she fought a Bindamu warrior draped in white robes. She managed to slay the man as she died, a better death than she deserved. But this was not the man Nandi saw, the man who led the Bindamu army. Apparently, he had not felt Zalika was worth his time. He would regret that decision.

By the time the Chuiku reached the river the stragglers had been gathered and pressed into service. They were a much larger force now, but still not as large as the army marching toward the river. The first time they attacked Awere their efforts were thwarted by the Rain Prayers; this time it threatened to be ruined by Zalika's stupidity. But there was no turning back. They had to fight with what they had. Nandi gripped the staff tight then placed it on the ground. She cut a strip of leather from her skirt, bound both ends of the staff then draped it over her left shoulder.

The nKu peered through the trees at the advancing army.

"Do we attack?" Etana asked.

"No," Nandi replied. Let them come to us."

She turned to the warriors.

"Archers forward!" she shouted.

The nKu archers came forward. To her surprise Siza and Abasi was among them.

"What are you doing here?"

"Fighting," Siza answered.

"Where is Goma?"

"With her mothers, as she will be if we do not return." Siza's voice ran with resolve. Nandi wanted to argue but they needed everyone. She looked at Abasi with a bow and grinned.

"Make sure you shoot Bindamu, not us," she said.

Abasi frowned. "I'm a good shot. Siza has taught me well."

"He's good enough," Siza replied. "With so many Bindamu it will be hard for him to miss."

Etana interrupted their brief respite.

The archers should cross the river and take position," he said.

"No," Nandi said. "They will stay here. We will let the Bindamu take the river."

Etana looked at her skeptically but said nothing.

Nandi looked at Siza. "Position the archers where they can get clear shots. Wait until the Bindamu are in the river before shooting."

Siza nodded then went about her orders.

Nandi pulled Etana close.

"Once the river is filled with Bindamu I will attack. Hold everyone back.

"You can't attack alone!" Etana said.

"I am not alone," Nandi replied.

"I won't let you do this," Etana said.

"You will," Nandi replied. "You forget who I am."

Etana stalked away. Nandi watched him leave. She wanted to tell him of her plan but it wouldn't do any good. He wouldn't believe her; none of them would. She would have to show them.

The Bindamu reached the riverbank then marched into the river, the white cloaked warriors leading them. As soon as the first warrior's foot touched the opposite bank Siza and the other archers let loose their arrows. A few of the white cloaked warriors avoided the volley and plunged into the woods, weapons at the ready. They were met by Etana and the marons and a furious battle took place. Though the warriors were skilled, they fell quickly to the Chuiku. Nandi took no notice of the skirmish; her attention was focused on the river. The Bindamu were pulling back and regrouping, their shield bearers forming a wall in order to advance against the arrows. In the distance they rolled some strange devices from within the city. She could wait no longer. Nandi sprinted from the trees. She glanced back for a moment to make sure she wasn't being followed before focusing on the Bindamu ranks.

"You told me to use my instincts," she whispered. "I hope you were right, Aziza."

Nandi closed her eyes as she reached inside herself. The staff burned against her back for a brief moment; when she opened her eyes, she looked down on the Bindamu, her large feet pounding the ground. Long tusks extended from her jaws. The laugh she planned to release became a loud trumpet. She trampled the terrified warriors as she swung her tusks from side to side. Some she grabbed with her trunk then tossed them away like toys. She had become the tembo.

Panic overwhelmed the Bindamu for a moment and they fell back in broken ranks. Nandi pursued them, trumpeting as she lifted the slow ones then threw them at their compatriots. The panic was short-lived; discipline prevailed and the Bindamu reformed ranks. Nandi shut her eyes then transformed from the lumbering tembo into sleek form of a duma. She sprinted into the ranks, slashing warriors with her claws and biting exposed skin. Then she turned and ran for the river. The Bindamu had enough of her attacks. They ran after her as fast as they could, ready to take vengeance.

Nandi bounded across the river and into the forest. She closed her eyes again then transformed into her true self. The others looked at her with expressions of awe. Etana approached her first, a slight grin on his face.

"Impressive. Do we get to fight now?"

Nandi smiled. "Yes, you do."

The handlers brought the farasi forward; Nandi and the others mounted. Nandi took the staff from her back then gazed at her warriors, hunters and marons joined together for battle. Though their ranks were bolstered by the other nKu, the fate of their land was in the hands of the Chuiku. She leaned her head back and roared. Her people responded. With a wave of her staff the nKu charged into the open.

* * *

A smile came to Akinbola's face as the NKulu charged into the open.

"There you are," he whispered.

He looked to Nzali, ignoring her worried face.

"The city is under your command until I return," he said.

"Bwa, maybe we should pull the warriors back into the city..."

Akinbola cut her off with the swipe of his hand.

"Nothing has happened that I did not anticipate. The battle ends here."

He folded his eyeglass then strode from the ramparts. The courtyard before the gates was filled with his cavalry, his elite warriors held in reserve for this moment. He mounted his horse then extracted his sword from its scabbard.

"Open the gates!" he shouted.

The gates swung aside and the Menu-Kash cavalry rode into battle, Akinbola at the lead. The foot soldiers scattered to make way for the charge, a few hapless ones trampled by the headlong rush. The NKulu mounts were smaller than the Menu-Kash horses, but what they lacked in mass they made up in agility. Instead of the clash the Menu-Kash expected, the NKulu darted between the gaps, their riders striking as they streaked by. Some managed to spring into the air with their riders, leaping over the startled Menu-Kash. Akinbola's attention was locked on the woman he'd waited to face ever since their mental encounter. She was the key to this battle. He did not wish to kill her; she would make a valuable prisoner and their marriage would seal his domination of these people. But the look in her eyes spoke of no quarter. This would be a fight to the death.

"So be it, priestess," he whispered. "So be it."

Akinbola pointed his blade at Nandi; the priestess raised her staff. He braced himself for the impact but the priestess disappeared. Something hard struck his head and he tumbled from his horse. He lost his breath as he struck the ground, gasping as he searched for his sword. His eyes cleared as he stood. A large bird landed before him then transformed into the Priestess. Akinbola managed to smile despite the pain in his chest, cursing himself for underestimating her transformation skills.

"Face to face at last," he said.

Nandi attacked. Akinbola deftly blocked her staff, jabbing and slicing at her when the opportunity appeared. The staff glanced off his elbow and he almost dropped his sword. He pushed out with his left hand, shoving the Nandi away. She stumbled, a look of surprise on her face. Akinbola laughed.

"You think you are the only one here with such power? You and I are not that different. As a matter of fact, we are exactly the same."

"We are nothing alike, Bindamu," Nandi said.

"You don't remember," Akinbola said. "None of you do. But that's understandable. Your memories were destroyed before you were imprisoned here. That took place so long ago even your jailers forget. But we never forgot."

Images flooded her mind without warning. She stood on the balcony of a massive building, staring down on a battle the raged around her. This was not nKululand; this was Menu-Kash. Yet it was not the empire she knew. This was an empire ruled by a different people; her people. But they were not nKu. They called themselves the NKulu. The army they fought was an amalgam of all the nations which had tired of their despotic rule and joined together to rid themselves of their enslavers once and for all. But there was one group among them that fueled the rebellion and made victory possible. Nandi's eyes swept the seething throng then focused on the faces of a determined few, faces familiar with those besieged in the palace, people draped in white robes furiously working their magic against their own.

The image shifted to the defeated NKulu being herded into large airships, their haughty clothes and spirits tattered, their arms and legs chained. The ships sailed far, finally landing on a distant island where they were discarded like refuse, their minds wiped of all but their basic memory by those same people in the white robes. The defeated ones were led into the deepest part of the island; then in a final show of ultimate power the robed ones raised massive mountains to surround their defeated foes creating a natural prison to insure they would never be seen again.

It was the story Aziza shared with her before. The image faded and Nandi stood before Akinbola once again.

"I thought should you know before you died," he said.

A memory was released in Nandi's mind, venom that had festered for centuries in the minds of priestesses long before her.

"The traitors," she said instinctively. "The traitors!"

Her attack was sudden, fueled by millennia of hate. The surge caught Akinbola off guard and he frantically guarded himself against the onslaught. Nandi swept him off his feet and he landed hard on his back. He rolled away, barely dodging a blow aimed at his head. He winced as she kicked his side, a crunching sound letting him know that ribs had been broken. Sharp pain laced his side as he stood and was struck in the mouth. He swung wildly with his sword hoping to drive her back. It was useless. Nandi pummeled him, the staff blurring as she struck his head, his legs, his arms, and his back. He was swallowed in a maelstrom of continuous pain, unable to use any of the spells he's saved for this moment. He finally collapsed, a mass of bruises and broken bones. Nandi stood over him, her chest heaving from exertion, her eyes filled with loathing.

"This . . . this is not over," he managed to say.

"It is for you, betrayer," she answered.

Nandi raised her staff then brought it down with all her might onto Akinbola's head. The staff split his helmet and skull. As Akinbola's life seeped from his body the rage that possessed her ebbed. Her legs wavered and she fell to her knees. She gripped her staff, feeding off its warmth and energy. She was covered with blood; some of it the Bindamu's; most of it hers. During their fight she thought his sword had missed its mark. She was wrong.

"Nandi."

She looked up to see Etana peering over his shoulder at her. He and a few other marons had formed a shield around her. Before them were Bindamu bodies piled on each other, a grotesque wall of bleeding flesh. Nandi closed her eyes and let the staff heal her.

"You are with me, Aziza," she said.

"I am," Aziza replied. "Your people are safe .. . for now."

Nandi's eyes widened. "It is not over?"

"Not yet," Aziza said. "You will never be free of the Bindamu. They will always fear and remember you for what you did to them."

"So, what is the use of all this?"

"It is the way of this world," Aziza said. "I have one more task for you, sister."

Nandi felt strong enough to stand. The Bindamu warriors had asked for no quarter and the nKu had not given it. The grasslands were covered with the dead. A battle raged on the ramparts, the Taiku finally joining their brethren and fighting for Awere.

"Should we help them?" Etana asked.

"No," Nandi replied. "Let them reclaim their honor. If they fail it is no consequence to us either way. The Bindamu army is defeated. There will be no other."

Etana looked skeptical. "How can you be sure?"

"Because I will make it so," Nandi answered.

* * *

Siris XXIII stood alone in his garden, still shaken by the message he's received from Kilinda. His best army had been defeated by the NKulu, destroyed by their witch and her rabble. Worse still was the news that Akinbola planned to betray him and slaughtered his Alchemists in the process. The Alchemists would eventually be replaced, but the loss of Akinbola was painful despite his motives. Without his clan Menu-Kash would struggle. Who would bring the wrath down upon uprisings? Who would check the NKulu? It went without saying that Akinbola's remaining clansmen would have to be killed. He'd given the order the same day he received the news. It would be a messy and costly affair but necessary. Traitors to the Stool could expect no mercy.

He shook his head as was his way, clearing his mind of morbid thoughts. It was between seasons, the daily rains diminishing before the onset of the dry season. His garden was in full bloom and his fruit trees were beginning to bear their bounty. Siris picked a green pear, inspecting the fruit's progress. It was then he noticed a hawk circling his garden, probably seeking one of the small rodents that occasionally made residence in the grove. To Siris's surprise the bird descended. He waited in anticipation to see what the bird had discovered but was shocked when the bird landed on the ground before him. By the time he realized what was about to happen it was too late. The bird transformed into the woman he'd seen long ago through another's eyes, the woman who had defeated his best troops and killed Akinbola.

"Do not attempt to summon anyone," Nandi said. "You would be dead before they arrived."

Siris forced down his fear. "You didn't come here to kill me. If so, you would have done so by now."

"You think too much of yourself," Nandi said. "Whether or not I spare your life depends on your next words. Some of your people are returning as we speak."

"Some of them?"

"Some agreed to stay on our terms. Others were too dangerous. They were dealt with. Those who were allowed to leave vowed never to return. I am here to make sure they . . . and you . . . keep the promise."

"Who do you think you're speaking to?" Siris raged. "I am Pharsa of Menu-Kash! I . . ."

Nandi pointed her staff at Siris and a sharp pain flashed through his chest. He collapsed to his knees.

"This is a personal threat," Nandi said. "If you feel your life is worth less than your empire then we can end our game now."

Siris raised his hand. "Please. No."

The pain subsided to a dull throbbing.

"Keep your word Bindamu or I will return. This I promise."

Siris lifted his eyes in time to see the priestess transform into the hawk then ascend into the sky. She circled twice then flew westward.

The garden gate flew open and Siris's guards hurried to him. Carna, his senior guard, was the first to reach him.

"I am sorry, bwa," he said. We could not open the gate."

Siris waved them away then stood. He dusted his clothes before speaking.

"I am fine," he said. "A ship will arrive soon from NKululand. Make sure the passengers are cared for then relocated to the interior. They are to speak to no one. Understand?"

Carna and the others bowed. "Yes Pharsa."

The guards hurried from the garden. Siris waited until they were gone before sitting on his stone bench as he rubbed his sore chest. As far as he was concerned the NKululand expedition was over. He was closing the tablet on that chapter. He would never open it again.

FORTY-ONE

Nandi would see no one after her return. She secluded herself in her mother's home refusing to speak about the last few weeks. Her mother relented after getting no responses to her questions. She watched her daughter with concern as she slept, ate, and labored on her beadwork. One misty morning Nandi emerged from her room dressed for travel, her staff secured across her back, sword and knives hanging from her waist belt. Her mother met her in their common room, a look of concern on her face.

"Where are you going?" she asked.

"To the priestess cave," Nandi said.

"So, it is time."

"Yes."

Her mother hugged her tight, so tight Nandi almost regretted her decision.

"I must tell you what the others are saying," her mother said. "They say you saved us and now the nKu are one. They say there will never be war again. They say there is no need for priestesses."

Nandi smiled. "One day what happened will be only stories and memories. Temboku will find themselves again, as will Simbaku, Taiku, Chuiku and the others. One day we will fight again. When that day comes the priestesses will need to save us again."

"You will live alone?"

"In the past those children abandoned and unwanted were sent to the priestesses. We will do so again."

"What about your own children?" Mama asked.

"I must go, mama." Nandi said.

They hugged once again. Mama kissed her cheek, making her feel like a child. In a way she wished she were.

Nandi exited the house, walking across the compound. She was halfway to the gate when Abasi and Siza met her, Siza holding little Goma in her arms.

"You're leaving us again," Siza said.

"You know where I will be," Nandi said. "You can come visit."

"We will," Abasi said. "Thank you for everything you've done, dada."

Nandi hugged them then hurried to the path. The further away she was from Jikubwa the better she felt about her decision. It was the right thing to do.

Etana was waiting when she reached the rocky creek, his arms folded across his chest.

"First I lost you to war, now I lose you to your calling," he said.

Nandi smiled. "No, Etana. You are not losing me. The others are, but not you."

She walked up to him then took his hand.

"It's a long walk to the caves," she said. "We have plenty of time."

-End-

ABOUT THE AUTHOR

Milton Davis is an award winning Black Fantastic author and owner of MVmedia, LLC, a publishing company specializing in Science Fiction, Fantasy and Sword and Soul. Milton is the author of twenty-three novels and editor/co-editor of seven anthologies. Milton's work had also been featured in *Black Power: The Superhero Anthology*; Skelos *2: The Journal of Weird Fiction and Dark Fantasy Volume 2, Steampunk Writes Around the World* published by Luna Press and *Bass Reeves Frontier Marshal Volume Two*. Milton's story 'The Swarm' was nominated for the 2018 British Science Fiction Association Award for Short Fiction. His screenplay, Ngolo, won the 2014 Urban Action Showcase Award for Best Screenplay. Milton Davis can be reached via his website, https://www.miltonjdavis.com/

Eda Blessed: A Ki Khanga Adventure

Raised in the streets of Sati-Baa, Omari Ket is a man that gets by on his wits and skills . . . and the attentions of a god. Eda Blessed shares the tales of the man and the mercenary as he roams the roads of Ki Khanga bouncing from one adventure to another surviving with his skills, wits, and Eda's blessings.
www.mvmediaatl.com

Ki Khanga: The Anthology

What is Ki Khanga? The answer lies in the pages of this amazing anthology. Balogun OjeAkinbola and Milton Davis define this fascinating world which forms the foundation of the Ki Khanga Sword and Soul Role Playing Game. Fifteen amazing stories will take you on an exciting journey throughout is intriguing world. Prepare yourself for stories of bravery, tragedy, love and adventure. Prepare yourself for Ki Khanga.

www.mvmediaatl.com

CPSIA information can be obtained
at www.ICGtesting.com
Printed in the USA
FSHW010402130220
66940FS